JENNIFER LYNN BARNES

Fate

DELACORTE PRESS

Published by Delacorte Press
an imprint of Random House Children's Books
a division of Random House, Inc.
New York

Delacorte Press and colophon are registered trademarks of
Random House, Inc.

Visit us on the Web! www.randomhouse.com/teens

Educators and librarians, for a variety of teaching tools, visit us at
www.randomhouse.com/teachers

Library of Congress Cataloging-in-Publication Data
Barnes, Jennifer (Jennifer Lynn)
Fate / Jennifer Lynn Barnes. — 1st ed.
p. cm.
Sequel to: Tattoo.
Summary: High school senior Bailey Morgan must choose between the
mortal world and the otherworldly Nexus, where each night,
as the third Fate, she weaves the web of life.
ISBN 978-0-385-73537-7 (trade pbk.)
[1. Supernatural—Fiction.   2. Fate and fatalism—Fiction.
3. Mythology—Fiction.   4. Best friends—Fiction.   5. Friendship—
Fiction.   6. Humorous stories.]   I. Title.
PZ7.B26225Fat 2008
[Fic]—dc22   2007049429

The text of this book is set in 11-point Galliard.
Printed in the United States of America
10 9 8 7 6 5 4 3 2
First Edition

For Erin and Alisa, who've been my friends since
before we could talk. From Bethany School
and baby ballet to our college graduations—
I can't wait to see what the three of us do next!

Chapter 1

Life.

    Life.

    Life.

    Love-hate-like-break-want-need-scared-no-yes.

    Miss her—want him—giggle-new-now.

    Life.

    Life.

    Life.

    The pressure of souls skating along the insides of my bones increased rapidly, until every human on the planet was as much a part of me as I was, every aspect of every person an open book for my eyes only. Their hopes and dreams, the things they wished for. The things they dreaded.

    In a state of divine ecstasy, I threw my head back. This was Earth, the mortal realm. These were humans. This was life.

I was Life.

Giving in to the unbearable pressure within me, I moved my hands in a silent, expressive dance, and soul light burst from my pores. I watched, mesmerized, as the light condensed into webs before my eyes. Some were so densely woven that they appeared as solid fabric; others were thin or sparse, a tangled mess.

It was time.

Like a pianist whose fingers knew a melody better than her mind did, I gave in to the familiarity and undeniable energy of the moment, allowing my hands to carry me through the mind-boggling task. Deftly, instinctively, I crossed this path with that, melded threads together and tore others apart. The fabric was cool to the touch, but white-hot sparks leapt off my body as I wove.

Life.

Life.

Life.

"Good morning, Oakridge! I'm Craaaaazy Mike, and you're listening to K-K-K-KHITS! It's seven in the a.m., and I a-m in the mood for some lovin', some badda bing, if you know what I mean. . . ."

I rolled over in bed and slapped at my radio alarm. I really didn't want to know what Crazy Mike meant any more than I already did, and I definitely didn't want to give him the chance to elaborate. I narrowed my eyes at the clock, and the time stared unapologetically back at me.

Seven a.m. Time to get up for school.

"Just five more minutes?" I asked. Since I'd turned

the alarm off, there was no beeping reply to my question, and I took that silence as permission to snuggle into my covers and close my eyes. This time, there was no weaving, no mystical plane to claim my spirit.

Peace at last.

"Bailey Marie, don't tell me you're still sleeping." My mom cruised by my bedroom door, not even bothering to stop as she made use of my middle name. It was a drive-by scolding, one of her many maternal specialties.

Mumbling under my breath about stupid Crazy Mike and my stupid alarm and my stupid middle name, I managed to get my body halfway vertical. A minute or so later, I actually made it out of bed and stumbled to the bathroom like some kind of deranged zombie in search of sweet, sweet brains. Once I'd managed to shut the door behind me and was positive that even my mom's superhearing wouldn't allow her to decipher my mumbles, I extended them to include two more subjects.

"Stupid Mom. Stupid ancient birthright."

I really wasn't a morning person.

I sought refuge from the horrors of things-that-happen-before-noon in the shower. After the water beat against my skin for a few minutes, I started to feel more human, which—given my nightly activities—was a wee bit ironic. I finished showering, and as my mood improved, little by little, I begrudgingly took back most of my "stupids." If I was being honest, I didn't really have anything against my alarm, my middle name, or what I'd just done in the Nexus between this world and the next.

Not ready to part ways with the shower but knowing I had to, I reached to turn it off. As I did, the overhead light hit my hand, casting a large, strangely fluid shadow near my feet. For a moment I stood there looking at the image, which wavered as I clenched the knob, shades of silvery purple fading to gray as I turned my hand. The stream of water pelting my face subsided, and I dropped my hand to my side and stepped out of the shower, leaving it—and the *très* creepy shadow—behind.

It was times like these that I regretted not dreaming anymore. Without a nighttime outlet, my subconscious and imagination had a tendency to go overboard during my waking hours; hence the funny shadows and the nagging feeling that something in the world (not to mention the shower) wasn't quite right.

I shook my head, and water flew off my sopping hair to join the steam beaded up on the mirror's surface. The condensation distorted my reflection, but I could still make out my not-brown, not-blond hair and my undeniably average body. For someone who held the fate of the world in her hands—literally—I sure wasn't much to look at. I probably should have been used to it by now, but even after two years of waking up to find that no matter what I did in other realms, I was just plain old me in this one, I still hadn't quite wrapped my mind around it.

Bailey Morgan, Third Fate. Not to sound too seventies, but that was just objectively trippy. Mythology wasn't supposed to be fact, and I wasn't supposed to be a part of it, but it was, and I was, and no matter how many days I woke up thinking the whole thing was crazy, it didn't change that it was all real.

I was the Third Fate, the Fate of Life.

"I'm single-handedly responsible for weaving the lives of the entire world," I said quietly, watching my lips move in the mirror as I said *world,* "and yet, I can't even fill out a B cup."

When it came to awe-inspiring power, I was good to go, but when it came to cleavage, I was hopeless. *Surreal* didn't even begin to cover my life.

"Bailey!"

This time my mom refrained from telling me that I was going to be late. She just yelled my name. I was pretty sure that in her über-Mom mind this passed for cutting back on the mothering and giving me a taste of the independence college would offer in another year.

"Bailey!"

I forced my eyes away from the mirror and my thoughts away from fleeting memories and awe-inspiring power. Forget the lives and destinies of the world as a whole. This was high school, and I wasn't even dressed yet.

Five minutes later, I was clothed and ready to go. Makeup was a luxury reserved for people who didn't mind getting up when their alarms told them to, and besides, I knew Delia well enough to know that even if my face was makeup free when I left for school, it wouldn't stay that way for long.

I grabbed my backpack and flew down the stairs, taking them two at a time. My mom was waiting at the bottom, and with pinpoint accuracy, she managed to land a kiss on my cheek as I rushed past.

"Have a good day, sweetheart. And don't forget to ask Mr. McMann if he thinks you should—"

I shut the front door behind me before my mom could finish telling me what exactly I should ask the school guidance counselor during our meeting that afternoon. My mom was what most adults referred to as "involved" and most teens referred to as "crazy." She was perceptive, she asked lots of questions, and she'd taught herself how to use internet search engines. Believe me, it was all downhill from there. Her obsessive Googling came in handy on rare occasions, but still. I was seventeen, and I was not a morning person. Now was clearly not the best time to be imparting life advice, especially the kind of advice that involved what the College Board recommended asking your guidance counselor during the application process.

"Don't forget to ask Mr. McMann if you should let me give you layers. On the DL, I think he's going to say yes."

That voice definitely wasn't my mom's, and even as I rolled my eyes at the unsolicited advice, I smiled at the way Delia had finished my mom's sentence. The idea of asking the school guidance counselor about hairstyles was patently absurd. Mr. McMann's idea of fashion was an oxford shirt and—if he was feeling particularly daring—suspenders. I was pretty sure he wouldn't have feelings one way or another about whether or not I should get layers.

"Morning, Delia," I greeted Delia Cameron: fashion goddess, connoisseur of boys, and one of my best friends for pretty much as long as I could remember. "Your car still broken?"

Driving wasn't really Delia's strong suit. As a general rule, the rest of us felt that the world was safer without Delia behind the wheel, but because we were friends and it was a somewhat sensitive subject, I used the term "broken" as opposed to "wrapped around a telephone pole somewhere."

"I prefer to think that my car is getting a makeover," Delia hedged. "But since it's not quite ready to reveal its new look to the world, I thought I'd catch a ride with you." Delia smiled charmingly, and as the two of us climbed into my car, she reached into her purse and pulled out her holy trinity of cosmetic products: lip gloss, powdered base, and mascara. I took the gloss and started the car.

As I backed down my driveway, Delia dangled the rest of the makeup in front of my face, clearly trying to tempt me.

"Come on, Bay. You know you want to."

"I can't put on makeup while I drive," I told her.

"Sure you can. It's easy!"

And that was why Delia's car was in constant need of a "new look."

"So, any news on the guy front?" I changed the subject from makeup to boys. One of the bonuses of being friends with the same people your entire life is that you know their weak points. Delia's were (in order)

7

fashion, boys, and sticky foods. She was a big fan of pudding.

"I actually had a revelation last night," Delia said, sounding for all the world like some yogi who'd spent the entire night meditating on the meaning of life.

"What kind of revelation?"

Delia was a fount of knowledge when it came to the opposite sex. If she'd had a boy-related revelation, it could very well affect the state of the world's dating circuit as a whole.

"Geeks." Delia shared her hard-won wisdom. I waited for her to elaborate, but she just sat there, smiling, thoroughly pleased with herself.

"Geeks?" I said finally.

Delia nodded, tucking a strand of chocolate-brown hair behind one ear. "Geeks," she confirmed.

I was overcome with the image of Delia meditating and chanting "Ommmmmmm," and then opening her eyes, having seen the light.

"Geeks." I said the word again, and Delia just smiled brightly.

Still not quite sure about her intended meaning, I pulled into the high school parking lot and drove down to the front, which was reserved for seniors, the exalted status my friends and I had finally achieved the month before. As I parked, Delia elaborated and allowed me another glimpse into enlightenment.

"Geeks," she said definitively, "are the new jock."

As I digested this piece of information and Delia and I climbed out of my car, an SUV flew past us and into the space next to ours. The driver didn't bother to slow the car until the instant it came to a complete and sudden stop.

"Zo's here," I announced needlessly. Delia snorted. Zo Porter had a need for speed that hadn't decreased since the days the three of us had spent riding our bikes around the neighborhood. Nowadays, Zo was a whirl-wind on the track and a thing to behold behind the wheel of a car.

"And you think *I'm* a bad driver," Delia said.

"You *are* a bad driver." Zo hopped out of the SUV and delivered the comeback at the same time. "I, on the other hand, am efficient."

"I think I can say with a high level of certainty that efficiency has never been so well and truly terrifying." Annabelle Porter was the fourth of our group, and the one of us subjected to Zo's "efficiency" most often since the two of them were first cousins and actually shared a car. "Nothing like a good brush with death to wake you up in the morning."

Zo ignored her cousin's sarcasm. "That's my motto."

"I thought your motto was *All sweatpants, all the time*," Delia said, tapping her chin thoughtfully and taking in Zo's current outfit with a knowing smile.

"Actually," Zo said, mimicking Delia's posture and tone exactly, "my motto is *bite me*."

There was a single-beat pause after that statement, and then I started laughing. Delia and Zo were in a con-stant state of argument, and they had been ever since the three of us were five years old. The absolute joy and affection with which the two of them exchanged barbs were as familiar to me as the ferocity with which they would demolish anyone outside our group who dared to do the same. Zo was fiercely protective, and Delia wielded more social power than the rest of us combined. Together, they were nearly combustible—and a force to be reckoned with.

"Speaking of mottos," I said, playing peacekeeper even though the two of them were as happy arguing as they were not, "Delia had a revelation last night."

"A revelation?" Zo was skeptical.

"Yes," Delia confirmed, deciding to enlighten them. "Geeks are the new jock."

Whatever Zo was expecting, it wasn't that. As for Annabelle, she simply blinked twice, took in the information, and processed it. In the years since the seventh grade, when Annabelle had first moved to town, I'd discovered that it was almost impossible to take her off guard. Of the four of us, A-belle was the sensible one, the reliable one, and the one most capable of going with the flow in her own uniquely Annabelle way.

Delia grinned at Annabelle's and Zo's reactions and continued lecturing with a solemnity that didn't match up with what she was saying at all. "Geeks are a virtually untapped subset of the male population, but if you think about it, they're really hot." Without pausing in her impromptu dissertation on geekitude, Delia reparted Annabelle's hair on the side instead of in the center and stepped back to appraise her work. "I mean, think about it, history is littered with hot geeks. Jason Mraz. Seth on *The OC* back before he got lame and the show got lamer. That one guy on *Beauty and the Geek*."

Delia's idea of "history" didn't exactly match up with the common definition of the word. Since she lived on the cutting edge of all things trendy, last year was "history" and three or more was practically ancient.

"Sarcastic," Delia continued decisively. "Soulful eyes. Mussy hair. Geeks are hot."

Delia, as befit her position as one of the most sought-after girls in the senior class, was a verifiable expert on hotness, and she had a slight tendency toward choosing boyfriends with the same trendsetter finesse with which she mercilessly designed each of our wardrobes.

"Let me get this straight." Zo's voice was absolutely devoid of inflection, but the look on her face was nothing short of incredulous. "You want a geeky boyfriend?"

"Geek is chic," Delia said. "And besides, it's different."

It was just like Delia to randomly decide to eschew A-list guys in favor of their comic-book-lovin' counterparts. It would be even more like Delia once the rest of the school decided that geek was definitely the way to go. I'd known Delia my entire life, and I still wasn't sure how she managed to put the It in It Girl without even trying.

It's the boobs. Zo offered a silent response to my question. She knew me well enough to know exactly what I was thinking, just by looking at the expression on my face. At any given moment, I could read her thoughts just as well.

Of course, the fact that I was actually psychic didn't hurt.

Delia's breasts have magical powers, Zo thought, knowing I would pick it up and smiling wickedly in my general direction. *If Queenie's ta-tas say that geeks are chic, then by next week, they will be. All hail the magic of her mighty C cup.*

I bit back a grin, not wanting to let on that Zo and I were having one of our by now infamous psychic conversations.

Delia, proving herself remarkably perceptive, was instantaneously suspicious of my grin stifling. "Are you guys having another silent conversation about my chest?" she demanded, placing her hands on her hips with characteristic dramatic flair.

"Ummmm . . . no?" I tried not to sound conspicuous and failed in a major way.

Zo fared slightly better. "Don't flatter yourself." She rolled her eyes and punctuated the movement with a poke to Delia's side.

"Translation," A-belle said wryly. "Yes. Bailey and Zo are indeed having another psychic boobies convo."

After a split second, the four of us started cracking up. Annabelle was the last person in the world anyone would have expected to utter a sentence involving the phrase *psychic boobies.* But somehow, she'd managed to say it with an absolutely straight face, as if *boobies* were a scientific term, right up there with *empirical* and *statistically significant.*

A group of freshman boys walked by and gave us some very strange looks. Well, technically, three of them gave us very strange looks, and the other two stared at Delia's cleavage, which just made me laugh harder.

"Come on," Annabelle said finally, recovering her composure before the rest of us did. "We're going to be late for class."

"You can tell us more about the geek thing at lunch," I told Delia.

"Only if the two of you promise to stop mind-talking about my boobs." Delia crossed her arms protectively over her chest.

"We promise," Zo and I chorused.

Delia's boobs. Delia's boobs. Delia's boobs. Zo sent me the silent message, and it was actually physically painful to bite back the laughter bubbling up in my chest.

"Oh. My. Gosh. You're doing it again!" Delia smacked Zo, who just kept laughing.

After a valiant effort at pretending we weren't, I finally let my giggles go, and as the four of us walked into the building and to our first hours, I couldn't help but wish that this moment and, more importantly, this year would last forever.

I so wasn't ready for high school to end.

Chapter 2

My first class was study hall, which just goes to show you how cruel life can be. The fact that the school required me to get up at 7 a.m. so that I could be there by 7:45 and sit around doing nothing for forty-five minutes was nothing short of sadistic. And the worst part of it was that I couldn't even complain about how unfair and cruel life was, because, well . . . I *was* life. Everything that happened in the world, every twist of Fate, that was me. My doing. My work.

So why exactly was it that I was stuck in study hall, instead of living it up in a mansion with a young Brad Pitt look-alike as my personal cabana boy? After two full years as the Third Fate, I'd come to accept my quandary. Technically speaking, I controlled the fate of the world, but in reality, *I* didn't control anything. Fate

Bailey and Real Bailey were like two separate people, and the second I crossed over to the Nexus and touched that metaphysical fabric, instinct and the power that ran in my veins took over. I couldn't consciously control what I wove. I just did it the way it had to be done. There was only one choice, only one dance meant for my hands each night. I didn't make up the movements.

They just came.

Hence me not having any cabana boys, any cleavage, or a date for the first dance of the year. Talk about déjà vu. Two years ago, before I'd ever heard of the Sidhe or paid any attention to Greek mythology, I'd been in more or less this exact same position. Then, a few days before the first dance of sophomore year, Annabelle, Delia, Zo, and I had gone to the mall, and unlike the other billion and one mall trips we'd made over the years, this one had changed everything, at least for a little while.

Absentmindedly, I reached for the small of my back, brushing my fingertips over the tattoo whose shape and appearance were forever burned into my mind: two crescent moons laid over a sunburst. The combination looked somehow simple, despite the intricate design. In a language that no living person today spoke, the symbol meant life. Separately, the moons and the sunburst had different meanings. The sun was a glyph that meant fire. The moonlike symbol was harder to define, but according to Annabelle's linguist (because of course A-belle had a linguist the way other seniors in high school had manicurists), it meant knowledge.

In practical terms, the tattoo was the mark of Life, the Third Fate. The symbols for fire and knowledge represented the powers that came with that position. Knowledge was the reason that Zo and I were able to have psychic boobies convos. I could hear people's thoughts and—if I really concentrated—make them hear mine. Occasionally, I could even control what other people were thinking, but I'd learned my lesson on that front. No more mind control for me. As for fire . . . well, let's just say that since I'd become the Third Fate, I'd had to keep my temper completely in check, because otherwise things had a tendency to get kind of heated. Literally.

"You have a tattoo?" The person in the chair behind me was apparently not studying any more than I was. Study hall was such a joke. "You don't seem like you'd have a tattoo."

I didn't know whether to take that as a compliment or an insult, so instead I just turned around, met the guy's eyes, and shrugged. Mr. Sits Behind Me in Study Hall didn't need to know that I hadn't exactly chosen to have this symbol permanently inked into my skin. Self-consciously, I tugged on the edge of my shirt, obscuring the tattoo from sight, and then turned back around.

Temporary.

The word echoed in my mind. Once upon a time (also known as two years ago), my friends and I had bought temporary tattoos at the mall, put them on, and acquired supernatural powers that we'd used to battle an evil fairy princess named Alecca. It was touch and go there for a little while, but ultimately we won, and as a result, I'd become the Third Fate. Eventually, my friends' tattoos (and their powers) had faded. Mine hadn't.

Temporary.

It was ironic. My tattoo wasn't supposed to last, but it did, and high school was supposed to last forever, but here it was, senior year. People were applying to colleges. My friends and I were thinking about our futures, and part of me couldn't deny the fact that after this year, the four of us might not be together. Annabelle was smart. Really, really smart, and lately she'd been talking about schools that didn't exist for me outside of *Gilmore Girls* reruns. Delia was daydreaming about New York City, and Zo and I were pretty much in denial about the whole thing.

Temporary.

Maybe that was just the way life was. The things that were supposed to last forever never did. Things were always changing. Every night, I wove, and life went on.

Bah.

"What's it of?"

"Huh?" I winced at the way the nonword sounded as it left my mouth. I wasn't exactly articulate in the morning. Or, you know, ever.

"Your tattoo. What is it?"

Was it me, or was the guy behind me inordinately interested in my tattoo? I turned around again to get a closer look at him, trying to remember his name and if we'd ever actually met. He didn't look all that familiar. He had mussy hair and a half-smile on his pale face. Thinking of what Delia had said that morning, I glanced at his eyes and wondered if they qualified as "soulful." If they did, I might just have found a new conquest for my geek-lovin' best friend.

"It's a symbol," I said, finally answering the boy's question. "It means stuff."

"Your tattoo is a symbol that means stuff," the boy repeated.

When he put it that way, it did sound kind of stupid, but I wasn't about to get into a discussion about what the symbol actually meant. I didn't want high school to end, but that didn't mean I wanted to get committed before I had a chance to graduate either. As a general rule, I was pretty sure that talking about destiny and my secret identity was a good way to get a one-way ticket to a room with padded walls. There were only three people (in *this* world, at least) who knew the truth about me, about my tattoo, and about what had happened two years before, and all three of them had been a part of it. They were with me when we defeated Alecca, and at the time, they'd had powers of their own.

Annabelle, Delia, and Zo knew the truth, and I had no desire to clue anyone else in. Not my parents, not my ex-boyfriend, and certainly not the guy who sat behind me in study hall (who may or may not have qualified as a chic geek).

Since I really didn't feel like talking any more about my tattoo or thinking any more about the fact that every day brought the end of the school year closer and closer, I did the unthinkable: I got out my physics book and started studying. This was a completely novel experience, and maybe not just for me. There was a decent chance that I was the first person to ever actually study in study hall at Oakridge High. I sort of expected the rest of the room to react, but nobody even noticed. They all just kept not studying in their own individual ways.

Friction is defined as—

Sidhe blue. Blood green.

The colors took over my mind, and I didn't get to see what the technical definition of friction actually was.

Sidhe blue. Blood green.

Not here, I thought, my body frozen to my seat with the force of what I was seeing. *Not now.* There was a time and a place for those colors, and study hall was not it. In fact, the entire high school was a Sidhe-free zone. That was how this worked. I was an average girl (maybe even a little *too* average) by day, and one of the Sidhe by night. Simple.

And that was when I heard the voices.

To you we call,
Our third of three.
Child of power
Who set us free.

Darn them. Did the phrase *public humiliation* mean nothing to the voices in my head?

Blood in your veins,
The barrier holds.
If balance wavers,
The bridge unfolds.

The horrible, unearthly beautiful voices sent a familiar shiver down my spine. I couldn't process the words, couldn't make my mind understand what they were saying because my body was focused entirely on the feel of their call in my blood. The words sat heavy and dormant in my mind, and I was quickly losing my grip on this reality.

We call you now
With earth and sea,
Air and fire,
So mote it be.

My blood pumped. My body throbbed. The world around me disappeared into inky blue nothingness, and then, I was gone.

I woke up in the Nexus, lying on the Seal. The etchings dug gently into my skin, cool on my lower back. My body sang, its connection to the stone beneath me strong. The Seal was my anchor here. Once upon a time, my blood had closed it, and now the power of the Seal brought me to the Nexus (which, by the way, was the supersmart Annabelle word for this Otherworldly place) every night to weave the web of life.

Lying on the Seal, I couldn't help but notice that it totally wasn't nighttime, and I so wasn't in the mood to work.

"What am I doing here? And what was with the whole 'we call you' spell thing?" I wrinkled my nose as I sat up. "In case you guys can't tell, this is me being not amused."

Immortal beings that they were, the man and woman who lived in this place were slightly less than intimidated by my Not Amused face.

"Welcome, Daughter," Valgius said, his deeply musical voice dishing out words specifically designed to remind me that in our cozy little threesome, they were the adults and, Seal or no Seal, I was the child.

"Bailey." Adea spoke my name softly, tempering the power of her voice and helping me to my feet. "This is your home as much as the mortal world is. You belong here, and you are needed."

Much like my earthly mother, Adea was a master of the guilt trip. Unlike my earthly mother, however, Adea was also a member of an ancient race of mystical beings whose world was magically separated from ours. The race itself had been called many things. To some, they were fairies. To the ancient Greeks, they'd been gods. To me, they were a royal pain in the tush.

Among themselves and a small number of humans, they were known as the Sidhe.

And each night, as the Third Fate, I was one of them: the only human-Sidhe hybrid in the history of either world. It was complicated and complex and a wee bit mind boggling, but basically, Adea and Valgius were my million-times-great-grandparents, and the whole Tattoo Escapade of Sophomore Year had awakened Sidhe blood that had been dormant in my family for centuries.

Hence my double life, which now apparently included

21

hearing voices, passing out in study hall, and waking up here.

"Bailey, child, are you listening?"

Eeep! I totally hadn't been, and if my nightly visits to this mystical place had taught me anything, it was that Adea and Valgius really didn't like being ignored.

"So," I said, offering them a weak smile, "what's up? Is there some fate that desperately needs fate-ing?"

I couldn't think of any other reason that they would have brought me here. The last time they'd summoned me like this had been during the whole Alecca fiasco. Since then, I'd only come to the Nexus at nighttime, to weave as part of our otherworldly trio, different facets of the same whole. Birth. Life. Death. Valgius. Me. Adea.

"Fate-ing can wait until tonight," Adea said, brushing my hair out of my face in a motion disturbingly similar to the one used by my mother, the founding member of the Bailey, Get Your Hair Out of Your Face Club. "Now we must talk about your Reckoning."

I recognized the tone of her voice and could only conclude that this did not bode well for me. Adea said "Reckoning" the way most adults said "college." In the past couple of years, I'd become an expert at spotting a "let's discuss your future" talk a mile off. I was also an expert at avoiding them. Unfortunately, my tried-and-true techniques for distracting my own parents probably wouldn't work on Adea and Val.

"Reckoning?" I repeated, overcome with the feeling that this would not end well.

Valgius smiled at my horrified expression. "Your

introduction," he clarified. "To the others and to the realm that lies beyond this place."

"What others?" I asked, my mouth dry with the implications of his words. "What realm?"

"The others," Adea said simply. "Those who dwell in the realm beyond. Those like us."

"Oh yeah," I said, trying not to audibly gulp. "Them."

I'd always known, at least logically, that there were more Sidhe than just Adea, Valgius, and me and that there was another world beyond the Nexus, connected to earth by what the three of us did each night. There was a big difference, however, between knowing something in a "yeah, that makes sense and sounds vaguely familiar" kind of way and in the way that involves actual thinking. It had never occurred to me—not even once—that I might have to meet these so-called others or go to their world.

Adea put two cool fingertips under my chin, lifting it so my eyes met hers. "You've been one of us for years, Bailey, and the equinox marks the second anniversary of your union with the Seal. You grow stronger every day, and your strength calls to the others. We must bring you to them, or they will—"

"Mabon is two days away, Bailey," Valgius said, swiftly interrupting his counterpart's words and leaving me to wonder what exactly Adea had intended to say.

Mabon, I thought, the word and its meaning taking up my entire brain. Mabon, the fall equinox, the day I'd destroyed Alecca and taken her place as the Third Fate.

"Mabon is a day of power, Bailey." Adea cut gently into my thoughts. "In the Otherworld, as on Earth, that means something. We can't shield you from what lies beyond this place forever. The beyond is your heritage, and those that dwell there are your blood. For better or worse, the three of us tie your world to theirs."

An odd look came over Adea's face then, as if the words she was about to speak didn't quite fit in her mouth. As if they weren't even hers.

"Such ties are fragile left unguarded, and with their fragility, your life."

Cryptic, *I thought*, thy name is Adea.

"And besides," Adea said, her voice more her own, though the cheerfulness seemed forced. "It'll be good for you to meet the other younglings. There are things about who you are and who you are to become that your mortal friends could never understand."

Clearly, Adea had never met my *friends*. Magical craziness didn't faze them in the least.

"Speaking of friends," I said, "they're waiting for me. Back on Earth. You know, that place where I'm supposed to be right now?"

That wasn't strictly true, but close enough. Delia, A-belle, and Zo were at school, even if they weren't in study hall and didn't know I'd left Earth for the Nexus.

"Can I go back now?" There was a slight chance I was whining, but I couldn't help it. Passing out has a way of causing a scene, and I didn't exactly want to wake up to see the entire class crowded around me.

Valgius sighed. "Go," he said, playing the mystical dad role to perfection. "Return to your earthly hall of study, but remember, tonight the Reckoning begins."

*   *   *

I woke up in a puddle of my own drool, my face pressed into my physics book. *Uggggggggg*. I sat up slowly, allowing everything to fall back into focus, and as I looked around the room, I realized that nobody had even noticed I was unconscious. I'd passed out on my physics book, and everyone around me, including the possibly chic geek, had been so wrapped up in not studying that they hadn't even noticed.

I wasn't sure whether to be grateful or insulted. The bell rang before I could fully decide between the two. As I gathered my books and walked out of the room, Geek Boy followed in my wake. "Hey," he called, hurrying to catch up.

"Yes?" I said, wondering why he'd chosen this day to talk to me when—in all likelihood—we'd been in study hall together for over a month.

"You know that symbol? Your tattoo?"

I nodded, even though the tattoo was the last thing I wanted to talk or think about right now.

"I thought . . . well . . . I just . . ." He struggled to figure out what he wanted to say. "I think it means life," he said, saying the words so quickly that they blurred together. "I just thought you should know."

My mouth literally dropped open, and I stood there, gawking at him. Geek Boy, the amateur linguist, had definitely just been upgraded to Geek Chic.

Chapter 3

"He recognized the symbol? Even Lionel didn't recognize it straightaway, and he's at the forefront of the field. The kind of archeolinguistic knowledge necessary to spontaneously translate something like that is just . . . wow." Annabelle was, to say the least, impressed.

Delia, on the other hand, was intrigued. "Now, when you say he had mussy hair, do you mean mussy like 'I don't know what a comb means,' or mussy like 'adorably tousled'?"

"I don't know," I said. "Maybe a little bit of each?" Then I turned to A-belle. "So it *is* a big deal that he knew what my tattoo meant, right? I'm not just imagining this. It's actually freaky?"

"It's amazing" Annabelle said.

"Personally," Delia put in, "I like to think of it as *hot*."

Zo had been remarkably quiet throughout our conversation, so I glanced at her, allowing her to weigh in on the topic.

"Are you going to finish those?" she asked, nodding toward my chili cheese fries.

For reasons I'd never fully understood, teeny tiny Zo, who didn't stand an inch over five foot, had the appetite of a three-hundred-pound linebacker and the metabolism of an underweight hummingbird. When it came to food, she was as single-minded as Delia was about fashion.

"The fries are all yours," I said, pushing them toward her. Normally, I relished the fact that seniors were allowed off campus for lunch, but today, sustenance didn't rank nearly as high on my list of priorities as the guy from study hall, or the fact that I was mere hours away from being Reckoned.

"You should ask him how he's familiar with the symbol's meaning," Annabelle told me.

"No," Delia corrected. "You should ask him if he has a girlfriend."

"Mmmshhhwammmpppp," Zo said, through a mouthful of chili fries.

"You guys don't think he, like, knows anything, do you?" Because we were in public (aka the mall food court), I kept my words vague. Saying stuff like, "You don't think he knows that I'm not entirely human, do you?" was just asking for trouble, especially since the mall and the high school were just a mile apart, making the food court the single most popular lunchtime destination for Oakridge seniors.

27

"He knows archaic languages," Annabelle said. "That's all." There was something in her tone that made me take a closer look at her face. Sensing my scrutiny, A-belle ducked her head and blushed.

OMG. This is a turn-on for you, isn't it? I kept the question silent to avoid embarrassing A-belle in front of the others.

Mayhaps, came the slightly abashed reply.

Annabelle Elisabeth Porter—you think linguists are hot!

Annabelle glared at me. *Shut up.*

Don't tell me you have a crush on Lionel. . . .

"Bailey," Annabelle yelped out loud. "Eww!"

"Do we want to know?" Delia asked.

Annabelle and I looked at each other. "Probably not," we answered together. Lionel, a linguist who worked with Annabelle's mother at the local college, was eighty-some years old and had a great deal of affection for his "Annie." Just not *that* kind of affection. I hoped.

Mmmmmmmmmm . . . chili.

I rolled my eyes at the stray Zo thought that entered my mind, and concentrated on turning my abilities off. At first, hearing thoughts, especially my friends' thoughts, had been as natural as hearing words, and I hadn't been able to control it at all, but it didn't take me long to realize that in high school, you never want to know what everyone else is thinking. For one thing it's too noisy, and for another, sometimes you hear the guy you like, the guy who's supposed to like you,

28

thinking about other girls. And sometimes you hear those other girls thinking things about you that make your stomach hurt.

Long story.

Luckily, the more time I spent with Adea and Valgius, the more control I gained over my powers. Unlike A-belle, who'd had this particular ability during our tattoo adventure, I could keep my will from bleeding over onto others, and as a general rule, I steered away from pulling mind melds. As my control had developed, I'd become able to focus the ability, to hear an individual's thoughts, or a group's, or nobody's at all. Figuring out how to make other people hear my thoughts had come last, halfway through junior year.

"Don't you ever think about anything but food?" I asked Zo.

She held a french fry in the air, poised for a fight. "You know how much I'd hate to waste this fry," she said, "but if you tempt me, make no mistake: I will throw it at you."

I stuck my tongue out at her. "Make my day."

Thirty seconds and one very brief food fight later, Zo and I were both a little worse for wear, Delia was shaking her head morosely, and Annabelle had an almost-smirk on her face because she'd managed to survive completely unscathed, despite the fact that she'd thrown a crumpled napkin at me in retaliation for the Lionel comment.

"I swear, you two," Delia chided Zo and me.

I pointed a finger at Annabelle. "She did it, too."

Annabelle sat there, looking angelically solemn, her best "who, me?" expression on her face.

"How many times do I have to tell you guys," Delia continued, "French fries are *not* accessories."

Because I could sense a conversation on what *did* count as an accessory coming our way, I changed the subject back to the guy from study hall. "So we've concluded that this guy has some major linguistics chops and that his hair may or may not be the good kind of mussy. You three have any other words of wisdom for me?"

Delia leaned forward, her expression earnest and intense. "If you had to rate him on a one-to-ten scale for self-deprecating sarcasm, what would he be?"

Zo narrowed her eyes at Annabelle. "You have got to stop teaching Delia words like *self-deprecating*."

Without missing a beat, Delia and A-belle looked at each other and then both launched pieces of their lunch at Zo.

Number of food fights this lunch period: two.

Number of people at nearby tables who were giving the four of us sketched-out looks: seven.

Number of food objects Zo caught and subsequently ate with little or no ado: both of them.

"I'm going to miss you guys so much next year." The words were out of my mouth before I could stop them, and the others groaned.

"No moping." The three of them spoke in perfect unison. We were only a month into senior year, and already my friends had made up a No Moping rule for me—no moping about ex-boyfriends, no moping about the fact that I didn't have a cabana boy, and especially no moping about the fact that life as we knew it was eight months away from over.

The punishment for moping varied, but based on the maniacal glint in Zo's eyes and the fact that I'd psychically teased Annabelle once already this lunch period, I could sense a tickling of epic proportions coming my way.

"No moping," I agreed quickly. "I just love you guys."

"Awwwwwwww," they chorused, but Zo wasn't looking any less evil.

"You're going to torture me no matter what I say now, aren't you?" I tried to resign myself to this fate.

"Yup."

"Totally."

"Indeed."

"Ack!" That last one was me as Zo started their collective tickling onslaught. Two minutes later, they finally decided I'd had enough.

"You're sadists," I said. "All of you. I see pop quizzes and awkward blind dates in your future."

Since they knew as much about my visits to the Nexus as I did, they took my threats somewhat less than seriously. After all, if I'd actually been able to change their fates—or mine—we wouldn't have needed a No Moping rule in the first place.

"So," Delia said, content to change the subject now that I'd paid for my moping crimes, "anybody else have a geek sighting to report?"

Zo glanced pointedly at Annabelle.

"Oh, you," Annabelle replied with a faux chuckle. "That's one of those witty insult things, isn't it?"

Delia let out an exasperated sigh. "Focus, people. Annabelle isn't a geek, and more important, she isn't male."

"Thanks," A-belle said. "I think."

"So far we have Cryptic Geek Guy," Delia continued, "and I've identified a possible Musician Geek Guy in my math class, as well as a geek of unknown categorization who looks exactly like that guy from that one show."

Specificity wasn't Delia's strong suit.

"That's three geeks, and there's four of us, so we need at least one more."

"How egalitarian of you," Annabelle said, a wry smile playing across her lips.

"You know, Queenie, this is going to be really hard, but I think I can do without my own geek." Zo did her very best to look self-sacrificing.

Delia snorted. "Nice try."

It would have taken a braver person than me to tell Delia that she couldn't just assign each of us a personal geek the way we sometimes let her play dictator with our wardrobes. As far as I'd been able to tell, the boy in study hall wasn't interested in me at all. He'd just been interested in my tattoo.

And that led me back to the thoughts that I'd been dwelling on all morning. Who was this kid? Why hadn't I ever seen him before? Our school was big, and I wasn't exactly observant, but shouldn't I have noticed him at some point over the past four years? And how in the world had he recognized the symbol? Oakridge High didn't even offer Latin, let alone more esoteric dead languages.

And yet . . .

If there was one thing I'd learned from being the Third Fate, it was that there was no such thing as coincidence. The pattern was what it was, and everything happened for a reason.

"You think we have time to run by Escape before fifth period?"

Zo groaned at Delia's question. Shopping wasn't Zo's cup of tea any more than chili cheese fries were Delia's. I glanced down at my watch. "Maybe," I said, offering Zo an apologetic smile.

Et tu, Bailey? came the silent remonstration.

"We've got seven, seven and a half minutes tops before we need to leave." Annabelle provided a more definitive answer. "Escape is a two-minute walk, so you wouldn't really have time to look at anything. . . ."

Delia was not deterred in the least. "Sold!"

We bused our trays, and the rest of us followed Delia, whose mall sense of direction was so honed that she could have made it to Escape blindfolded. We were halfway there when, all of a sudden, I felt a familiar tingle at the back of my neck.

Sidhe.

The feeling caught me totally and completely off guard. It was subtle, the kind of thing you might not notice if you hadn't felt it before, but I couldn't ignore it. It was a feeling of sameness, of innate recognition. It was the kind of feeling you get when you meet some-one's eyes and, for a split second, you know that they're thinking the exact same thing you are.

It was a feeling I'd only had in this world once be-fore. At this mall. The day we'd bought the tattoos.

"OMG."

"Delia, if we stop anywhere else, we won't even make it to Escape."

"No, A-belle, like seriously—OMG. Look."

There, directly in front of us, was a small kiosk filled with accessories.

"Is that . . . ?" Zo trailed off.

"Morgan." I said the name softly, my eyes meeting hers across the room. She had bicolored hair and un-earthly blue eyes the exact same crystalline shade as Adea's. Two years ago, this woman had sold us the tat-toos that had changed our lives, then unceremoniously disappeared. She was Sidhe, one of the oldest, and she was here.

Again.

I stood there, frozen, even as my own thoughts came back to haunt me. There was no such thing as co-incidence, and if Morgan was here, this whole Reckon-ing thing was much, much bigger than Adea and Valgius had led me to believe.

Of the four of us, Annabelle was the only one who didn't go into some state of shock. Instead she just calmly appraised the situation, taking in every last detail and, more likely than not, attempting to categorize it and commit it all to memory. Zo, Delia, and I were momentarily silent, each of us staring at the familiar face.

"Hello, girls." Morgan's voice was hypnotically musical. That, more than anything, identified her as something greater than she appeared.

"Hello." Annabelle's voice was soft, respectful but cautious, as she returned Morgan's greeting. Zo didn't bother with pleasantries and instead just grunted. As for Delia, she completely recovered from her shock, and the shopping genes that dominated her DNA took over. "So what do you have for us this time? Because personally, I've been looking for some kind of locket. Preferably a very classic style, but with some small, modern twist. And if it could give me my transmogrification back, that would be awesome."

"Hello, Bailey." Morgan somehow managed to say those words without seeming like she was ignoring Delia altogether.

As hard as I tried, I couldn't quite bring myself to respond. This was crazy. Morgan. Here. She was Sidhe. She was Poseidon, Neptune, *whatever*, and she was here. First Adea and Val put the whammy on me during study hall, and now Morgan reappeared after a two-year absence, with nothing more to say than "Hello, Bailey." And the crazy just kept on coming.

Morgan reached out and put her fingertips beneath my chin, lifting it up and angling my eyes toward hers. "You've grown up."

Somehow, I didn't think that one of the oldest and most powerful Sidhe in either world had come to the mortal realm to channel my aunt Margie and her trade-mark "Bailey Marie, look how you've grown!"

Zo, sensing that I wasn't exactly jumping for joy at this turn of events, took a step forward and narrowed her eyes at Morgan, the implication clear. Zo had no powers, and Morgan was probably the most powerful being any of us had ever met, but Zo wasn't about to shy away from kicking some fairy butt if she thought she could protect me by doing so.

"I wanted to see you," Morgan told me, ignoring Zo as easily as she had Delia, "before you met the Others."

"To warn me?" I couldn't help the question.

"No." Morgan's voice was high and clear, so pure that it almost hurt to listen to it, but at least this time I was able to resist the thrall of her unearthly blue eyes. "To give you something."

The last time Morgan had "given" me something, I'd wound up with a tattoo on my back and the world's most unusual part-time job.

"You may be Adea and Valgius's blood, Bailey, but don't forget who it was that brought that blood to this world. I watched your family for centuries, waiting. You carry my name."

Was it weird that it had never occurred to me that my last name was her first? It was right there, plain as day. Bailey Morgan.

Seriously, though, I was already dealing with an übermother, an earthly father, two mystical parental types, and three best friends who wouldn't let me mope, even when a good moping was really and truly called for. I didn't exactly have a lack of guidance in my life, and the last thing I needed was a fairy godmother.

"So." Delia tried a second time to get Morgan's attention. "Got any hoop earrings?"

If Morgan heard Delia, she didn't give any indication of it, which was an even bigger clue to her nature than the voice or the eyes, because there wasn't a human being alive who could resist, let alone ignore, Delia Cameron.

"I have something for you."

It would have been so easy to allow the sound of her voice to overwhelm me, but I nibbled on my bottom lip, trying not to give in to the depth of her tone.

"I don't give gifts lightly, Bailey," she continued. "Things are changing, and they will continue to do so whether you consent to the changes or not. It's only natural that you'd be thrown off balance."

Was she *trying* to make me mope?

"Take these." Morgan held out four chains, each with a single pendant on the end. The four pendants were identical, tiny circular mirrors surrounded by a thin ring of metal.

"Not exactly what I had in mind . . ." Delia mused.

"What do they do?" Zo phrased the question bluntly. "Because if these things do something, I want the one that does something cool."

Two years post-tattoos, Zo was still complaining about how everyone else had gotten a cool power, while she'd been stuck with something as passive as premonition.

"Bailey." Annabelle said my name. "She's waiting for you to take them."

Part of me wanted to say no to the gift. The other part of me realized that was stupid. If it hadn't been for Morgan and the tattoos, Alecca would have destroyed the world, and we wouldn't have been able to stop her. As far as fairy godmother types went, Morgan had already proven her bibbidi-bobbidi-boo chops. At the same time, taking the necklaces felt like saying yes to something, like if I took them, I was giving the world/my destiny/whatever permission to change.

You don't have to take them if you don't want to.

Zo's thoughts penetrated my shields. I could keep the rest of the world out, but my friends' thoughts had a way of sneaking past the barriers, even when I wasn't listening for them. Something about Zo telling me that it was okay to say no to Morgan's offer gave me the last push I needed to say yes. Things were changing, and this time, I was going to be ready.

I expected images to flash through my mind when my hand closed around the chains, but instead I was rewarded with a single moment of pure, peaceful nothingness. No worries. No thoughts. Silence.

"Wear them," Morgan said, her musical tone never changing. "Always."

With shaky hands, I turned to the others and held out the necklaces. One by one, my friends took them until each of us was holding one. Silently, we undid the clasps, and then we stood there, staring at one another. Their thoughts came into my mind without words, and as I clasped the necklace firmly around my neck, I knew that whatever happened, there wasn't a force in either realm that could tear my friends from my side. They put on their necklaces, willingly accepting whatever risk came along with entering the magical world once more.

As we stood there, Delia verbalized what we were all thinking, in her own uniquely Delia way. "One for all, and all for accessories."

Zo snorted.

Annabelle smirked.

I smiled.

And Morgan disappeared.

Chapter 4

"I can't believe she just disappeared," I grumbled as the four of us headed back to the food court en route to my car. "I mean, who does that? Seriously, who lays in wait for someone at the mall, tells them stuff that makes absolutely no sense, thrusts jewelry into their hands, and then disappears?"

"I like her," Delia said decisively. "And if you're actually complaining about free jewelry, I may have to disown you as a friend. At the very least, there's going to be some kind of intervention."

Zo shuddered. As the recipient of more than one fashion intervention over the past few years, she recognized the validity of Delia's threat.

"It's not that I mind the necklaces," I amended quickly. "It's just . . ."

That I didn't like what these gifts represented? That I hated that Morgan had come right out and told me things were changing and there was nothing I could do to stop it? That I was starting to suspect that the chance of death involved with being Reckoned might actually be a nonzero number?

"It's unsettling," Annabelle said, vocalizing what I could not. "Not the jewelry per se," she amended quickly, lest she incur Delia's wrath, "but that the very idea of Bailey meeting the other Sidhe seems to have provoked a visit from Morgan."

"What about the fact that we have no idea what these suckers do?" Zo offered, hooking her pinkie through the chain around her neck. "If that isn't disturbing, I don't know what is."

"Argyle socks with plaid minis?" Delia suggested, straightening her own necklace so that the pendant was dead center, just above the neckline of her low-cut top.

The conversation continued as we walked toward the food court, but I found myself falling uncharacteristically quiet. We'd all spent so much time together over the past few years—heck, over the course of our lifetimes—that my friends were very good at reading me, but somehow none of them had caught on to what bothered me the most about Morgan's words, and these gifts.

It wasn't the nonzero chance of death.

It wasn't the fact that *cryptic* and *Sidhe* were practically synonymous.

It wasn't even that Morgan had very conveniently

neglected to give us so much as a smidgen of an idea about what the necklaces were for and why we would need them.

The thing I just couldn't get past was that Morgan had looked me in the eye and confirmed the fear that had been nibbling away at me since the last day of junior year. Things were changing, whether I wanted them to or not. And as Delia, Annabelle, and Zo discussed the myriad of potentially disconcerting aspects of our encounter with "the other side," I just kept thinking that the next time something like this happened—if there was a next time—there might not be four necklaces or four tattoos or—I don't know—four enchanted nose rings. If Morgan came back a year from now or two or five, she might come bearing one gift. Just one.

"We'll figure the necklaces out," I said, confident of that, if nothing else. "That's what we do. We figure things out."

Delia beamed. "One for all, and all for—"

"Milkshakes!" Zo interrupted Delia's proclamation, and when Annabelle started snickering, I let myself join her and forced the paranoid depresso–Bailey part of my brain back into hibernation. Yes, we were seniors. Yes, we'd be going out into the big bad world soon. No, I didn't even want to think about what it would be like to get a one-on-one visit from Morgan, and no, I wasn't going to pay any attention to her "things are changing" speech.

Instead, I turned my attention to Zo's request for a milkshake. "Sorry," I told her, "but we don't have time. As it is, we'll probably be late getting back to school."

"Unless, of course, these necklaces hold the secret to time travel," Zo said, wiggling her eyebrows and making dramatic *dum dum DUM* sounds under her breath. Beside me, Annabelle seemed to be seriously considering Zo's tongue-in-cheek suggestion about time travel, but Delia waved it away with a flick of one hand. "If there were time travel involved, Morgan would have given us watches."

None of us dared to challenge Delia's logic on that one, so we opted for hurrying through the food court and out to the parking lot as quickly as we could. We'd have to hit every light on the way back to avoid being late, and sadly, most of our teachers didn't see seniority (or conversations with ancient beings of power) as an excuse for tardiness. Go figure.

As the car came into sight, I began digging for my keys. Out of the corner of my eye, I saw Delia slide her sunglasses from the top of her head to the bridge of her nose, and my brain latched onto her movement, processing in slow motion as the glasses cast a fleeting shadow that slithered across her face and disappeared into her smooth skin a moment later.

I turned to look more closely at Delia's face, but in doing so, I stopped watching where I was going. When you're as much of a walking· disaster as I am, that is never, ever a good thing.

"Oamph!"

Annabelle may have been the linguistic prodigy, but I was without question the one who excelled at making up nonsense words and sound effects to punctuate my dismay at—for instance—falling over a giant pile of

43

gravel that came out of nowhere for the sole purpose of tripping me. I hurtled face-first toward the ground, but Zo—her reflexes fueled by the vast number of calories she'd just consumed—managed to catch me before I went completely splat.

"Thanks," I said.

Zo shrugged. "No problemo."

I was overcome with a sense of déjà vu, because the two of us had definitely had this exact exchange on multiple previous occurrences. Trying and failing miserably to look inconspicuous, I took a deep breath and concentrated on getting the instinctual postfall embarrassment under control. Being a fire starter meant that burning cheeks had the potential to lead to actual sparkage, and the last thing I wanted was to draw any more attention to my tragic lack of grace.

Unfortunately, even as I managed to clamp down on my pyrokinesis, I couldn't shake the feeling that my little performance hadn't gone unnoticed. Someone was watching me. I was sure of it. A wave of mortification at being gawked at by the entire senior class washed over my body, until I had convinced myself that there really wasn't anyone in this town who *hadn't* seen me flailing around like an infant octopus with too much energy and not nearly enough coordination. I worked up the courage to glance around, but found that aside from the four of us, the parking lot was eerily empty.

Mark the calendars, I thought. *This may be the first time I've made a fool of myself and not run into the Ex-Boyfriend Who Shall Not Be Named immediately thereafter.* Still, I couldn't shake the sense that someone, somewhere was watching.

Not quite trusting my senses, I spared a single glare for the gravel I'd tripped over, but didn't dwell on it or the imaginary heat of someone else's eyes on my body. Instead, I went back to looking for my keys and resolved to keep my paranoia to myself.

"Found them!" I punctuated my words by jingling the keys.

"If you'd carry that Kate Spade tote I got you, you wouldn't have to dig for them," Delia scolded. "There's a side pocket, perfect for keys, compacts, and—"

I climbed into the driver's seat and didn't get to hear the rest of Delia's lecture, but whatever she said, it must have started with a *c* sound, because the first thing Annabelle said as she buckled herself into the backseat was, "Impressive alliteration."

Delia unceremoniously claimed shotgun for herself and then turned to smile at A-belle. "I try."

"Well, Queenie, got any alliterative ideas about what these necklaces do?" Zo asked. Of all my friends, Zo could be the most single-minded, which, given Delia's consistently one-track mind, was really saying something. Once Zo got the bit in her mouth on something, she didn't let go until the answer was found and the problem solved. Zo didn't like mysteries, which made me wonder why exactly she hadn't set her mind to solving the Big Problem (also known as "graduation," "college," and "future, the").

"These pieces are simple, but definitely funkier than

anything Morgan gave us before," Delia mused. "Circular, which is totally classic, but the mirror adds a touch of self-reflection, for that postmodern you-are-what-you-wear kind of feel."

"Forget I asked," Zo said, having neglected to abide by her own cardinal rule: never get Delia started talking about clothes, pudding, or boys.

"The four necklaces are identical," Annabelle added, curtailing Delia's dissertation on the stylistic attributes of our newest possessions. "Maybe they connect us to each other somehow?"

"Little round walkie-talkies?" Zo asked.

"Seriously, Zo, what is with you and walkie-talkies?" Delia rolled her eyes. "You're obsessed with them!"

Zo immediately shot back, "First of all, that was before we had cell phones, and second, we were seven."

Annabelle—who had no idea what the two of them were referring to, since she'd been living abroad at the time—continued musing aloud about the possibilities the four of us were currently wearing around our necks. "I was thinking more along the lines of a psychic connection," she said.

Been there. I broadcast the thought to all three of my friends. *Done that.*

"But they could connect us in some other way," Delia said. "I mean, maybe they meld our emotions together or something. Or oooohhhhhh, maybe these things will let us go with Bailey to do her fancy Nexus whatsits."

That was a thought. A surprisingly good one, actually.

Meeting the other Sidhe would be a lot less intimidating with my friends to back me up. What if these necklaces would bring their spirits to the Nexus along with mine? What if I didn't have to face the Reckoning alone?

What if splitting up didn't really have to mean splitting up?

The more I thought about the idea, the more I liked it, but at the same time, part of me couldn't imagine Morgan telling me I couldn't stop things from changing and then giving me a magic necklace that helped me keep the important things exactly the same. Maybe it was because she was an adult and I'd gotten into the habit of thinking of them as the enemy in the Bailey Versus the Future campaign, but . . .

I groaned—loudly and for a long time—as I remembered something that I'd managed to put out of my mind all morning.

"What?" the other three asked at once.

"I have a meeting," I said. "Right after lunch, with Mr. McMann."

"Told you we should have stopped for milkshakes." Zo reached over from the backseat to poke me triumphantly in the shoulder.

I half-expected Delia to repeat her request for me to ask Mr. McMann what his opinion was on layering my hair, but she proved to be otherwise occupied.

"Satin scoop-neck top, preferably in blue," I heard her whisper. "Pink Juicy sweatpants. Tiffany earrings."

"What are you doing?" I asked her, stopping at a

red light that I would have run before I'd remembered my meeting.

"Nothing," Delia said completely unconvincingly, and then she mumbled something else under her breath.

"What did you just say?" Zo asked.

Delia sighed. *"BabyblueLouisVuittonearmuffs,"* she said, rushing the words out so fast they blurred together.

"What?" Annabelle, Zo, and I repeated.

"I said 'Baby blue Louis Vuitton earmuffs,' " Delia repeated, and I noticed that she was holding a straw wrapper in one hand and waving her other hand above it.

"Hate to break it to you, Dee," Zo said, "but those aren't earmuffs."

"Well, they aren't earmuffs *yet*," Delia admitted, "but you never know. I mean, they could be, if . . ."

"If these necklaces gave you guys back your powers," I said, finally understanding why Delia had suddenly developed a tic that involved talking to the trash in my car. Sophomore year, her tattoo had given her the power to turn one object into another, just by concentrating on what she wanted it to be. Budding fashionista that she was, those three days had quite possibly been the best (and best-dressed) of Delia's life so far.

"It's not working," Zo said. "Is it?"

The edges of my lips turned up at the wary tone in her voice. Transmogrification had allowed Delia to perform makeovers of fantastic proportions without so much as breaking a sweat. From Zo's perspective (and mine, for that matter), this wasn't necessarily a good thing.

"It's not working," Delia confirmed with a melo-dramatic sigh. "But hey, a girl can dream."

"Nightmare," Zo coughed into her hands.

"Fashion disaster," Delia coughed back.

"And proud of it." Zo ditched the coughing and spoke the words plainly.

Annabelle ignored the familiar squabbling alto-gether, talking over them. "You know, we may want to look into the traditional role that jewelry plays in a variety of ancient cultures. Taking into consideration the fact that the tattoos had their basis in languages throughout the world, there's a chance that Morgan has again molded her gifts after something from this world and that the answer to all of our questions lies in history, archaeology, mythology, or . . ."

Annabelle stopped to take a breath, and I stared at her in the rearview mirror. Forget what I said about Zo being the most single-minded. When it came to ques-tions and answers, Annabelle, who'd been raised in aca-demia and was pretty much an expert herself, definitely had the rest of us beat.

"I know that look," Zo said, switching her attention from Delia to A-belle. "That look means trouble."

"Trouble?" Annabelle asked, her tone way, way too innocent.

"Trouble," Zo confirmed. "I know the way your twisted little mind works." Her words took on an accu-satory tone. "Admit it, the second you get back to school, you're going to start making graphs."

I had no idea what exactly Annabelle would graph, given that the grand total of what we knew right now was not much, but I was pretty sure that Zo was right. Annabelle had Graph Face, and that meant that whatever Morgan had set in motion by giving us these necklaces had well and truly begun.

After all, it wasn't an adventure until A-belle broke out the graphs.

Chapter 5

"So, Bailey, have you given any more thought to your future?"

There was only one right answer to that question. It wasn't "Why, no, Mr. McMann, I haven't," and it wasn't "In the future, I hope not to be killed by fairies."

"Sort of," I said. Since the right answer was "yes," Mr. McMann gave me an encouraging smile, hoping to prod me into saying what he wanted to hear.

"I know I'm going to college." That much really wasn't up for debate. School and I got along pretty well (excepting study hall), and I definitely wasn't ready to brave the real world yet. Besides which, I was somewhat attached to my life, and if I'd even thought the words *no college* in my mother's presence, she would have killed me.

"That's good, Bailey. Very good!" Mr. McMann was all about the positive encouragement. I wasn't entirely convinced that he actually knew anything about the college application process, but the man definitely knew upbeat like the back of his own disturbingly hairy hands.

"So have you thought any more about where you'd like to go?" Mr. McMann asked in the chummiest of voices. "With your scores, you'll have *options*." To punctuate his point, he pumped his fist victoriously in the air.

From the way he was acting, you would have thought I was headed for valedictorian, but the guidance counselor and I both knew that I had pretty good scores and pretty good grades, just like I had pretty good hair (minus the color) and a pretty good body (minus the cleavage, or lack thereof). I was smart, but compared to other smart people, I was average. I wasn't unfortunate-looking, but when it came to looks, I fell closer to cute than pretty. I wasn't all that athletic, I didn't do student council, and though most of my teachers liked me well enough, I didn't inspire fist pumping in anybody but Mr. McMann, and five years from now, even he probably wouldn't remember me.

Still, I had *options*. Of course, it would have been easier if I didn't, because if you only have one choice, you can't possibly make the wrong one.

"Bailey?" Mr. McMann prompted, goofy smile still fixed to his face.

"I'm not sure," I said. "I guess I wouldn't mind going to school close by."

When I'd pictured college, I'd always pictured Delia, Zo, Annabelle, and me hanging out in dorm rooms and eating pizza at midnight. The realistic part of me knew that college wasn't one giant sleepover, but when I tried to imagine something else, all I could see in my mind's eye was a giant white screen, glaringly blank.

"I guess I wouldn't mind going farther away either." A new city could be fun. Or, you know, terrifying.

"Well, that's certainly a start," Mr. McMann said. I stared at him incredulously. I'd officially narrowed it down to colleges that were either close or farther away. If that was a start, then I didn't want to know what absolute stagnation looked like.

In abject fear of another fist pump, I continued talking. "I'm not really sure what I want to major in."

"Nobody knows!" Mr. McMann was practically singing, but I didn't believe a word of his impromptu song. Delia wanted to major in business, with a minor in fashion design. Annabelle was going to double in classical languages and literature and archaeology. Zo, in the greatest irony of all time, was leaning toward nutrition.

Sure, Mr. M, I thought. *Nobody knows.* He made college sound like one of the great unsolved mysteries of our time.

"Would you rather go to a big college or a small college?" Mr. McMann asked in a tone that would have been more appropriate for saying "oohhhhh, ahhhhhh" than for the words he actually uttered.

"Medium-sized?"

"Now we're getting somewhere!"

Now I was just guessing.

We went back and forth like that for another ten minutes, and the entire time, I couldn't decide which freaked me out more, talking about my future with the one-man pep squad, or trying to prepare myself for whatever it was that had Morgan thinking that I'd need extra help. Absentmindedly, I played with the chain around my neck until my fingers came to the pendant. I toyed with it while Mr. McMann asked me how I felt about all-girls schools. I tried to phrase my answer diplomatically, and ran my thumb over the edges of the charm.

"I'm not sure about an all-girls sch—*yeeoowwww!*"

Mr. McMann blinked several times, shocked at my outburst and momentarily speechless.

"Sorry," I said. "My thumb." It was bleeding, cut by the sharp edge of the pendant. I said a silent, sarcastic thanks to my Sidhe benefactress for giving me a necklace that could slice hairs and possibly cut through metal as well. It had sure done a number on my thumb.

"Oh," Mr. McMann said, his voice working its way back to upbeat. "I have Band-Aids!"

I found it a little unsettling that he talked about Band-Aids with the same level of enthusiasm with which he considered my scholastic future. As he fished around in his desk for a bandage, I grabbed a tissue out of a nearby box and pressed it to my thumb. I took a few seconds to glare down at the pendant, and even from this angle, the reflection in the small, circular mirror caught my eye.

The first thing I noticed was the color, a brilliant blue-green.

Sidhe blue. Blood green.

The words were a memory, an echo of something I'd heard and seen before. I knew this color, knew it as well as I knew that tattoo on my lower back. This was the color of Sidhe blood, the ink with which the symbol of Life had been laid into my skin.

I angled my head to get a better look at the mirror around my neck, and the image became clearer: the tissue, the thumb, the blue-green color spreading out from the point of contact between the two.

My blood, I realized. *It's blue-green.*

"Ah. Here you go, Bailey," Mr. McMann said, offering me a dinosaur Band-Aid. I didn't spend a single second thinking about the fact that a forty-year-old man who dressed like an upscale lumberjack had dinosaur Band-Aids in his desk. I was too busy trying to hide my thumb from his guidance counselor eyes. With my luck, he'd take one look and then attempt to convince me that blue-green blood made me some kind of "underrepresented minority" in the college application process.

"Bailey?"

Carefully, I took the Band-Aid with my left hand, keeping my right under the desk and out of his view.

But when I looked down at my thumb again, my blood was red, making me wonder if there was such a thing as college-stress-induced hallucination. Fumbling clumsily with the wrapper, I finally managed to secure the bandage into place, and as I moved to throw the bloodied tissue away, I caught the barest glimpse of it in the mirror around my neck.

Blue-green.

Red in reality, blue-green in the mirror.

Okay, I thought, relieved, *so that's a no go on the hallucination front.*

"So, Bailey. About all-girls schools." Mr. McMann cleared his throat. "Was that a no?"

Thankfully, that question brought an end to our meeting, and I was excused to go back to class. As I walked down the hallway, taking my time and feeling sorry for my throbbing thumb, I thought back over the past few hours.

A cryptic geek had accurately translated my tattoo.

Adea and Valgius had put in a rare daytime appearance to tell me that tonight was the beginning of my Reckoning.

Morgan had appeared out of nowhere to give me necklaces that she insisted my friends and I would need.

I'd cut myself on one of the aforementioned necklaces and discovered that my blood turned blue-green in the pendant's mirror.

And last, but certainly not least, my meeting with Mr. McMann had just confirmed what I'd long suspected: everybody except me had plans for next year, or plans for making plans, or at least an idea of what they'd like those plans to be, whereas all I knew was that I didn't particularly want to go to an all-girls school.

Probably.

How was it that I could go two years without anything freaky happening (except fate-ing, which wasn't freaky so much as it just *was*), and then all of a sudden, boom—everything went completely nutters at the exact same time?

I made it back to class without an answer to my question, and as I slipped into my seat, all I could hope was that there weren't any more surprises out there, waiting to spring themselves on me at the last minute.

"Miss Morgan?"

The teacher said my name, and for one terrifying instant, I couldn't even remember what class I was in.

"Yes?" I said, my voice very small.

"Could you explain to us the definition of friction?"

Well, that solved one mystery. Clearly, I was in physics class, and clearly, whatever Sidhe beings fancied themselves the gods of irony were messing with me, because that was the exact piece of information I'd tried to study in study hall that morning.

Operative word: *tried*.

"Friction is . . . ummmm . . ."

"Friction is the force generated when one object moves along another, generally defined by the equation f equals μmg, where μ is a friction coefficient, m is mass, and g is the force of gravity."

I couldn't believe it! Somebody had actually come

to my rescue, and Annabelle wasn't even in this class. Though if she'd been here, she wouldn't have spoken out of turn anyway. At most, she would have metaphorically looked the other way while I probed her mind for a silent hint.

"Thank you, Mr. Talbot-Olsen, but I was asking Bailey."

I could feel "Mr. Talbot-Olsen" (whose name did not seem to fit his voice at all) shrugging beside me, but I didn't look at him until the teacher turned her attention elsewhere.

"How is the equation for friction modified if you have an object moving along an incline?"

Nobody volunteered the answer, and the teacher focused in on another of my unsuspecting and borderline-unconscious classmates. As the chosen pupil sputtered out an answer that made mine look somewhat articulate, I tuned out again. Class went on, and after a few minutes, I finally dared a peek at my knight in shining physics armor.

Mussy hair.

Too pale to be classically good-looking.

A little on the skinny side.

Dark brown eyes that might have been soulful.

It was the boy from study hall. When Delia said that geeks were an untapped subset of the male population, she wasn't kidding. They were, apparently, as close to invisible as you could possibly get without being actually transparent, because even though I lived in the middle of the social stratosphere and nowhere near the top, I couldn't remember ever seeing him before today.

I don't know if it was because Delia's "enlighten-ment" was contagious, if it was because he'd risked physics-teacher wrath to come to my rescue, or even if it all went back to the fact that there was something distinctly mysterious about the way he'd read my symbol, but no matter the reason, I couldn't look away from this boy.

His hair was definitely the "adorably tousled" kind of mussy.

No, I told myself. *Bad Bailey.* His hair wasn't the point. The point was that something weird was going on here. And besides which, I wasn't looking for a boy. Been there, tried that, had the broken heart to prove it. All I wanted was to spend as much time with my friends as I could before they left for good.

For once, I was glad that physics was one class I didn't have with any of the others. For the next fifteen minutes, I could mope as much as I wanted, and no-body could tickle me out of it.

I stole another glance at the mussy hair, and the boy smiled at me. It is a testament to the fact that I might be pathetic (and that even I wasn't immune to the power of Delia's trendsetting C cup) that holding the memory of that smile in my mind, I couldn't even muster up a good mope.

Chapter 6

After the final bell rang, I avoided stopping by my locker on the way to my car. Delia's locker was right next to mine, and when it came to crushes, pseudo-crushes, and not-quite crushes, she was pretty much as psychic as I was. She'd take one look at me, go "You have crush-face!" and insist on hearing every last detail, even if it made her late for cheerleading practice. I loved her to death, but this time I wanted to figure out what I was feeling, or what I wasn't, before she did.

To be fair, Delia had a lot more experience recognizing the symptoms of crushdom than I did. It had been so long since I'd been in a maybe-yes-maybe-no state of mind that I wasn't any surer of Cryptic Boy than I was of what was in store for me with the other Sidhe tonight. In my entire life, I'd had exactly two crushes, one of whom became, somewhat briefly, the only legitimate boyfriend I'd ever come close to having.

Kane and I had dated on and off my sophomore year. We hung out (and made out) just enough that I was sure that something was going on, but not enough that I knew whether or not he actually considered me his girlfriend. I was too afraid that the answer would be no to ask. Junior year, he'd started "hanging out" with other girls at the same time, and when I'd told him (okay, when *Zo* had told him) in no uncertain terms that he couldn't just play with me when it suited him, he'd stopped seeing the other girls, and we'd been together, really together, for four months.

Looking back, I wondered if Kane had ever actually wanted to be with me, or if I'd wanted it enough for the both of us: Maybe he'd just liked being wanted, or maybe, as I secretly feared, his being with me had more to do with my subconscious mind-control powers than anything else. Over time, I'd learned to control them, and over time, he'd gotten less and less interested in me. Coincidence?

No such thing.

"No moping." Zo walked up and flicked the side of my neck with her finger, and I jumped. "Seriously, Bay, for someone who's got mind-boggling superpowers, you spend a lot of time as Depresso Girl."

"You love me anyway," I grumbled.

"Course I do," Zo answered, and then she thumped me again. "It's called tough love."

"Very funny," I said, but my mouth, proving itself a traitor to the rest of my body, smiled at her manner. Zo and I were both only children, and some days, she was as much a sister to me as a friend. On those days, I spent a significant amount of time in headlocks and getting thumped, and she spent more time than was humane listening to me whine. Since she had apparently decided that today was one of those days, I obliged by whining.

"I cut my thumb." I held the offending appendage up and let my bottom lip poke out in classic puppy dog fashion. "It hurts."

"Awwww . . . poor Baiwey." Zo put on a baby voice. I stuck my tongue out at her.

"Brat," she said.

"Brat," I returned.

"Wanna be brats together?"

"Is that your way of asking for a ride home?"

Zo hooked an arm through mine as we began walking toward my car. "Do I even have to ask?"

Since A-belle took classes at the local university two days a week and Delia had cheerleading practice on those same days, Tuesdays and Thursdays, it was just Zo and me after school. I always gave her a ride home, because Annabelle had their car, and most of the time, our "car pool" turned into the two of us cruising around for hours, talking and goofing off and conducting highly important experiments, like driving to every gas station within a five-mile radius of the high school so that we could compare the quality of their slushees. The two of us usually ended up at my house, where my mom always and without fail invited Zo to stay for dinner. Since Zo's dad's one and only culinary specialty was pancakes so fluffy they should have been illegal, Zo had a long history of getting most of her home-cooked meals at my house, while I got all of my fluffy pancakes at hers.

"You want me to drive?" Zo asked, her voice almost comically hopeful.

"Let me think about that for a second. . . ." I tapped my chin thoughtfully. "What was Annabelle saying this morning? Something about being terrified with you behind the wheel?"

"What was I saying this morning? Something about A-belle biting me?"

"I'm drawing a blank on what you said to Annabelle," I said. "Also, I'm pretty sure you told *Delia* to bite you."

Zo shrugged and made her way to the passenger side of the car. "Any chance on you drawing a blank the next time Dee asks whether or not I've done my share of scouting for geeks?"

The two of them really were the least compatible people ever.

"I'll see what I can do," I said, thankful that Zo didn't have Delia's sixth sense about crushes, because the second the word *geek* left her mouth, I started thinking about Cryptic Boy, my physics savior with the mussy hair. Half afraid that Zo would pick up on it anyway, I climbed into the car. She settled herself into the passenger seat as I started the engine.

"Where to?" I asked.

"Is today Cookie Day?"

My mom was always good for an afternoon snack, and she baked at least once a week. Truthfully, if it hadn't been for Zo, I think Cookie Day would have stopped when I was about eight, but my mom never got tired of Zo telling her how good her cookies were, and Zo never got tired of eating them. The two of them had a wonderfully symbiotic relationship. My mom was an überparent. She would have mothered a rock if the rock had let her, and even though Zo wouldn't have admitted it under threat of torture, my tough-as-nails friend kind of liked being mothered.

"Rumor has it that it's double-chocolate-chunk day," I said, knowing I was sealing both of our fates with the mere mention of chocolate.

Zo's eyes rolled back in her head a little at the thought of cookies.

"Okay," I said. "My house it is." I put the car in reverse and backed out of the parking place.

"So what's the deal?"

It took me a second to realize what Zo was asking.

"With the moping. Twice in one day. What's the deal?"

Because I knew she wouldn't have asked if she didn't actually want to know, and because I was out of thumping range should she decide that my explanation qualified as moping again, I answered her. Once I started talking, it all poured out at warp speed: worrying about the four of us splitting up, the Reckoning being all ominous, my torturous college counseling session, the green blood, and the fact that the boy from study hall was also in my physics class. Toward the end of my explanation, I didn't even bother to mask my distinctly crushlike descriptions of Cryptic Boy's mussy hair.

I'd always sucked at hiding things from Zo.

"Okay," Zo said, when my explanation finally ended.

"Okay?" I wasn't sure whether I was asking her to elaborate, or just trying to get her to tell me again that everything would be okay. Since kindergarten, Delia had been my stylist, and Zo had been my bodyguard. Delia made things fabulous; Zo chased the monsters and/or bullies away. I expected her to somehow make this better, even though a large part of the problem was worrying about what would happen when she wasn't there to do the chasing anymore.

"Okay," Zo confirmed. "The senior year thing you'll just have to deal with. You're a big girl, Bay, and you couldn't get rid of the rest of us if you tried. Do you really think that's going to change?"

Did I?

"The blood thing is freaky"—Zo didn't give me time to process my thoughts before plowing on to the next issue—"but since the necklace came from the Accessory Stand of Great Power and Responsibility, I'm not really surprised. We just need to figure out why it turned your blood green, so we'll know what else it does."

Huh. I'd been so distracted by real-world drama that I hadn't spent much time wondering about the implication of my blood turning colors in the mirror. *Note to self*, I thought: *work on that*.

"But what about the fact that Morgan is here at all?" I asked. Since we'd gone from sister mode to friend mode, I made an effort not to sound like I was whining. Considering that I was letting the whole "deal with it" thing slide, I thought I was doing pretty well.

"Morgan being here just means things are going to get interesting." Zo looked down at the pendant on her chest, and when she looked up, the expression on her pixie face was absolutely unholy. "Admit it, last time, with the tattoos . . . ."

"It *was* kind of cool," I said. "If you forget the part where Alecca almost killed us."

Us. Just saying the word made me feel like there was an us and like Zo was right and I was stupid for worrying, even for a second, that not too far in the future there might not be. We'd faced down the ultimate evil together, and here I was worrying about college.

"Bay, Alecca never stood a chance." Zo seemed very sure of this. Perfect confidence, aggressive to a fault. That was Zo to a tee. "As for the boy . . . ," she continued.

"Yeah?" So far, Zo was doing a decent job of making me feel better (even if part of making me feel better entailed making me feel like an idiot for feeling bad in

66

the first place). Listening to her talk about it, things seemed simple, so even though boys weren't exactly her forte, I was definitely open to her suggestions.

"I say go for it. If he hurts you, leave 'im to me."

The expression on her face transitioned from unholy to deadly. When it came to my feelings, she was a bit overprotective.

I mulled over Zo's boy advice. Could I really just go for it? I mean, when did that ever work out for people like me?

"Don't tell Delia," I said after a few minutes. "About the boy."

"And convince her that there's something to this Geek Theorem of hers?" Zo snorted. "Never."

By the time we made it to my house, I was feeling a whole lot better. Liking Cryptic Boy (if I did actually decide to like him) didn't have to be a bad thing. I was good at crushing on people. It was the whole being-a-girlfriend part I was questionable at. Ultimately, I decided that with each of my problems (except for the one that I was going to "deal with" by ignoring), I needed more information. And that meant . . .

"Research," Zo finished glumly.

That was more A-belle's area than it was either of ours.

"Cookies first," I said as I opened the front door. "Research later."

"What are you girls researching?"

My mom was probably a ninja in a former life. She's just that stealthy.

"Ummmmm . . . boys." I said the first thing that came to mind.

My mom looked from Zo to me and then back again. "Where's Delia?"

Had I not been in the process of being extremely sketchy and lying quite badly, I would have started cracking up. My mom knew my friends way too well.

"Cheerleading practice," Zo said with a completely straight face. "Annabelle's at the university."

At first, I was grateful to Zo for covering for me, but then my mom's eyes lit up at the word *university*, and I was briefly overcome with an intense but short-lived desire to toss my friend out the window.

"I'd forgotten she was taking classes there this year," my mom said. "You girls should sit in on one of them sometime."

Zo seemed to have realized what she'd done. She should have known not to mention anything related to c-o-l-l-e-g-e around my mom.

"And her mother works there, too, doesn't she? I bet Dr. Porter could arrange for a private tour of some kind. I wonder if she knows anyone at Wellesley. . . ."

I didn't need to be psychic to predict that Annabelle's mom was going to be getting a call from mine very soon. With my luck, the four of us would end up spending fall break visiting colleges together, with special tours set up by whomever Dr. Porter knew at each one.

I seriously needed to figure out how to control my

fate-ing just enough to make sure that didn't happen. The moping penalties I would inevitably incur if it did would probably result in my hospitalization.

"What is that wonderful smell?" Zo's words side-tracked my mother.

"Cookies," my mom said, and the two of them stood there for a second, grinning at each other. I could barely remember what their relationship had been like back when Zo's mom was around, but these days, Zo and my mom were both downright gleeful in their mutually beneficial relationship. In no time at all Zo had a cookie in each hand and I was nibbling around the edges of one of my own.

"So," my mom said, "anything interesting happen at school today?"

Zo and I met eyes.

A boy in one of my classes recognized the tattoo you don't know I have. I sent the thought in Zo's direction, and she sent another response we wouldn't be saying out loud back my way.

Some lady at the mall gave us magical necklaces, Zo thought, *but we don't know how they work yet.*

I'm going through some rite of passage in the fairy realm tonight, I thought back to her.

Bailey has a new crush, Zo continued.

I gave her a horrified look. As bad as talking about the Sidhe would be, talking about a potential crush would be a million times worse! My mom *loved* getting the lowdown on my love life (or lack thereof) a little too much.

"Interesting?" I repeated my mom's word choice. "Nope."

Zo paused just long enough to make me nervous. "Not a thing."

Fifteen minutes, several probing questions, and a half-dozen cookies (two for me, four for Zo) later, the two of us escaped to my room.

"What have I told you about thinking about anything that falls under the heading of *romance* in my mom's presence?" I said once the door was shut behind us.

Zo rolled her eyes. "Bailey, your mom isn't that perceptive. You're just really bad at bluffing."

"And which one of us has a secret identity?" I crossed my arms over my chest.

"The same one of us that could use her mind-control powers to make her mother do whatever she wanted."

Clearly, Zo had lost her mind. I couldn't mind meld my mom. It wouldn't work. She'd know, or somebody would smite me for even thinking of doing such a thing. This was *my mom* we were talking about.

"Let's research," I said, letting my mental shields down just enough to let some of my power leak over onto Zo.

"Cool," she said. "Research!"

I smirked, and she threw a pillow at me.

"Darn you, Bay!"

"I thought you wanted me to use mind control," I said, the picture of innocence.

"Not on me!" She threw another pillow. "Brat."

I sent her a mental image of me sticking my tongue out. *Brat*.

Zo took a defiant bite of the cookie she'd brought upstairs with her, and then we both snorted.

"Soooooo," I said, drawing the word out. "Google?"

Chapter 7

In the time it took me to actually navigate my way to Google (because, of course, I had to check my email first, and then a couple of my favorite websites, and then my email again), Annabelle probably could have skimmed eight encyclopedia entries on Greek mythology, four on Celtic traditions, and two on the historical role of jewelry in ritualistic mysticism. Unfortunately, I didn't exactly have A-belle's skills, which was why I had options for college and Annabelle had Options with a capital O.

"Bailey," Zo said, and the one word carried an entire sentence with it, one that simultaneously warned me about moping, told me to concentrate on the task at hand, and suggested that I would need to supply her with more cookies soon.

"Right," I said. "Research. This is me paying attention."

This was me having no idea what exactly I should research. My fingers hovered over the keyboard. Three or four times, I moved to type a word, only to jerk my hands away from the keys at the last second. Did I really want to see what the internet could tell me about Morgan? It would be easy to run a search for some of her older aliases, but at the same time, I wasn't sure how much learning about Poseidon or Neptune would tell me about the real Morgan.

Mythology never got things quite right. The Sidhe weren't who the Celts thought they were, the Fates weren't who the Greeks thought they were, and Morgan wasn't Poseidon or Neptune, even though she had once answered to those names.

"Bay. Lee."

Zo broke my name down into two words this time, which basically meant everything that she'd communicated before, but with more urgency on the cookie front. She was getting antsy, and I knew from vast amounts of experience that an antsy Zo was not a good thing.

"Why don't you go get us some more cookies," I suggested. "And I'll get started up here."

"Likely story," Zo said, tweaking my ponytail with one hand. I couldn't help but note that her skepticism didn't stop her from taking my advice and heading back down to the kitchen for round two of Cookie Day.

Once Zo left the room, I tried to make good on my

end of the deal, but I honestly didn't know where to start. I stared at the screen until my eyes started burning, but I refused to blink, hoping that something—other than the constant niggling reminder in the back of my mind that sooner or later, I'd have to learn to do all of this on my own—would come to me. Slowly, painstakingly, my fingers typed a single word.

R-e-c-k-o-n-i-n-g.

I hit enter, knowing as I did that there probably wasn't a website that explained an ancient Sidhe ceremony that took place in the world beyond the Nexus.

The first thing that popped up in the search results was some movie I'd never heard of about a crime-solving priest. Then there were a couple of e-zines, a page about zombies, and finally, a simple definition. I clicked on that last one, and words soon filled my screen.

Reckoning: noun.

Counting or computing a specific sum.

An itemized bill.

A settlement of accounts, as in "a day of reckoning."

"Okay," I said, as I processed this information and came to three very important conclusions: first, that there was a distinct chance that I'd be spending my first night in the world beyond doing the equivalent of Otherworldly math homework; second, that the phrase "a day of reckoning" was distinctly creepy and made me think of cheery things like the end of the world and Judgment Day; and third, that there was a distinct chance that watching the movie with the crazy priest might have been more helpful than what I was doing now.

Since I didn't have a copy of the movie, I settled for moving on and trying again, this time with a different word, one that I didn't really expect to tell me anything more than *Reckoning* had.

N-e-x-u-s.

It was Annabelle's word. I'd spent months referring to the place I went each night to weave as "the place I go each night to weave," but Annabelle had started calling it the Nexus, and the name stuck. I probably could have just asked her where she got the word and what exactly it meant, but for some reason, I wanted to see for myself.

Nexus: noun.
The connection between items in a series.

A little more digging told me that it came from a Latin word meaning "to bind," and with that single piece of information, I found myself flashing back to the first time I'd gone there, and the second, and the third. Everything I knew about that place and Sidhe history hurried busily to the forefront of my mind, each detail elbowing the others for room in my thoughts.

Once upon a time, the two worlds—the one the Sidhe lived in and the human world—were just barely offset from each other in metaphysical space. Over time, the barrier between the two became harder and harder to cross, and the more complete the separation between the worlds became, the more the Sidhe began to fade away, their power weakened by their distance from our world.

I tried to remember how the rest of the story went. I'd only heard it once, back when I'd first found out that the entities we were dealing with during our tattoo crusade were actually the mythological Fates. The specifics were a little fuzzy in my mind, but some details—like the fact that the barrier between the worlds had become harder to cross—were as solid and firm as they would have been if someone had spoken them to me just a moment before.

"As their connection to the human world weakened, so did their powers," I murmured, trying to remember if that was the exact phrasing the woman who'd told me this particular tale had used. "So they did something to make sure that they'd never lose that connection completely." I paused and gave up on repeating the story word for word, settling for my own version of what had happened. "They built the Nexus—the realm in between two realms—and they sent three small Sidhe children there, to watch humans live and to become permanently connected to those lives in the most intimate way possible."

That was how Adea, Alecca, and Valgius had become the Fates. That was why, when I went to the Nexus each night, the Sidhe in me connected with the human souls in this world. Because in the Nexus, Adea, Valgius, and I were the connection between this world and the world of the Sidhe. The power inherent in human lives ran through us, and that made the rest of the Sidhe more powerful too.

Hadn't Adea said something about connections? Or maybe she'd called them ties. I couldn't really remember.

I cursed my memory, but part of me had to admit that maybe it wasn't so much a matter of not being able to remember as it was a matter of not paying that much attention the first time. Adea had used her "let's talk about the future" voice, and then she'd gotten all cryptic and I'd zoned out. It was a perfectly natural response—one that had gotten me through many college talks with my mom (not to mention my meeting with Mr. McMann earlier today), but unfortunately, I was beginning to suspect that in this case, this particular method wasn't exactly what you'd call helpful.

"I'm back, and I come bearing cookie."

I glanced toward Zo, still caught up in my thoughts. "Cookie?" I asked on autopilot. "As in singular? Don't you usually come bearing cookie*s*?"

Zo shrugged. "There might have been a few casualties on the way up the stairs."

Translation: She'd eaten them.

"You come up with anything good while I was gone?" she asked, handing me a cookie, which I set gingerly aside, because some of us didn't have stomachs the size of Montana and metabolisms that made warp speed look slow.

"Maybe," I said. "I was thinking about the story that Keiri told us."

"Keiri? As in Daughters of Adea, Sidhe-worshipping, told-us-about-the-Fates Keiri?"

I nodded. "That would be the one. She said that Adea and Val were the connection between humans and Sidhe."

Zo nodded.

"Nexus means connection," I continued, realizing even as I said it that I wasn't properly communicating the depth of my thoughts. Luckily, with Zo, it didn't matter, because she could read me as well as Annabelle read Latin.

"If Adea and Val connect the two worlds," she said, "that means you do too. Right?"

I nodded.

"And this whole Reckoning thing is supposed to be you going to . . . what do they call the other world again?"

What *did* people call the Sidhe world? I'm sure Annabelle could have given us an alphabetized list of mythologically correct names, and I was pretty sure that Adea and Valgius had referred to it simply as "the place beyond," but I settled for something a little more self-explanatory.

"I don't know," I said slowly. "I guess people call the other world . . . ummm . . . the Otherworld."

"Clever," Zo opined.

I grinned at her. "I thought so." After all, the other Sidhe lived there, and it was a world other than the one I spent most of my time in.

"What do you think it will be like?" Zo asked, her head tilted to the side and her voice softer than usual.

"I don't know," I said. "The Nexus is pretty."

The words sounded moronic to my ears, but Zo just nodded. "I think I remember that," she said. "I was kind of concentrating on the evil fairy trying to kill us at the time, but I remember things being very . . ." She trailed off.

Now it was my time to nod. "Yeah."

The Nexus was hard to describe. Something about it defied description.

"Are you scared?" Zo's words caught me off guard. Our therapy session in the car aside, Zo wasn't exactly known for her sensitivity. She was more of a hit-now-ask-questions-later kind of girl.

"A little," I said. "Adea and Valgius tried to make it seem normal, like of course I'm going there and I'm going to meet others just like me, but at the same time, something about the things they said made it sound like there was more to it than that." I paused, because up until then, I'd concentrated on what Adea and Valgius had told me, rather than the way they'd told me.

For a long time, Zo and I sat there, both of us quiet. I wasn't sure what she was thinking, and I didn't probe her mind to find out. Instead, I thought about what had been said in the Nexus and what had gone unsaid and about the fact that Morgan had definitely done some saying and unsaying of her own.

"I'd go with you if I could," Zo said finally. Her words were sweet, but her tone was more disgruntled than anything else. She didn't like the idea of not being able to protect me from whatever the Reckoning entailed.

Come to think of it, I wasn't so fond of that idea myself.

"I'd take you with me if I could," I said, and I

refused to say the rest of the sentence—*but I can't*—because it felt like admitting something awful that was true in more ways than one.

It was official: the world was conspiring to make me see everything as a metaphor for the end of high school.

"So what now?" I asked Zo, half-expecting her to have answers that had nothing to do with the next half hour and everything to do with the next few years.

"The way I see it, we have three options." Zo was clearly in the mood to take charge, and I (a) knew better than to stand in the way of *any* of Zo's moods, and (b) didn't, in general, have any objection to following.

"Option one: We try to research the necklaces." Zo made a face. Clearly, she realized that of the four of us, she and I were the least apt to do any kind of research on mystical jewelry. A-belle was research girl, and Delia was the fashion expert; the two of them would be all over this soon enough.

"Option two: We forget about the research and go for a trial-and-error kind of thing for using them."

I considered that one for a moment, thinking about what the necklace had shown me earlier and wondering what I'd see if I probed things more.

"What's option three?" I asked, hating that I couldn't just jump on option two, which was quite obviously the best choice.

Zo picked up the charm on her necklace and held it out and away from her neck, assuming a fighting stance as she did. "I challenge you to a duel!" she said.

I held out my own necklace and grinned back at her. "I accept."

The two of us launched ourselves into option three: using our necklaces in a twisted pendant sword fight, careful not to do any actual damage with the sharp edges.

Productive? Maybe not, but it was exactly what I needed.

As we circled each other, completely concentrated on the task at hand, I barely noticed that the shadows in the room seemed to move with us—even the ones that should have been standing still.

Chapter 8

On some level, I must have seen the shadows when Zo and I were attempting to duel, but it wasn't until I laid down to sleep that the image—slithering, scattering, shifting—made its way into my conscious mind. The entire scene played against the backdrop of my eyelids, over and over again, the movement of the shadows so subtle that I wondered if it was real or if this was just another example of Things That Happen When Bailey Doesn't Get Enough Actual Shut-eye.

Given everything I had on my mind, I should have had trouble falling asleep, but I didn't. One second I was lying there thinking about shadows and Zo (and college, which was never far from my mind), and the next, I was out.

*   *   *

The Seal was cool under my back. I lay there for a long moment, my eyes closed, feeling as comfortable as I did in my own bed. More than anything else in the Nexus, the Seal was home.

"We are connected."

Adea's voice broke into my thoughts, and I flashed back to my mom's "Bailey Marie" that morning. Adea wasn't big on middle names. She preferred eerie lectures. At least this time, I knew what she was talking about.

Sort of.

"The three of us are part of one whole, and the Seal represents that whole. It was forged out of man, out of Sidhe, that we might connect the two. In a time when the worlds were separating, our birth brought them closer together, that this Seal and the balance it represents might hold the worlds, separate but entwined, the powers from one rejuvenating the other."

"Four score and seven years ago . . ."

For some reason, my mind decided that it would be productive to imagine Adea delivering the Gettysburg Address, rather than actually trying to connect her words to my earlier ponderings about the role I played in connecting the worlds.

". . . our fathers brought forth on this continent . . ."

Sigh. I was hopeless—either my subconscious didn't want me probing the issue of connectivity, or it had the attention span of a kindergartener.

"You are very young." Valgius's voice was deep and held just enough of a hint of disapproval that I wondered if either of them could see past my shields to my wandering thoughts. The first time I'd come to this place, I'd been an open book, but over months—now years—my power had grown, and they'd become less and less able to use theirs on me.

"I'll be eighteen in a couple of months," I said. With a little huff that made me sound closer to the mental age of my subconscious, I finally opened my eyes, which I'd resisted doing in an attempt to stay snuggled down on the Seal for as long as possible, safe and sound and waiting for mortal souls to flood my body with knowledge, power, and the desire to weave.

"Eighteen." Adea's voice held a great deal of amusement. "Sometimes I forget you live in their years, Bailey." She paused, and I could sense her debating whether or not to say more. "You might not always."

"Then whose years would I live in?"

Adea and Val remained suspiciously quiet. Like I wasn't hesitant enough about this Reckoning thing already.

"Come," Val said finally.

I looked around me at the Nexus, the place that Zo and I had agreed was "pretty." I was clearly outdoors, but the space gave the impression of being enclosed. The grass underneath my feet was lush and just barely damp, always touched by a morning dew no matter what time I came here. "Where are we going?" I asked.

I couldn't begin to imagine what the Otherworld would be like, any more than I could describe the Nexus when I wasn't there. At that second, the Nexus seemed so simple and clear in my mind: the Seal, the grass, the morning sun, and flowers, lots of them, so large and colorful that they seemed to belong more to prehistoric Earth than the world where I spent my days.

Maybe that was what Adea meant about time passing differently here. Sidhe lived so long that most humans considered them immortal, and their world, just offset from the mortal plane, hadn't aged the way ours had.

Neither of my companions answered my question about where we were headed. They took it as rhetorical, since I vaguely knew the answer before I'd asked the question. Instead, Adea issued an order, her tone light, but impossible to disobey.

"Take our hands." Her voice sounded the way that honey looked dripping off a spoon: light and golden, thick and flowing.

Knowing I didn't have a choice, I lifted my hands and slowly took one of theirs in each of mine.

Birth. Life. Death.

Our hands warmed until they were so hot that I expected my fingers to melt. It hurt, but not as much as it should have, and in a strange way, the pain felt good. Right. Familiar.

Birth. Life. Death.

We were three, and as we stood there, memories washed over me. Memories that weren't mine, but weren't theirs either. Memories of what it meant to be born, to live, and to die. Memories of the Earth itself, memories of this place. Memories of the Seal, forged by human and Sidhe.

And something older than all of that. Older than the Nexus. Older than Adea and Valgius and the blood in my veins.

"Do you feel them?" Adea asked me. "Do you feel their call?"

Each night I came here and, as I wove, became one with the mortal realm. This time, the connection stretched out in a different direction, and their voices—unspoken, but somehow musical—echoed in my mind.

Sidhe. Sidhe. Sidhe.

In that moment, we stopped being the three Fates. We stopped being Birth and Life and Death, and our connection to the world I lived in faded away, drowned out by something bigger, something that came from so far inside of me that I was half-afraid that it would turn me inside out trying to reach the surface.

Sidhe. Sidhe. Sidhe.

"This is their call," Valgius said. "Can you answer it, Bailey?"

I had to. I had to answer it or it would kill me, but I didn't know how.

"Shhhhhhhhh." Adea's comforting murmur made me realize that I was emitting a pained, low-pitched whine.

"Remember, Bailey," she said. "That's all you have to do. Just remember what it was like before we were three, when we were simply one with our world and the others like us. Remember what it was like to be Sidhe."

I squeezed my eyes shut, as much in fear of this moment as anything else, and as I stood there, their hands in mine, I remembered, and then I knew.

Feral beauty. Unforgivable power. Everlasting light.

That was what it meant to be Sidhe.

I felt the change even with my eyes closed and knew

that we were suddenly and inexplicably elsewhere, as distant from the Seal as the Nexus was from the mortal realm. The air was crisp and cool, but my body warmed itself from the inside out, until the combination of the two was near divine in its perfection, like stepping out of the pool on a warm summer day, body covered with water and the sun shining down on me. Every inch of my flesh was alive with contrasting sensations, and I was overcome with the thought that until this moment, my body had been little more than skin I was forced to wear.

"Welcome home, Bailey."

For the first time, Adea's voice didn't strike me as musical or powerful; the echo of her thousands of years didn't hurt my ears or fill me with awe. Without even opening my eyes, I knew that voices such as hers belonged here, and when I spoke, the sound came from a place inside of me that I hadn't known existed. "Where are we?"

I couldn't bear to open my eyes for fear that seeing this place would somehow tarnish the beauty I felt in it.

"Faerie. Olympus. Avalon. The Beyond. This is a place of many names."

Those words were familiar, and whatever part of me was still human remembered that I'd given this place a name of my own—the Otherworld—but standing there, eyes closed, the true name echoed through the recesses of my mind, two words melded into one.

Sidhe. Home.

I opened my eyes.

At first, all I saw was colors, each so rich and distinct from the others that my memory of the mortal world melted away, as gray as Dorothy's Kansas in comparison to Oz. Slowly, the colors became shapes: rolling hills and lush vegetation and a perpetual sunrise or sunset—I couldn't tell which—painting the sky in shades of pink and purple and orange. Somehow, I knew that this place was unchanging, that even in the darkness of night, if there was such a thing, the colors would be there, as rich in black as they were in golden white light.

It took me a moment to realize that the light wasn't coming from whatever passed for this world's sun. Instead, it radiated from our skin. I looked down at my hands, wondering at their unearthly glow.

If Delia could see me now, *I thought*, she'd want to strap me on a chain and wear me around her neck.

The thought was fuzzy, and the contrast between it and the strength of my impressions of this place—so lyrical that they should have felt alien in my head—reminded me that this was the one place my friends could never follow.

"Are you ready?" Adea's voice came out as barely more than a whisper, and it was unclear whether she was speaking to me, Valgius, or herself. There was something urgent in her tone, some frenetic need to do something, be somewhere.

"I'm ready." My answer should have surprised me, but it didn't. There comes a point when something is so true that whether or not it was expected simply doesn't matter.

Adea laughed then, and the sound was visible in the air around us, the way warm breath is on a cold winter day. Her joy at being here, at being Sidhe, hung in the air, the exact color as the horizon of the Otherworld sky. She ran then, straight forward, into the vast landscape before us, and I found myself immediately on her heels, tearing through the land with speed that should have been impossible. The world around us settled back into a blur of colors as we ran, and I savored each sensation: each time my bare feet hit the ground, each flower that reached out to caress me, welcoming me as one with the land.

And as we ran, the colors and the scene around us changed, until mountains grew under our feet, erupting out of the ground in purples and grays that were more silver than anything else. I kept running, and the growing mountains thrust us higher and higher toward the sky, into the clouds and a light, pearly mist that tasted sweet on my tongue.

And then, without warning and without planning to do so, I stopped running, knowing beyond any human understanding that we had arrived at our destination. I stood very still, my heart pumping viciously behind my rib cage, my hair in my face, and my brain suddenly aware that we were being watched. Big time.

I could only see a few dozen of them, but I could feel more, staring at me from great distances, from the tops of other mountains, from down in the lush green valleys, from underneath brilliant blue-green waters.

The entire Otherworld was looking at me and into me, and for the first time since I'd left the Seal, I felt horribly and utterly human.

When we were little, I was always the shy one, and Delia, who didn't have a shy bone in her body, and Zo, who wasn't exactly a cowering miss herself, had developed a *game that they called "everybody look at Bailey" to help me embrace my inner diva. The game went like this: once or twice a year, when we were in a big crowd of people, the two of them would meet eyes and then as loud as they could yell, "Everybody look at Bailey!" And everybody would look at me, and I would want to die until I remembered that they were standing there beside me, smiling at me like I was the type of person people* should *want to look at.*

For a moment, the memory was clear in my mind, but as quickly as it had come, I lost it. Earth and mortals had no place here, even in memory, and every thought I might have had about my friends was quickly replaced with longing.

Need, *I thought, not knowing what it was I needed. Adea put her hand on my shoulder, and a pleasant shiver ran through my body at the physical contact.*

Then, just as I was starting to regain my mind, or at least some semblance thereof, a woman stepped forward from the many beings who watched us. Her hair was the color of an opal, a pale pearly white that reflected pink as she moved. "Welcome, Bailey. We've been waiting for you. . . ."

"For a very, very long time." A man finished her sentence, and I searched for him, scanning the crowds of beings with two-toned hair, iridescent skin, and eyes every shade of blue. Finally, my gaze settled on a man who was in every way the woman's opposite. She was small; he was broad-shouldered and gave the impression of being even bigger than he actually was. Her skin was the color of caramel; his was the white of untouched snow. The rest of him—eyes, hair, and expression—was dark.

Beside me, Adea and Valgius inclined their heads. It took me a second to figure out that they were bowing.

Why hadn't anyone told me that I'd need to know how to bow?

"I am Eze," the woman said, and I couldn't keep from thinking that her hair looked like it belonged more on a unicorn than on a woman, Sidhe or no. There was something mythical about just standing in her presence. "Queen of Light."

That would explain the bowing. I glanced at the man who had spoken earlier, wondering if that made him the King.

"I rule the night," he said, deigning to answer my unasked question. "I am Drogan, King of Darkness."

If I'd been watching this scene in a movie, I probably would have thrown popcorn at the screen to protest the cheesy dialogue, but somehow their words carried a kind of depth I couldn't explain based on their meanings alone. The part of me that had recognized Morgan at the mall recognized the same thing in the two of them, something ancient and familiar, horrible and awesome, and I found that my body wanted to bow to them.

King of Darkness, Queen of Light.

"Leave us," Eze said to those watching us, her words screaming command, *even though she wasn't speaking all that loudly. For a moment, I thought I'd displeased her, but Eze smiled warmly at me, the expression at odds with the biting chill in her voice as she spoke to the others. "She is new to our world, and you will overwhelm her. Adea and Valgius, you may stay."*

No sooner were the words out of her mouth than the

eyes all around me disappeared, their owners fading back into the mountains, until there were only a handful of sets left: Adea and Valgius, Drogan and Eze, and six others, who stepped forward, summoned by an order I couldn't hear or a lure I couldn't feel. A fire appeared in front of me, and I stared into it, wondering if the others were still watching.

And then, without warning, Eze was beside me, and the light from her skin was almost more than my eyes could bear, her hair flashing the palest of pinks as she moved. She reached a hand out and touched my face. "Poor child," she said. "Lost for so long. How you must have longed for us, not knowing what it was that you were missing." Her fingers trailed lightly over my skin. "How lonely you must have been, how scared in a world in which eternity means nothing."

I wasn't lonely, I wanted to say. I've never been alone. But somehow, the mention of eternity brought to mind my realization from earlier that day that nothing lasts forever, and I couldn't push back the feeling that I'd been moving inexorably toward loneliness my whole life and just hadn't gotten there yet.

"You'll never be lonely here, Bailey." Drogan's voice was heavy and deep, as much a contrast to Eze's as his appearance was to hers. "You'll never be alone." He took my hand in his and began tracing his fingers across the back of it in light, deliberate movements.

"You are welcome here, Bailey."

"You are home."

The King and Queen spoke in tandem, and after

another eternity, Drogan let go of my hand and Eze drew hers back from my face. The two of them turned and walked slowly and imperiously away.

"Adea, Valgius, come," Eze called over her shoulder.

"Yes," Drogan said, his voice washing over me, the sound of it at once caressing and beating at my skin. "Do."

There was something hard about the words. Something frightening.

"Let the young ones talk amongst themselves."

Young ones? I tore my eyes away from the most royal of the Sidhe and turned toward the others I could feel in this space.

Oh, I thought, taking in their appearances. Young ones.

As Adea and Valgius disappeared with our lieges, I tried to remember the way I'd felt running through the Otherworld to get to this mountain, but I couldn't muster any kind of unadulterated emotion—let alone the kind of physical and mental grace I'd managed effortlessly before. I was Sidhe, I was home, and I was scared out of my freaking mind, because the only thing more intimidating than full-blown royal Sidhe were Otherworldly teenagers.

And as I stood there in front of the fire, six of them advanced on me at once.

Chapter 9

I was a good friend, but I wasn't good at making friends. There was a big, big difference between the two, and other than Annabelle, I hadn't put my friend-making skills to the test since preschool. I hadn't needed to.

"Hello," I said. My voice still had a certain amount of power to it, an age more in line with the memories I held of this place than the number of years I'd lived on Earth.

"Hello." All six of them spoke at once, and the combined effect of their voices was paralyzing.

"You needn't be afraid," one of the girls said.

"We won't harm you." A second girl, nearly identical to the first, finished the sentence. Two other girls, who looked slightly older and slightly more like they were considering devouring me whole, said nothing, instead choosing to segregate themselves on the other side of the fire. They whispered behind pale hands, and something about the pointed glances they were shooting my way reminded me of the popular girls at my high school.

Great, *I thought*. I'm a dorky Sidhe. Because being part of an ancient fairy race isn't difficult enough on its own.

The girls who had spoken to me met my eyes again, and there was something about the tilt of their pearly pink mouths that seemed vaguely familiar. Before I could quite sort out what it was, one of the two males stepped forward.

"I'm Xane," he said, "heir to the Unseelie throne."

Xane, *I thought*. Rhymes with Kane. *Like my ex, Xane held himself with a certain amount of confidence that I'd come to identify over time as arrogance, absolute certainty that whatever he wanted, he would be able to have. Including me.*

"I am Axia." One of the pearly-mouthed girls spoke again, and even though the expression on her face never changed, I couldn't shake the feeling that she was rolling her eyes at Xane's airs. "This is my sister, Lyria. Our mother is Eze." Axia added that last bit almost hesitantly, as if she wasn't quite sure whether she wanted to claim her mother, let alone the throne, for herself.

For her part, Lyria said nothing and offered me a shy smile. I wondered how Eze had given birth to daughters like these.

"I take after my father," Xane said, lifting the thought from my head with a smirk that made me wonder whether he was perceptive or able to get past my psychic shields. "Axia and Lyria are not so clearly begotten."

"We will one day share the Seelie throne," Axia said.

"If there's still a Seelie throne to share," Xane scoffed.

Lyria frowned at him, but said nothing.

While the heirs argued among themselves, I turned the words I'd heard over and over in my head. Seelie. Unseelie. Light and dark, two parts of the same whole. I found that I didn't have to ask for definitions of these terms, the same way that I'd always known instinctively how to spell Sidhe, even though it wasn't written at all the way it was pronounced.

"They'll be at it for hours," a voice whispered directly into my ear.

If I'd been in my world and not theirs, I would have jumped, but I was a different Bailey here, and I found that his presence didn't surprise me, that I'd known he was next to me, edging closer all the time.

"Drogan and Xane don't venture forth from their domain very often," the voice continued, "and when they do, Xane makes it a point to argue with Eze's daughters the way Eze typically argues with his father."

I turned to meet my whisperer's eyes. Like all of the Sidhe (except for me), his were blue, so light that there was barely any color in them at all. His hair was an odd combination of brown and red, the kind of hair color the sidekick on an afternoon television show might have. His skin glowed, but it made him look more sunburnt than ethereal. His features were even and perfect, but the myriad of expressions that danced across them as I surveyed him looked comfortingly commonplace.

"I'm James," he said.

"James?" I asked. Adea, Valgius, Eze, Drogan, Axia, Lyria, Xane, and . . . James. Something about that seemed just a little off.

"Is there something wrong with my name?" James asked, the edges of his lips quirking upward as I tried to think of a diplomatic way to answer his question.

"There's nothing wrong with it," I said, grateful for his cheerful disposition and the fact that in this incarnation my voice was incapable of squeaking. "It just seems kind of . . . human."

James's face changed at the word human, almost as if I'd said a deliciously naughty word or made a dirty joke.

"It was my name first, you know," James said, his tone completely conversational. "It's not my fault that I may have allegedly crossed over to the mortal realm one solstice and told a pregnant woman my real name." A look of faux innocence replaced the mischievous glint in his eyes as he continued. "It's certainly not my fault if aforementioned woman liked my name—allegedly, of course—so much that she used it for her firstborn son."

I caught on, quicker than I might have if this conversation had been taking place on Earth. "And if the name spread across the world and became very popular for generations afterward?" I asked.

James shrugged, looking just the tiniest bit sheepish as he did. "That would not be my fault," he said. "Allegedly."

I should have been weirded out that I was talking to the first James, especially as that meant he was at least a few thousand years old, but something about him felt so wonderfully normal that I couldn't quite accept that fact, and I chose to ignore it—and his reaction to the word human—entirely.

Unconsciously, my gaze flitted toward Xane and Eze's girls, as I wondered if all Sidhe would have the same reaction. I found the three of them still in a standoff, the girls silent and Xane pontificating enough for all three of them. On the other side of the fire, the cliquey girls were still whispering and snorting to themselves, content to pretend that I'd never dared to tread on this sacred place or their sacrosanct little social circle.

"You wanna sit?" James asked.

"Where?" I replied, fascinated by how very human he sounded, and by the fact that he seemed to have no interest in the other girls, including not one but two future queens.

James took my hand and led me closer toward the fire. As the warmth jumped off the flames, clamoring for my skin, a deep pool of ice opened up inside of me, sending chills down my bones and allowing the fire to warm them. I shivered, more with pleasure than with cold.

"We're creatures of balance," James said. "Never too hot, never too cold." He started to sit down, and I watched as the mountain contorted itself to provide him with a bench of sorts. Hesitating for just a moment too long, I sat down beside him.

"Where you come from, things that aren't hot or cold are lukewarm or cool or neutral," James continued, paying no heed to the accommodation the mountain had made for us. "Here, we're always hot and cold, in equal parts, and we feel them both in everything we do. Being

98

Sidhe means having that in all things: light and dark, night and day, water and blood."

I didn't exactly follow on that last one, but his voice sounded like laughter, and I liked it. It wasn't a chuckle or a giggle or a tentative tee-hee. It was indelicate, snorting laughter, and I could have listened to it forever.

"We have forever here," James said. "And ever and ever and ever and ever . . ."

I felt vaguely like he was seconds away from breaking into "The Song That Never Ends."

"Good things never end here," James said, "and bad things disappear the moment we will them away." He reached toward me, and when he put his arm around my shoulder, it seemed like the most natural thing in the world for my skin to touch his.

"It's nice here," I said, unaware that the words were planning to exit my mouth. Still, I couldn't stop them. Sitting there, on top of a mountain that bent its will to ours, breathing in clouds that tasted sweeter than cotton candy, listening to a boy who sounded like laughter, I let myself indulge in a moment of pure oneness with everything around me. I closed my eyes, and I could feel Xane and Axia and Lyria, could feel the girls sitting across the fire, and Adea and Valgius, attending the Queen and King. I could sense the rise and fall of the hills, could hear the sun setting, little by little. More than anything, I could feel that scattered throughout the land, there were others like me, others whose ancient blood was interwoven with my own to the extent that I could feel their bodies as extensions of my own.

"It's nice," I said again.

"It's home," James said simply. "We've missed you."

Me? They didn't even know me.

"We've always known you. All Sidhe know all others: we're born with the knowledge of those who came before us and those who will go after. It's obvious when someone is missing, when our world is unwhole."

It pleased me to think that this place might miss me once I left. That James might have missed me.

As this thought took up residence in my mind, a muscle in my neck twinged, and as I reached up to rub it, my hand brushed against the chain around my neck.

"What's that?" James asked, eyeing my necklace with interest.

I went for a quick subject change and somehow came up with a question to sidetrack him. "How can your world miss me," I said, "when I was born to live separate from it?"

I wasn't sure where the words came from, but the second they were out of my mouth, they triggered my memory of the story I'd been thinking about earlier that day, about a race whose power was faltering until they set aside three children to know human beings, three children who wove the Fate of the mortal world and were never given the chance to live in their own.

Wasn't that why Alecca had gone all Evil Bitca on the world? Because she and Adea and Valgius had lived separate from the rest of the Otherworld, a living sacrifice for the power that fueled this land, and when Adea and Valgius had fallen into very human love with each other,

Alecca, the Fate of Life, had had nothing left except a very human hatred.

"I'm the Third Fate," I said. "I belong to the Seal, not to this place."

Darn it! I didn't want the words to be true. I didn't want to be saying them. I didn't want to be remembering these things or asking these questions.

"You belong where you choose, Bailey," James told me. "This place could be yours, if you'd accept it." He reached out, and the mountain morphed again to provide a small stone cup, filled with an amber-colored liquid that smelled like maple syrup and daisies and incense all at once. James brought the cup to his lips.

"Nectar of the gods," he said, and I couldn't tell whether he was joking or not. "You want?" He held the cup out to me, and my thumb throbbed where I'd cut it on the necklace earlier that day.

"No," I said after a long moment. "No, thank you."

James shrugged. "No big," he said, lowering the cup to the ground. "So what do you want to know?"

The question took me by surprise.

"You must have questions," James said, wiggling his eyebrows. "I have answers. Ask away."

"Okay," I said finally. "If Adea, Valgius, and I are the Fates, who's everyone else?"

For a moment, I wondered if James would even know what I was talking about. The Sidhe hadn't given themselves these names, hadn't (as far as I knew) fashioned themselves into gods for the ancient Greeks. I wasn't even sure that any of them, aside from Adea and Valgius, knew

101

as much about the mortal realm as I knew about this one—even if James had allegedly *crossed over back in the day. For all I knew, James might not even know what I meant by* Fate.

"*Got any guesses?*" *James asked.* "*Come on, start with Eze.*" *I took his response as an indication that he did know what I was talking about, but that didn't make guessing any easier. My knowledge of Greek mythology was sketchy at best, and given the degree to which myths usually ended up being wrong, I had no idea which portions of what I knew I could count on to be reliable.*

"*She's the Queen of the Seelie Court,*" *I said.* "*The Queen of Light.*"

"*And that would make her . . .*" *James seemed to enjoy seeing me squirm. For someone who wasn't human, he did a darned good impression.*

"*You tell me.*" *I wasn't about to risk a guess that might somehow insult Eze, because I got the distinct feeling that her being out of sight meant nothing about whether or not she was out of earshot.*

"*The Greeks liked to think of her as a man,*" *James said.* "*They just couldn't see that much power as female.*"

Eze, *I thought.* Eze.

And then it came to me, from where I had no idea. "*Holy freaking cow in a box,*" *I said.* "*She's Zeus!*"

"*Very good,*" *James said.* "*And yes, she is.*"

I silently thanked him for not commenting on the fact that I'd just used the phrase "*holy freaking cow in a box.*" *The expression on his face told me quite explicitly that part of him had wanted to.*

I forced myself to focus. "So if Eze is Zeus, that makes Drogan . . ."

"Zeus's brother, of course," James said. "If there was one thing the ancient Greeks did well, it was familial relationships. There were three siblings, who divided the world between them. Zeus ruled over the heavens, also known in this realm as the World of Light. Hades took the underworld . . ."

"The World of Darkness," I finished. Drogan as Hades. It was a creepy image. "What about the third sibling?"

James clamped his mouth shut.

"What?" I poked him in the side and blushed the second I realized I'd done it.

"There is no third," James said. "There are only two. Seelie and Unseelie, King and Queen. So it has always been."

Brainwashed, *I thought*, party of one, *but I didn't say it out loud.*

"And the others?" I asked.

"Xane doesn't make any appearances in that particular mythos himself," James said, obviously amused by that fact, "but you can think of him as a smaller, younger Hades. Axia was once known as Artemis, Lyria as Aphrodite."

Somehow, it was hard to picture shy-smiled Lyria as the goddess of love.

"And those two?" I asked, gesturing across the fire. I realized a second too late that the girls were no longer there.

"It's generally considered ill-mannered to point." The

girls appeared on either side of the bench, seemingly out of nowhere. They had pale skin and lips the color of blood. Like James, they were redheads of sorts. The one who had spoken was a true strawberry blonde, her hair both pale and red. The other looked more like a lion, her mane a darker shade of James's red-brown. The two of them were incredibly thin—to the point that I felt easily twice as wide as the two of them together. Their eyes were deep-set, and their piercing blue gazes dug into me like talons.

"Uhhhhh . . . hi, girls," James said. I got the feeling that he wasn't so much caught off guard that they were there as he was uncomfortable with their proximity to me.

"Hello, James," the girls said in unison, and then they began to pet him, running their hands up and down his triceps and occasionally burying their fingers in his hair. If my entire life had been a movie, this moment alone would have been enough to change its rating to PG-13. Heck, I was almost eighteen, and I didn't feel old enough to be watching this.

"Girls," James said patiently, ignoring the fact that they couldn't keep their hands off of him, "this is Bailey."

"We—"

"—know."

They finished each other's sentences, their bloodred lips savoring the words.

"Bailey, this is Kiste." James gestured to the girl with the darker hair. "And this is Cyna."

Kis-tee. Ky-nah. *The pronunciations hung in the air.*

So who are they? *I thought, trying to figure out which Greek goddesses would most likely be redheaded vampires.*

As soon as the word vampire *crossed my mind, I spent several seconds wondering if there was such a thing as a vampire Sidhe, and if Kiste and Cyna were staring at me like that because I was on the lunch menu. With James beside me, I didn't feel scared, but the possibility still creeped me out.*

"We're—"

"—thirsty."

With that pronouncement, the girls reached down and the mountain provided them each with a stone cup filled with the same liquid James had offered me earlier.

"You want something, Bay?" James asked, and I couldn't help but notice that he shortened my name the way Delia and Zo did.

"I'm fine," I said, even though my tongue was suddenly doing its very best imitation of cardboard.

"You're—"

"—human."

"We—"

"—can—"

"—smell it—"

"—on you."

I wondered if this was what Eze had pictured when she'd left me to get to know the others.

"She's Sidhe," James said. "She belongs here."

His words were so emphatic that he attracted the attention of the others.

"James is right. Our blood runs in her veins, hers in ours." This was from Axia.

Kiste and Cyna did everything but hiss at her.

105

"She hasn't done anything wrong," Lyria said, her voice barely more than a whisper. She wouldn't meet my eyes or theirs, but her words seemed to carry some weight with them.

"She's here on my father's invitation," Xane said. "And as much as it pains me to say it, Lyria's right. She hasn't done anything wrong."

Kiste and Cyna sulked, burrowing into James until it was hard to tell that they were three separate people.

"Bailey, you look thirsty," Xane cut in, his tone so weighted down with superiority that I wasn't sure how he fit any words into the sentence to begin with. "Would you like some water?"

Suddenly, I was being offered three cups of water at once, one each from the heirs to the Otherworld thrones.

I reached out to take the one Axia offered, but at the last second, I saw something in her eyes that made me drop my hand. Maybe it was nothing. Maybe it was my imagination.

Maybe it was a warning.

"Bailey, it's time to go. It will be morning soon in the mortal world, and you have yet to weave."

I'd never been so glad to see Adea and Valgius. Eze and Drogan stood behind them, watching me, their expressions gentle and their features heartrendingly beautiful. As I looked upon them and thought about what this man and this woman had once been to the Greeks, I felt like I was staring at two stone statues, like their smiles were carved into faces as old as this mountain itself and didn't reflect anything except the carver's intent.

My hand went again to my necklace, and words flooded my brain from all directions.

She reeks of mortality.

We will have her.

I will have her.

Will she drink?

I dropped the necklace.

"Sometime you're going to have to tell me where you got that thing." James leaned forward as he whispered.

"Sometime," I whispered back, "you're going to have to tell me who you were to the ancient Greeks." And, for that matter, who Kiste and Cyna were supposed to be.

James offered me a lopsided grin, but said nothing.

"Bailey," Valgius said, his tone vaguely amused. "We must go."

"Good night, Bailey," Drogan said. Xane echoed his father.

"Good morn," Eze corrected, and her daughters, their voices light, did the same.

"Good to meet you." This was from James.

"Good—"

"—bye."

Kiste and Cyna were all too happy to see me depart. I wasn't sure what to expect as I left the mountain and the beings I'd met, but soon all of my questions faded away, because Adea, Valgius, and I were running again, down the mountain, through land and forest, until all I could hear or think or remember was the sound of my own feet hitting the ground and the unadulterated, ecstatic joy of being who and what, where and when I was.

Sidhe. Home.

Nothing could temper the beauty of this place. Nothing could stop the pull I felt toward it, and as Adea, Valgius, and I finally stopped running and the three of us joined hands, I knew deep down that nothing could keep me from coming back. I refused to close my eyes this time, not wanting to cheat myself out of the wonders I might see by keeping them open.

"Think of the Seal, Bailey. Think of the two of us. Think of what it means to be born and to live and to die."

Birth. Death. Life.

Valgius. Adea. Me.

And suddenly, we were back. Knowing what I had to do, I walked like a zombie to the Seal and let the connection take hold, funneling all mortal souls and destinies into my body and into my hands. And then, because I had to, I wove and secretly wished I was running instead.

Chapter 10

"Good morning, Oakridge! I'm Craaaaazy Mike and you're listening to K-K-K-KHITS. It's seven a.m., and I'm thinking about the seven deadly sins. Which one are you? Give us a call here at the studio, and the craaaaaaaziest answers will make it on air."

I was pretty sure that by "craziest answers," Crazy Mike meant "people who say lust." I was equally sure that I wasn't about to stick around to find out. I reached out with one hand, and when I swiped air instead of alarm, I threw my pillow in the general direction of the sound. When that proved useless, I narrowed my eyes and allowed a warm feeling to spread out from my body and attack the offending appliance, which promptly burst into flames.

In retrospect, that probably wasn't a good idea.

"Bailey Mar—*aaaaaaaaaaackkkk!*" My mom's drive-by scolding jerked to a stop, and she let loose an ear-piercing shriek. Proving that her completely unsupernatural Mom abilities were more useful than my superpowers, she almost instantaneously acquired a fire extinguisher from our utilities closet and made quick work of my blazing alarm.

Crazy Mike wasn't going to be bothering me again.

"Are you okay?" my mom asked, still wielding the fire extinguisher like a madwoman, as if the radio might reignite any second.

"I'm fine," I said, but the words fell flat. I wasn't fine. I was lost. Lonely. Alone. I missed the Otherworld the way I'd never missed anything in my life, the way I knew deep down that I would miss my friends once they went off and started living their exciting post–high school lives.

My mom seemed to sense that I was less than chipper, though she could have never, in her wildest dreams, come anywhere close to guessing why.

"You'll feel better once you have a plan," my mom said, imparting what passed in her mind for words of maternal wisdom. "You just need to narrow down your list a little and decide where you want to apply. Those deadlines will sneak up on you before you know it, and I think not applying anywhere early is part of what's stressing you out."

If I took the Otherworld out of the picture, my mom was simultaneously almost right and horribly wrong. The fact that I didn't have a plan for the future *was* stressing me out, but the fact that I hadn't opted for early admission was my one saving grace. At least this way I could still live in denial, much as I was still coming to terms with the fact that I'd spent the night in a world that made the Nexus seem like the redheaded stepchild of mythical places.

"You'd better get a move on," my mom said, cutting our heart-to-heart surprisingly and mercifully short. "At this rate, you won't even have time to wash your hair." With those words, she lifted the fire extinguisher higher and squirted it again, just to be safe, and then exited my room, leaving my alarm clock and my dresser covered in weird foamy stuff that made my eyes burn.

This was why it wasn't a good idea to use pyrokinesis in your bedroom.

I took a shower, and as my mom had predicted, I didn't have time to wash my hair. I was moving so quickly that I even forgot to take off Morgan's necklace, and I wondered briefly if this was taking what she'd said about always wearing it a little too far. After I'd lathered and rinsed, I turned off the shower and stepped out. I toweled off and then reached for my body splash, spraying a liberal amount on my hair, just in case.

Despite being in hurry mode, the second I stepped out of the shower, my eyes zeroed in on my reflection in the mirror, and I couldn't help but stare at it, looking for some hint of the person I'd been the night before. My hair was close to honey-colored, but in the most unremarkable way imaginable. In the Otherworld, it was both brown and blond at the same time, but here, it didn't quite manage either one, and sadly, my trip to the great beyond had done little to give it volume or bounce. My summer tan was already long gone, and even covered in steam, my body didn't let off any kind of glow.

She reeks of mortality. The words from the night before taunted me, and I wondered whose thoughts I'd inadvertently heard. I wanted to think it was the vampire twins, but I couldn't shake the feeling that it was Eze, that her stony smile didn't reach her eyes for a reason, and this was it. But even thinking that, part of me didn't want to wait until nightfall to go back. I wanted to be there, with the colors and the smells and the tastes and the wonderful, horrible feeling of being near others like me.

I didn't want to be standing in this world, naked and unsure of myself.

A sharp rap on the bathroom door startled me. At first, I thought it was my mom, but then the mystery person opened the door just far enough to thrust in a manicured hand holding my least favorite pair of jeans (they were too tight and made my legs itch) and a V-neck top. "Wear this, and hurry up. If we get to school early, I can bring you up to speed on Geek Watch."

I knew that I had only a small window of opportunity before Delia charged into the bathroom and took over all aspects of my personal appearance, so I grabbed the clothes and changed into them as quickly as I could, hopeful that at least I'd be dressed by the time she started her full-out fashion onslaught.

I had the shirt halfway over my head when Delia got restless. The next thing I knew, she'd grabbed a brush and was twisting my hair into some kind of knot that nobody except for Delia and a handful of sailors knew how to tie.

"Your hair smells like Country Apple," she said.

Astute, was Delia.

Either because I was lucky or as a matter of mercy, she didn't mention anything about the slightly un-washed nature of said hair, and by the time she was done, twenty-eight seconds later, I actually looked halfway decent. Not bothering with my makeup bag, Delia brought out her own trifecta and managed to make me over before I could utter even half of a refusal.

"Okay, let's go. Chop-chop. There are geeks to be watched and flirt strategies to be . . ." Delia searched for the right word. "Strategized."

I followed her out of the bathroom, my mind else-where, running over hills and drinking the sweet, cool nectar I hadn't so much as brought to my lips the night before. I looked at my feet as the two of us walked down the hallway, my eyes drawn again and again to my own shadow. As I clunked my way down the stairs—sans any grace whatsoever—I suddenly realized that I hadn't seen a single shadow in the Otherworld. Stuck on that notion for absolutely no reason whatsoever, I zoned out and lost track of what Delia was saying right around the time we headed out the front door. Delia, however, was not a person to be ignored, and when I got to the car, she snapped me out of it, primarily due to the numerous pieces of poster board leaning against the car's side.

"What are those for?" I asked suspiciously. Delia plus arts and crafts meant trouble. There was an incident with poster board when we were eight from which the neighborhood had never quite recovered.

"Trust, Bailey," Delia said. "That's all I'm asking." And then, because she was on a roll, she smiled charmingly at me. "By the way, can I drive?"

I didn't even dignify that question with a response. Completely unfazed, Delia picked up the poster board and climbed into the passenger side. As I buckled my seat belt, I caught the barest glimpse of the top of one of the pieces of poster board.

GEEK WATCH 2009.

This was so not good.

"You can't look yet," Delia told me, hugging the poster board to her chest. "I need to attach the pictures."

"Pictures?"

Delia smiled. "On a totally unrelated note, I need you to get a picture of the guy from study hall, the one who recognized your tattoo. Just take one with your phone. The quality might not be great once we blow it up, but—"

"Blow it up?" I tried to get another look at the poster board. "You do realize you're crazy, right?"

"Which one of us hears voices?" Delia asked. "Oh. Right. That would be you." She paused. "And speaking of, what happened last night with the Reckonmawhatsit you told us about at lunch?"

"Reckoning," I corrected, then nibbled on my bottom lip. For reasons which I couldn't have explained, more words than just that refused to come out of my mouth. Maybe because there weren't any that would describe things quite right, or maybe because there were, but I wanted to keep them for myself.

"It was . . . interesting," I said finally.

"Whoa, TMI." Delia raised an eyebrow. "There is such a thing as oversharing, Bay." And then, just in case I didn't catch it myself, she leaned a little closer and shared another tidbit with me in a conspiratorial whisper. "Sarcasm is the new perky."

Delia was probably the only A-lister at our school who could actually manage both.

"I'll tell you more once the others are here," I promised, knowing that this wasn't something I'd be able to keep from them forever. There was nothing I didn't share with my friends. My brain just wasn't wired for keeping secrets.

"Just tell me this much. Those others you met? The ones you were all nervous about yesterday?" Delia's voice dropped to a reverent whisper. "Were any of them hot?"

James. His name flashed immediately to mind, and I tried to remember what he looked like. Glowing skin, red-brown hair, blue, blue eyes. He was Sidhe, but something about him felt human. *Hot* wasn't the right word, and he wasn't even geek chic, but something about him stuck in my mind like toffee in freshly brushed teeth. There was just something about that boy . . . fairy . . . Greek god . . . whatever.

"Oooohhhhhh," Delia said, interpreting my facial expression with the skill of a professional profiler. "One of them *was* kind of hot. Does that mean you're not still crushing on the guy from study hall?"

I really didn't know how she did it. I hadn't even seen her since physics class the day before, when I'd decided that I might have possibly been interested in That Guy, and yet somehow she'd picked up on it. Probably before I had.

"I'm debating," I said, but even saying it made me feel a little bit silly, because I wasn't normally the kind of girl who had options in the crush department—especially not options who seemed like they were maybe kind of sort of interested back.

"No moping." When I snapped out of my reverie, Delia was giving me a very stern look. Luckily, without Zo there, she didn't pursue it further. "Honestly, Bay, when are you going to realize that you are one hot mama?"

I parked the car and turned to look incredulously at Delia. "Did you just use the phrase *one hot mama*?"

Delia looked momentarily abashed. "Absolutely not."

"Liar."

Zo and Annabelle were already waiting for us in the

parking lot. Both of them took in sharp breaths when they saw Delia's poster boards.

"This cannot end well," Zo said.

Delia turned to Annabelle. "You're on my side, right, A-belle?"

Annabelle, having not been there for the poster-board incident when we were eight, wasn't quite sure what she was supposed to be taking sides about. "I am Switzerland," she declared.

"What if I said there were graphs involved?" Delia knew exactly how to tempt Annabelle, who immediately turned to Zo and, with a completely straight expression on her face, said, "I'm on her side."

"Blood is supposed to be thicker than water." Zo grabbed her heart in mock betrayal.

"Yes, well, perhaps graphs are thicker than blood."

Water. Blood.

The memories of the night before were there, just below the surface in my mind, and hearing the right words brought them out. My blood. The water they'd offered me to drink.

"Speaking of blood," Zo said, sounding disturbingly cheerful, "I told A-belle about the slice and dice with your necklace yesterday."

Before Delia could pick up on the fact that there was something about our accessories that everyone knew except her, I quickly filled in the gaps with trademark Bailey babble. "Yesterday, I cut my finger on my pendant—you should totally watch out because they're really sharp—and the pendant's mirror showed the reflection of the blood, only it was Sidhe blue. Blood green. The color of our tattoos."

Luckily, Delia spoke fluent Bailey and didn't need a translator. "Gotcha." Without pause, she turned to Annabelle. "Any theories?"

Annabelle, being Annabelle, obliged. "Bailey said it herself: blood green. Our tattoos were made out of Sidhe blood."

Delia made a face.

"Bailey is part Sidhe, so even though she bleeds red in this world, it makes sense that the mirror might show her blood as a different color. Maybe the mirror shows things the way they really are. Or . . . ooooohhhhh! Maybe it makes the unseen seen, or reflects intangible mystical properties as easily processed visual stimuli."

I was overcome with two feelings. The first was double sided: Annabelle was a genius and I was an idiot (why hadn't *any* of those explanations occurred to me?); the second was a pang at the way Annabelle said *Sidhe*. She pronounced it correctly, but the word just didn't sound the same on her lips. Whenever Adea or Valgius or any of the others said it, they said it like it was the single most important word, the defining aspect of their being. It was their everything.

To Annabelle, it was just another word.

"I'll see what I can look up on magicked mirrors," Annabelle continued, thinking out loud. "There must be some way to distinguish between the different nuances of possibilities here. Anything else you want me to look up?"

Delia opened her mouth.

"Anything else that doesn't involve fashion or boys," Annabelle clarified. Delia closed her mouth. A-belle's eyes fixed on mine, and I was reminded of the fact that even without powers, Annabelle was mighty perceptive. "Anything about last night?"

I looked at my watch. First period started in less than two minutes, so I didn't have time to go into any details about the night before. I could hoard the memories in my mind for a while longer, probably until lunch, but because this was A-belle and I knew that not only would she find what I asked her to, she'd actually enjoy finding it, I gave her what I could.

"Anything you can get on Greek mythology would be good. I need info on all of the major players." If I could figure out who James was supposed to be . . .

"She's thinking about hot fairy guy," Delia announced.

"Am not."

"Are too!" All three of them spoke at once.

"He's not hot. He's just . . . James."

Zo wrinkled her forehead. "Adea, Valgius, and *James*?"

Zo's words managed to break through a dam in my mind, and more information came pouring out of my mouth as we walked. "Then there were these two girls who were, like, all over him. They kept stroking his arms like this." I demonstrated on Delia.

"Kinky."

Zo, Delia, and I turned to stare at A-belle, who looked sufficiently horrified.

"Yesterday it was psychic boobies, and today it's

kinky," Zo commented. "You're kind of turning into a pervert, A-belle."

The very idea was so patently ridiculous that I had to bite back a smile, which I only did for A-belle's sake, because her cheeks had turned bright, bright pink the second the word left her mouth.

Giving Zo a look that told her in no uncertain terms to stop teasing her cousin, I continued babbling. There were some things Delia and Zo just couldn't understand, and blushing was one of them. Of the four of us, Annabelle and I were probably the most alike, and babbling was my way of showing Shy Girl solidarity.

"And then there were these two girls named Axia and Lyria, and they're supposedly Artemis and Aphrodite, so anything you can find out about the two of them would be great. And Drogan is Hades, and his son is kind of full of himself, and Eze is totally Zeus."

Not that Eze could be partially Zeus, but this fact seemed so noteworthy that I had to add the "totally" in there, just for good measure.

"You met Zeus," Annabelle said, somewhat dazed.

"She has pink hair," I replied solemnly.

"Pink hair?" Delia seemed to be torn between being horrified and intrigued.

"Zeus is a girl?" Zo was nothing if not skeptical, but Annabelle simply noted this information and tucked it away in her mental filing cabinet for future reference. "I'll see what I can dig up," she said. "I'll also look up Morgan. She was Poseidon, right?"

I nodded, and thinking of Morgan made me bring

my hand to my necklace, even though I knew just how hazardous for the thumbs that could be.

"Light pink or dark pink hair?" Delia was still fixated on this point.

"Light. It was more white than pink, but sometimes, if light caught it the right way, you could make out the second color."

"Kind of unicorny?"

Sometimes Delia and I were on the exact same page as well.

"Yeah," I said, a smile creeping over my lips. "Kind of unicorny."

"We're going to be late for first period," Annabelle announced, and we picked up the pace. Some people wore watches. I didn't need one. I had an Annabelle instead. "Anything else I should look into?" she asked me.

I hesitated. Saying the words here seemed almost sacrilegious. I knew before I said it that it would sound wrong on my tongue, the same way that *Sidhe* did on Annabelle's. In the Otherworld, my voice was ancient, but here, I was seventeen, and it sometimes bordered on squeaky.

"The Otherworld," I said. "That's what Zo and I decided to call the . . . you know . . . other world." I paused, trying to work my way up to telling Annabelle the names Adea had mentioned when we'd first crossed over the night before.

Sidhe. Home.

The words weren't words so much as a memory of a feeling that I couldn't begin to articulate, so instead I

121

parted with the other, less personal—and less true—names.

"The Otherworld," I repeated. "Also known as Faerie, Olympus, Avalon, and the Beyond."

Sidhe. Home.

The feeling receded to the back of my head as I said the other names of the place that after only one night, I held very close to my heart.

A place where I would never be lonely.

A place for running and beauty and tasting clouds on your tongue.

"Faerie, Olympus, Avalon, and the Beyond," Annabelle repeated. "You know, there are probably at least a dozen other names in cultures across the world that refer to the exact same thing. I'll do some digging online and see what I can pull up."

A few minutes later, the four of us split up to go to our fourth hours. Delia left me with very firm instructions for mine: "Get a picture of your geek."

I rolled my eyes, but got the distinct feeling that my friend wouldn't be taking no for an answer.

"And remember, Bay," Delia said, in the tone of someone imparting great and sought-after wisdom. "It's totally possible to have two crushes at once."

Chapter 11

I slid into my seat in study hall five seconds after the bell rang, but the proctor didn't notice. A certain amount of obliviousness was a necessity for anyone proctoring study hall, given that the job required them to continuously overlook the hordes of students not studying. As I knew from personal experience, this particular teacher didn't even notice when, for example, you passed out on your physics book. A just-barely-tardy wasn't going to rank much higher on the notice meter.

Feeling vaguely wicked for getting away with something that at least two of my teachers considered a cardinal sin, I pulled out one of my textbooks and offered my appreciation to the proctor by at least pretending to study. I flipped through the pages, looking at the pictures, and with each one, I traced my finger over its surface, thinking how the contrast between photos taken in the seventies and the modern world was in some way similar to the differences between the Otherworld and Earth. It wasn't just a difference in color, and it wasn't just a difference in sheer size. It was a difference so great that the two didn't even occupy the same number of spatial dimensions. The real world was 3-D; these pictures were trapped on the two-dimensional page.

If time was the fourth dimension, then the Otherworld was 5-D. At least.

After a while, I got bored with the pictures, and I glanced around the room, looking for the mysterious Mr. Talbot-Olsen, he of the mussy hair and physics gallantry. Today, he was sitting beside me instead of behind, which meant that I only appeared mildly (as opposed to massively) sketchy trying to look at him without letting on that I was doing so. Like me, he was pretending to study, and he had a notebook out. I squinted, forgetting about subtlety in favor of potentially parsing out what he was writing. I'm not sure what I expected to see in his notebook, because it wasn't like he was likely to have conveniently spelled out the origin of his knowledge about ancient languages, and I doubted that he was sitting there daydreaming about me and doodling "Mr. Bailey Morgan" in the margins of his notebook.

Despite my best squinting efforts, though, I couldn't make much sense of his scribbles from this distance. His handwriting was pretty much as messy as his hair. Thinking hair thoughts distracted me for a few seconds because I kind of wondered what it would be like to touch his, and then I thought about running my hands through it, and that led me to thinking about James and the vampiric redheads petting him the night before.

James or my mystery geek? James or Mystery Geek?

Delia had claimed it was possible to have two crushes at once, but I was skeptical. In the years before I'd dated Kane, my devotion to him had been absolute. I hadn't even indulged in celebrity crushes; I was just that focused on my dream boy. So the idea of developing not one but two new crushes was a little unfathomable, especially considering that one of the boys wasn't human and that the other one definitely knew things he shouldn't.

Before I could fall into a black hole of self-conscious daydreams, I snapped myself out of it and tried to approach the situation with a little more objectivity. I needed more information about this boy, and that required getting a better look at his notebook, which required leaning over ever so slightly, which I did, and then it required leaning over just a little bit more . . .

Whap.

I fell out of my chair.

Oh, the horror. The absolute never-ending horror—but at least it wasn't for nothing, because as I tumbled out of my chair, my head came just close enough to his desk to make out the words written at the top.

Alec Talbot-Olsen.

Okay, I thought, *I have a name.* It wasn't much. A little Facebook sleuthing probably could have told me the same thing, with less humiliation and fewer bruises, but at least the throbbing in my knee provided me with an ache that wasn't in any way related to Otherworld withdrawal. And my geek had a name. Granted, he was looking at me kind of sideways, and my chances of fulfilling Delia's mandate and stealthily snapping a picture weren't looking too great, but I had bigger things to worry about. Like the fact that every single person in study hall, none of whom had noticed me passing out the day before, were now looking at me like I was the lead freak in a sideshow.

I felt a blush rising in my cheeks and tried to push it down. I couldn't afford to lose control of my emotions; I was already at my "one fire a day" limit. I scrambled to my feet and tried to pretend that the whole falling thing hadn't happened. I tried to think happy thoughts: puppies and kitties and cotton candy and unicorns . . . but thinking about unicorns made me think about Eze and her eerie-colored hair, and that led me back to the words I'd been trying not to think about for most of the morning.

She reeks of mortality.

I couldn't even survive in the mortal realm without almost concussing myself in a lame attempt to spy on a boy. How could I possibly expect to be a part of things in the Otherworld? It was beautiful. Perfect.

Home.

Okay, I thought, *what is wrong with me?* I'd just taken a nosedive in front of twenty-five other kids, and all I could think about was my not-a-dream the night before. I'd spent seventeen years in this world and only one night in the Otherworld. How could I miss it when twenty-four hours ago, I hadn't known the first thing about it? My mental image of the world of the Sidhe had always been the Nexus. I'd never understood that compared to the real Otherworld, the Nexus was practically earthly. Human. Mortal.

She reeks of mortality.

As the words entered my mind again, it occurred to me that in my rush out the door that morning, I'd forgotten to put on deodorant. I squeezed my arms tight to my sides in a gesture meant to guard my armpits from the world—or possibly the world from my armpits. Either way, as I sat there my paranoia escalated until I was absolutely positive that despite my not having so much as broken a sweat, mortality wasn't the only thing I reeked of.

"Are you . . . I mean . . . errrr . . . I guess . . ." Next to me, Alec tried to put together a coherent sentence. I figured he was probably trying to ask me if I was having some kind of armpit-clenching seizure, but when he finally got the words out, what he said was, "Are you cold?"

"Ummm . . . yes." I'd go with that answer over pit paranoia any day.

Alec gave me a small, tentative smile and then he started unzipping his jacket. The zipper got stuck halfway down, and as he battled with it, the meaning behind his actions finally sank in.

He was taking off his jacket to give it to me because I had said I was cold. Boys just didn't do things like that, and if they did, they were suave and smooth and expected something in return, but Alec . . .

He was getting all kinds of frustrated with the zipper. With an audible huff, he attacked it once more, and it finally gave way. Unfortunately, the effort propelled him sideways, and I watched as he struggled to catch his balance, lost, and fell out of his chair, exactly as I had a few minutes earlier.

Was it weird that I found that strangely endearing? And maybe even a little bit attractive? He fell out of his chair . . . for me.

I glanced around the room, wondering if his fall had garnered as much attention as mine had. Sure enough, everyone was staring at the two of us, but this time I didn't blush at all. He was blushing enough for the both of us.

It was a very nice blush.

Stay away.

The thought came unbidden, and it sounded foreign in my head. Sharp. Uncompromising. Dangerous. In fact, I'm pretty sure the correct word would have been *sinister*.

Stay away from him.

"Okay," I murmured under my breath. "That's a little bit scary."

The voice in my head wasn't Adea's, it wasn't

Valgius's, and it definitely wasn't mine. Someone or some*thing* was warning me away from Alec. But why? What could anyone stand to gain by keeping me away from a boy whose claim to fame was that he blushed as much as I did?

Unless, of course, Alec's real claim to fame was something else. It was so easy to forget that he'd recognized my tattoo and known what it meant. One look at his hair pretty much did that for me. Still, cute mussiness aside, the fact remained that Alec knew something that he probably shouldn't.

And based on the voices in my head, I could only conclude that somebody out there didn't want me to find out why. Either that, or they didn't want me to discover whatever else Alec knew.

OMG, I thought, processing these conclusions fully. Alec might know something else. About the Otherworld. About the Reckoning.

About me.

I glanced over at him, as if the answer to all of these questions and more lay in his expression, but his face was buried in his notebook again. From what I could see of his cheeks, he was still blushing. Despite the whirlpools of emotions swirling around in the pit of my stomach and the forefront of my mind, I found myself wanting to offer him a word or two of comfort, something along the lines of "I know how it feels" or "Been there, done that," but then I caught sight of his jacket still lying on the ground. He'd fallen out of his chair trying to take it off for me, and while he'd been trying to regain his composure, I'd become totally and completely sidetracked by the presence of someone else's hissing voice in the private recesses of my mind.

Maybe I was wrong, I thought, unable to tear my eyes from the jacket and what it represented. *Maybe he was never going to give it to me. Maybe the voices in my head haven't messed everything up this time.*

Or maybe Alec lost the courage to give me his jacket when I'd zoned out, every aspect of my conscious being concentrated on the warning I'd been issued and the possible reasons behind it. Maybe Alec took my zoning out as an indication that I wasn't interested, and now he was hugely embarrassed that he'd tried to give me his jacket in the first place.

After all, if I'd been him, I could guarantee that would be exactly what would have happened.

Slowly, I reached down to pick up the jacket, completely disregarding the warning I'd been given and the fact that I could still feel another presence flickering in and out of my head, like I was a television set with bad reception. I paused, as much because of the feeling as to look up at Alec and gauge his reaction to my actions.

"Still cold?" he asked, forgiving me for the perceived brush-off he'd probably been berating himself over for the past few minutes.

I nodded in answer to his question, took the jacket, and slipped it on. I wasn't actually cold, but I wasn't about to turn down such a sweet offer, and I couldn't bring myself to let the voice in my head threaten me out of making a nice guy smile.

Alec had a really nice smile.

Stay.

Away.

From.

Him.

The words were more emphatic this time, delivered with an odd, staccato rhythm that would have freaked me out even if the message had been "Have a nice day."

Completely creeped out, I grabbed for the chain around my neck, as if I expected the necklace to protect me from whoever had pushed their way through my psychic barriers. Nothing happened. I could still feel the presence in my mind, quiet and waiting.

I froze in my seat, my body going perfectly stiff as I remembered my tongue-in-cheek mental rant about the nonzero chance of death involved in the next few days. Of course, at the time I hadn't realized that Alec was a player, that for whatever reason, he mattered enough for somebody to warn me away.

I shook my head once, trying to clear it of inter-lopers in a way that felt completely natural, but didn't prove to be effective. The movement of my head, com-bined with the stiffening of my upper body in response to the sheer freaky quotient of what was happening to me, resulted in my losing my balance yet again. This time I managed to catch myself before I fell out of the chair, but I still garnered a few chuckles.

Darn those girls, I thought, never too caught up in Otherworldly troubles to focus on the fact that the popular crowd at my school enjoyed laughing at me more than they would have if I weren't Kane's pathetic little ex.

We could take care of them for you, the voice in my head promised. *We could make them stop laughing.*

Was it me, or was there a "forever" implied on the end of that sentence?

No, I thought back vehemently. *Leave them alone. Leave* me *alone.*

This was almost as effective as shaking my head had been.

The sound of the bell signaling the end of study hall surprised me—mainly because, for a split second, I mistook it for a shrill scream that only I could hear. With great effort, I forced myself to stand up, and as I stood, the feeling of wrongness slid away from my body, until I realized that whoever had been in my head a moment before wasn't there now.

As I bent down to grab my backpack, dazed and confused, I realized two things. First, that I was still wearing Alec's jacket, and second, that the chair I'd been sitting in a moment before was covered by a shadow. I glanced toward the window, where a filing cabinet, responsible for the shadow, peered back at me.

Were the shadows I'd been seeing somehow connected to the sinister voice in my head?

I made myself take off Alec's jacket. I fumbled with the zipper, but didn't have too much trouble with it, and as I handed the jacket back to Alec, I unzipped my bag with my other hand and pulled out my cell.

A girl had to have her priorities, and right now I really couldn't take thinking about shadows or voices or the strong possibility that if I didn't stay away from Alec, things might get ugly.

Instead, I flipped open my phone, expertly switched it to camera function, and took his picture just as he turned to leave the room. In what amounted to nothing less than a miracle, he didn't seem to notice.

Feeling somewhat satisfied (and still on edge from the morning's events), I closed the phone and stuck it in my bag, lest the oblivious proctor come out of her reverie long enough to confiscate it. Right before he reached the classroom door, Alec turned and smiled at me once more, before walking slowly away.

Completely light-headed and still more than a little *off,* I made my way to the door, barely processing the many conversations going on around me. There was a good chance at least one of them was about me and my freakishness, but the dialogue that managed to break its way through my daze had nothing to do with my performance in study hall.

"I love him."

"Me too. I love him so much."

"I'm totally going to be Mrs. Him."

I cast a sideways look at the speakers of those sentences, wondering who their *him* was, and why October seemed to be the new spring when it came to l-u-v.

"Nice haircut."

I didn't have to look in the direction of those words to know that they were spoken by one of Alexandra

Atkins's cronies, the very same girls, coincidentally enough, who'd enjoyed laughing at me so very much. This time, however, the insult wasn't aimed my way (for once). Instead, it seemed to be targeting one of the l-u-v girls, who finally stopped romanticizing long enough to process it.

"In fact," Jessica (the Alexling in question) continued, "that haircut is just adorable. It reminds me of my dog, you know? I just want to pet you. Or hit you with a rolled-up newspaper or something."

This was one part of high school I most definitely wouldn't miss.

"Maybe next time," the Mean Girl continued, "you can just shave your head. Believe me, bald is beautiful, at least compared to *that*."

With that, Jessica flounced out of the room.

Hair Girl (who really didn't look that bad or canine at all) stood there, her eyes dull and shell-shocked, and her friends just shook their heads.

"Don't pay attention to her. She's a witch."

"Yeah," Hair Girl said. "And she gets away with it."

The other two girls began walking out of the classroom. As they stepped over the threshold and turned back to their friend, an expression that struck me as vaguely familiar and utterly alien settled over their faces. "That's just so wrong," the two girls said in unison, their voices—dangerous and oddly sultry-sounding—burning themselves into my memory. And then the girls stepped through the doorway and out into the hall, and continued their conversation, the oddness that had descended on them a moment before suddenly gone.

I hurried out of the classroom, shivering as I stepped through the doorway, wondering if my imagination was going overboard, or if Alec wasn't the only one involved in this mystery.

Chapter 12

Lunchtime could not come soon enough. And when it finally did roll around, I'd come dangerously close to convincing myself that the study-hall creepiness had been just another twisted daydream. You know—long for the Otherworld, think about James and Alec, imagine a sinister voice in my head warning me away from the latter. The daydream theory made perfect sense, except for the fact that this wasn't the first time I'd heard voices. Honestly, I was starting to think that I needed to write NO VACANCY on my forehead in permanent marker.

Really, though, what I needed was to find out who had invaded my psychic space and why they had warned me away from Alec.

Awww, I thought, temporarily distracted. *Alec.*

Apparently, the mystical weirdness surrounding Alec didn't detract from my desire to act on Delia's Geek Theory. If anything, the mystery added to Alec's allure. I didn't know whether it was because I was part Sidhe or because I was one hundred percent teenage girl, but I couldn't put the mystery—or Alec—out of my mind.

My mind was still in the clouds when I met my friends in the school parking lot. There was so much to tell, but before I could ask them to weigh in on the Alec mystery, I had to bring them up to speed. I had major explaining to do, and I wasn't exactly sure where to start. As the four of us piled into A-belle and Zo's car, I cleared my throat. "Hey, guys? Did anything weird happen to you during, I don't know, first hour?"

I didn't expect the answer to be yes, because the only psychic voice any of my friends had ever heard was mine, but the question seemed like a good way to segue into the Guess-What-Happened-to-Me-in-Study-Hall topic.

"First hour," Zo said, mulling over my question. "It sounds vaguely familiar in that 'happens before noon' kind of way."

Zo was even less of a morning person than I was. I turned to Annabelle, knowing instinctively that Delia's version of *weird* would likely involve color coordination or flirtations gone bad.

"I had English," Annabelle said. "We talked about *Beowulf*."

"And you enjoyed it," Zo said.

Annabelle grinned.

"Now, *that's* weird."

Annabelle looked straight at Zo and said something in a language that wasn't English. Because she'd lived in about a dozen different countries growing up, A-belle knew more languages than the rest of us combined, and for the past couple of years, she'd been really into studying ancient languages. As a result, though her English was strictly PG, she often got the last word by saying something a little more profane and a lot more insulting in a language none of us could understand.

"I'm just going to pretend you told me what a wonderful, witty cousin I am," Zo maintained, but we all knew that Annabelle had won this round.

"Your question raises another interesting one, though, Bailey," Annabelle said.

"Where are we going for lunch?" Zo guessed.

"Did you take a photo of your geek?" That was from Delia.

"No," Annabelle said. "If Bailey's wanting to know if something weird happened in our first hours, that probably means something weird happened in hers."

I knew I could count on Annabelle to pick up on that. She was Old Reliable *and* Miss Observant, and I loved her for it.

"Something did happen," I said, and my mind went straight to the way Alec had smiled at me, even though I'd meant to express the eerier aspects of my study-hall experience.

"Well, don't leave us hanging, Bay," Zo said as she

started the car and pulled out of the parking lot. "And where do you guys want to go?" It occurred to me that if the rest of us didn't get our bids for lunch in soon, with Zo behind the wheel, we'd inevitably end up at Coney, a restaurant where everything came with a side of chili and two sides of cheese.

Annabelle intervened. "Let's go to Fifties," she said decisively, and Delia and I groaned in protest, my news and the fact that I had yet to dish it temporarily forgotten. There are some things in life that take precedent over just about anything. Our joint Fifties-related trauma was one of those things. The summer we were sixteen, all four of us got jobs as carhops at Fifties, a drive-in restaurant where your food was delivered directly to your car by girls on roller skates.

Needless to say, I'd spent the entire summer as one giant bruise, and the fifties-style burgers and fries had lost most of their appeal over the course of our carhop tenure.

"We've got a lot to discuss." Annabelle explained her logic, turning around to give me a look that clearly stated that she was still waiting to hear what had happened to me during first hour. "And these discussions are probably ones we shouldn't have in public." She paused. "Right, Bay?"

I nodded. The last thing I needed was for someone to overhear me saying something about the voices in my head. The popular crowd already thought I was a loser; I didn't need the rest of the school thinking I was clinically insane, too.

"Annabelle's right," I said, for probably the eight millionth time in the past few years. "We need privacy, and things don't get more private than staying inside the car." Fifties was hands down the fastest, easiest option that ruled out the possibility of eavesdroppers.

"Done." Zo was pleased—the summer we'd worked at Fifties, she'd easily eaten her weight in onion rings.

Delia wasn't as enthused, but she tried to stay positive. "I hear they're serving salads now," she said, tactfully not mentioning that a Fifties salad was, in all likelihood given the rest of the menu, a bunch of deep-fried lettuce. "And speaking of salads, Bailey, talk!"

Delia didn't bother with actual segues. She just didn't have to.

"Okay," I said, dragging out the word to give my mind time to process bits and pieces of memory from this morning: the sound of the voice in my head, the words it had spoken, the way Alec had looked at me, the weirdness I'd felt in the room just before walking out the door.

My friends didn't interrupt my thought process—not even Delia, who had trouble staying quiet more often than not.

"There were voices," I said. "In my head."

My friends took this news quite well.

"No offense, but aren't there always voices in your head?" Zo asked. "I mean, you're psychic. It kind of comes with the gig."

"Not that kind of voice," I said. "This wasn't someone's thoughts. This was someone talking to me, the way that Adea and Val do."

"And you're certain it wasn't either of them." Annabelle's words were a statement, not a question, but I confirmed them anyway.

"I'm positive. When Adea and Valgius talk to me, their voices are . . ." There were so many words. *Bone-shattering* and *mind-boggling* and *wonderfully terrible*. "Trust me. This wasn't them. It sounded . . ." It took me a second to find the right word. "Younger."

At the time I'd heard the words, my impressions had centered on the venom in the tone, but as soon as my mouth picked *younger* to describe it, I knew it was true. Adea and Valgius never sounded hateful. Even Alecca, who'd been a Big Bad in every sense of the term, didn't resort to mean. There was enough power in her voice that she didn't need to.

Once you reach a certain point on the evil scale, mean just looks kind of silly.

"The voice warned me away from Alec," I said. "And whoever it was"—with my realization about the speaker's age, the suspect list had just gotten a whole lot shorter—"they really meant it."

"Who's Alec?" Zo asked.

I sensed, rather than saw, Delia rolling her eyes. "Alec's her geek. Obvi."

"The one who knew what your tattoo meant?" Annabelle asked.

I nodded.

141

"And now one of the Sidhe . . ." She paused. "We are working on the assumption that the voice was a Sidhe, yes?"

I nodded. Maybe there were other possibilities— another psychic, some mystical creature I didn't even know about—but given who and what I was, Sidhe was our best bet. And besides, if what James had said the night before, about Sidhe innately knowing their own, was to be believed, it made sense for me to trust my instincts. I'd felt Morgan near before I'd seen her. I'd felt the other Sidhe the moment I'd entered the Otherworld.

I'd felt that same familiarity, only less so, with each cutting word the voice in my head had spoken.

"Alec knew what your tattoo meant, and now one of the Sidhe is warning you away from him. Either he's dangerous and someone's warning you off for your own good, or somebody doesn't want the two of you together because it interferes with their plans."

"I think he knows something," I said. "Something that somebody else doesn't want me to know." I just couldn't imagine what that could be. I'd been to the Otherworld. I'd met other Sidhe. What could a high school geek know that would set one of them on edge?

"You have to talk to him," Delia said. "Trust me on this one. If someone is telling you to stay away from him, what that really means is that he's worth having. Every guy I've ever dated has come complete with a 'back off, he's mine' memo. Apparently, your geek is a desirable." She smiled. "The movement is growing."

Zo snorted. "Delia, I seriously doubt that the Sidhe want Bailey to stay away from Geek Boy so that they can date him themselves."

"But they could want him for something else," Annabelle said thoughtfully. "In some mythologies, the fair folk enjoy playing with humans. Making them their pets. Some people even believed that fairies stole human babies and replaced them with their own."

"So either the Sidhe want Alec for something, in which case Bailey needs to be his personal bodyguard, or he knows something, in which case Bailey needs to get the information out of him. Either way, I stand by my original assessment. The two of them totally need to date. Bailey can guard his body all she wants." Delia delivered that last sentence with a tone that had me fighting off a blush.

Still, it wasn't the worst idea in the world. . . .

"Was there anything else?" Annabelle asked me.

"She wants something she can research," Zo said, interpreting for her cousin. "Apparently, now that she's looked up everything you asked her about this morning, she's lusting after a new assignment."

"I do not lust," Annabelle said.

Delia reached up to pat A-belle's arm consolingly. "That's just because you haven't found the right geek yet. Don't worry, Delia is on the case!"

Delia referring to herself in the third person was never a good thing. Trying to head off disaster, I gave Annabelle what she'd asked for. "When I heard the voices, I was sitting in shadows. And I keep feeling like someone is watching me, like there's something more to a shadow than there used to be. And then there was this weird thing as we were leaving class. I can't even describe it, but it felt distinctly creepy."

"Shadows," Annabelle murmured. "I'll add it to my research queue. And I'll look for information about the Sidhe crossing into our world, too. Even if they're just here psychically, it might help us figure out how it's done."

About that time, I noticed that the car wasn't moving. "How long have we been at Fifties?" I asked.

"Five minutes," Zo said proudly. "We made great time."

I was grateful that I'd been so caught up in our conversation that I hadn't noticed the driving techniques that allowed us to make it to Fifties in half the time it should have taken.

"We should probably order," Annabelle said. "And then I have some things we need to discuss."

We ordered, and I tried to figure out what exactly the next discussion would entail. When Annabelle pulled out a three-inch-thick binder and started handing out packets of paper, I flashed back to what Zo had said about Annabelle finishing her research assignment and wanting a new one.

A-belle was nothing if not efficient.

"This is the best overview I could find of Greek mythology," she said. "It's pretty comprehensive, and covers the Olympians, lesser gods, and heroes." All business, she handed us each another, smaller packet. "This one has information on the specific entities you asked about, Bailey, compiled and paraphrased from a variety of sources and color coded by god. Aphrodite is yellow, Artemis is green, Poseidon is blue, Hades is red, and Zeus is pink."

Taken out of context, Zeus being pink would have seemed weird, but thinking about Eze, it made perfect sense.

When Annabelle started handing out a third packet of printouts, I thought Zo was going to have a heart attack. This was probably more reading than she'd done all of last year.

"This is everything I was able to come up with on the Otherworld, also known by a variety of other names, all of which refer to a place inhabited by fairy races and offset from the mortal plane in some way." Annabelle paused for a breath and then rattled on. "Incidentally, one of the terms for the Otherworld is *Faerie*, which is also used to refer to the creatures who live there. This term has its root in the Greek *fata*, which was originally used in reference to the three Fates."

Normally, when A-belle started a sentence with "incidentally," the rest of the sentence was the kind of thing that she found interesting but I didn't even understand: boring with a side of over-my-head. This time, however, I followed her point surprisingly well. Even though the Greeks and the Celts hadn't melded their mythology in any way that approximated reality as I knew it, somehow, the word *fairy*—however it was spelled—came from the way the ancient Greeks had referred to Adea, Alecca, and Valgius.

Maybe on some level someone had figured it out. The Fates were faeries, the creatures who lived in the Otherworld. Sidhe.

Having successfully imparted that interesting tidbit, Annabelle continued summarizing her findings. "From what I've been able to tell, it appears as though most myths have the Otherworld as home to a variety of different kinds of supernatural creatures, including fairy varieties other than Sidhe."

Wrong, I thought. The Otherworld was for Sidhe, and only Sidhe. Power and beauty. Nothing else.

"Some stories divide the Otherworld into two parts, so I've divided this information into sections as well. The Seelie Court, which you'll find on pages three and four of this handout, traditionally houses the more benign fairies, and the Unseelie Court—on pages five and six—seems a lot more sinister."

Wrong again. If there was one thing I was certain of, it was that Eze and Drogan were matched on many levels; neither of them was more dangerous than the other. They were equally wonderful and equally horrible and even thinking their names generated in me a bone-deep desire to bow.

A tap at the window made me jump, as much as I could with my seat belt still on. Zo rolled down the window, and a poor, beleaguered carhop, who was probably thinking about how much she hated roller skates and hamburgers and us, handed over a large bag bulging with food. It took us a few minutes to get the money right, and the entire time I kept one eye on the carhop, wondering if we'd be the ones to push her over the carhop edge.

After we'd paid, she begrudgingly handed us some napkins and a single packet of ketchup to share, and without another word or, heaven forbid, a smile, she skated away.

Zo rolled up the window and, like some kind of fast-food Santa Claus, began happily doling out our food. I accepted my cheeseburger and then craned my neck to look at Delia's salad, which appeared to be impressively green, aside from a liberal splattering of croutons half the size of my fist.

Downright jovial now that she was surrounded by edibles, Zo spared a thoughtful look for the thick wad of papers Annabelle had handed her. "You want to give us the condensed version of this, A-belle?"

Annabelle, after chewing a dainty bite of onion ring, agreed, and the rest of us dug into the food and tuned in to the Annabelle Porter Show. "Most of the individuals Bailey asked about were Olympians, senior gods who were thought to dwell primarily on Mount Olympus."

I remembered the mountain I'd stood on the night before and the way it had morphed to meet our needs, the way it had literally grown beneath my feet, catapulting me into the sweet mist of the sky as I ran.

"The Olympians came to power after overthrowing an older generation of gods called the Titans. If we assume that this reflects something that actually happened in Sidhe history, I can only guess that there was some kind of power struggle and that the current rulers emerged as victors during or before the heyday of ancient Greece."

I nibbled around the edge of a Tater Tot. A-belle in scholarly mode was a thing to behold.

"After the war with the Titans, three of the Olympians, brothers, emerged as leaders and divided their world among them. Zeus became ruler of the heavens, Hades inherited the underworld, and Poseidon got the seas."

I tried to interweave this information with what I'd learned the night before. Mythology never got things quite right, so I didn't expect what I'd seen to line up exactly with what Annabelle was saying, but decided I'd settle for making as much sense out of the overlap as I could.

Eze, who was once known as Zeus, ruled the heavens, which had to refer somehow to the Seelie Court, since Eze was the Seelie Queen. Drogan was Hades, meaning he had inherited the underworld, also known as the Unseelie Court. An image came to my mind as I thought about the kind of place that the so-called King of Darkness would call home: dark and cavernous, but somehow every bit as beautiful as the land of light. That just left Morgan, who was Poseidon. James hadn't mentioned her, but he had told me that there were three rulers before he'd cut himself off, leaving me with the impression that mentioning Morgan's existence, let alone her name, was forbidden. According to mythology, Poseidon ruled the seas.

The ones in the Otherworld, and the ones on Earth.

The second that last thought occurred to me, I knew it was true, but I wasn't entirely sure how I'd arrived at the conclusion, or even if it was a conclusion, or if it was some kind of memory, carried by my Sidhe blood to my human brain, slumbering there and waiting to be recalled. This insight came to me all at once, but I needed a few seconds to process it. Luckily, Annabelle broke from talking to take a bite of her chicken sandwich.

A few seconds later, she was back in action. It took more than a chicken sandwich to keep our resident Research Girl from imparting wisdom to the masses (read: Delia, Zo, and me). "There are numerous myths involving Zeus, to the extent that there isn't really a definitive myth. He was thought to have many children: the Muses, Artemis, Apollo, Hercules . . . the list goes on and on, but it does not, interestingly enough, include Aphrodite, whom some consider to be older than Zeus himself."

"Must be a clerical error," I told her. "Because Lyria—that's Aphrodite—she's definitely Eze's daughter, and she's definitely a teenager. Though I guess the Sidhe version of a teenager is still probably thousands of years old. At least."

I wondered how old James was, or Xane or Lyria or

Axia or any of them. If they'd played a role in Greek mythology, then they'd been around in the heyday of ancient Greece, and if James was to be believed, he was the first James. In other words, the "young ones" among the Sidhe were a *lot* older than I was. At this rate, I'd be sitting at the kids' table at "family" gatherings until I died.

If I died.

"In mythology, Aphrodite sprang to life fully formed from the foam in the sea," Annabelle continued. "She's the goddess of love and beauty, though the love side of that equation seems to tend more toward lust than anything else."

Zo stopped shoveling food into her mouth just long enough to whistle when Annabelle said *lust*.

Annabelle blushed and glared at Zo, in that order, and then continued. "Aphrodite was known as a jealous goddess. She was moody and vengeful and very aware of her own beauty."

I tried to picture Lyria. She'd been so quiet, quieter even than Annabelle, and she'd come to my rescue when Kiste and Cyna were playing the bitca game with me. *Timid* was a word I'd use to describe her, and maybe *graceful*, but *moody, jealous,* and *vengeful*?

The ancient Greeks had apparently been smoking something when it came to the myths they'd constructed for Lyria.

"What about Artemis?" It was hard to think of Lyria without thinking of Axia. Of the two sisters, Axia was dominant, though hers was a quiet strength, diametrically opposed to Xane's arrogance and even her own mother's steely, regal air.

"Artemis was the goddess of the hunt," Annabelle replied. "She was often depicted carrying a bow with arrows. She was strong and sleek, the ethereal huntress, and was also considered to be the goddess of the moon. Her twin brother, Apollo, was the sun god."

Sun and moon: the symbols intertwined on my lower back. Together, they meant life.

"There was no Apollo," I said, sorting things out as I talked. "Just Artemis and Aphrodite, Zeus and Hades."

Then again, just because I hadn't met Apollo didn't mean he didn't exist. For all I knew, James could be Apollo.

"What about Hot Fairy Dude?" Delia asked, practically (though not, I was sure, actually) reading my mind.

I considered the possibility. James as Apollo. The sun god, James.

It just sounded wrong. Then again, I was deeply suspicious that "James" wouldn't sound quite right with anything.

"I actually think James might not be an Olympian," Annabelle said. "From the way Bailey described her experiences in the Otherworld, it sounds as if the Olympians she met have all been pretty high up in the Sidhe hierarchy. Zeus and Hades rule the two courts; Artemis and Aphrodite are Zeus's heirs. If James was Apollo, I think you would have gotten some sense of his status, Bailey."

151

I definitely couldn't see James as a prince of any-thing. He seemed too normal, too goofy, too border-line human. Lyria, Axia, and Xane had identified themselves as heirs to the thrones from the get-go. James hadn't been involved in their political squabbling at all.

"So if he's not an Olympian, what does that leave?" I asked. Now that my earthly crush was shrouded in mystery, I felt more compelled to figure out everything about my Otherworldly one, especially who he was to the ancient Greeks.

"Unfortunately, James not being an Olympian doesn't narrow down our choices that much," Anna-belle said. "The Greeks had gods for pretty much every-thing. James could be anyone."

For once, my hormone-driven brain didn't zero in on the part of that sentence that focused on a cute male. Something else about Annabelle's words jumped out at me, grating in my ears. In lecture mode, A-belle was saying the word *god* just enough for it to bother me. It was one thing to talk about Greek gods and myths, but when the characters from those stories were people I'd met . . .

It just seemed wrong. Axia and Lyria, Drogan and Eze . . . they weren't gods. They just weren't. They were Sidhe, a proud, ancient race whose world was off-set from ours. They were powerful, but they weren't *all*-powerful. They were beautiful, but they weren't necessarily good, and the part of me that had grown up in this world couldn't shake the feeling that if there was a god, a real one, he was something else entirely.

Annabelle, oblivious to my silent philosophizing, took another bite of her sandwich and then continued, happy to lecture indefinitely now that she'd sunk her teeth into the subject. "Just to give you a familiar example of some non-Olympians, the Fates, also referred to as the Moirai, were considered separate from, and to some degree lower than, those who dwelled on Olympus."

You reek of mortality.

Lower than the Olympians, through my association with this world and the mortals who lived here. Separated from the Otherworld; exiled to the Nexus.

"Other non-Olympians included the Muses, the Graces, and the Furies. Tangentially, the number three seems to hold a great deal of significance in these myths, though there were, of course, nine Muses."

"What about cupids?" Delia asked. "That's Greek mythology, right?"

"Cupid," Annabelle corrected, "as in singular, and that name is actually Roman. To the Greeks, he was Eros."

My mind went again to James, and I tried to picture him as Cupid. From there, my thoughts progressed (or maybe digressed) into a rather elaborate daydream involving James setting his sights and his arrows on me.

"Eros was quite easily distinguishable among the Greek gods," Annabelle continued, "due to his wings."

I knew better than anyone that the Greeks had gotten a lot of things wrong, so I didn't let A-belle's words burst my daydream bubble quite yet, even though I had to admit that James didn't seem overly romantic,

153

at least not toward me. Still, James could have been Eros. If quiet, timid Lyria was Aphrodite, anything was possible.

"Speaking of Cupid," Delia said, refusing to use the Greek name, probably because the Roman one made her think of Valentine's Day, which most girls loathed but Delia actually adored, because red was one of her best colors and she had a weakness for those candy hearts that pretty much no one else liked but everyone handed out each year anyway. "Can I fold down the backseat so I can spread out my supplies?"

Delia saying the words *Cupid* and *supplies* in close proximity to each other could not possibly be a good thing.

"That depends," Zo said suspiciously. "Are we going to have a repeat of the poster-board massacre?"

Massacre was probably overstating things. A little.

"I was *eight*," Delia retorted, "and it's not like anybody died!"

"Answer the question," Zo deadpanned.

"Fine," Delia said pertly. She lifted one manicured hand into the air. "I do solemnly swear that I have my poster board under control."

"And no part of this secret project involves putting streaks in my hair?" Zo continued, suspicious as always.

"For the last time, they're called highlights," Delia huffed, "but I promise to leave your hair alone."

"Deal."

Delia climbed out of the car and opened the back, letting down the tailgate and manhandling the rear seats into a folded position so that she could spread out the suspiciously large amount of "supplies" she'd brought.

"Okay," I said, trying to stay focused and not allowing myself to think too much about Delia's project. "Cupid, Zeus, Hades, Artemis, Aphrodite, the Fates, etc., etc. Anything else?"

I could tell just by looking at her that Annabelle was dying to correct my et ceteras, but instead she just glanced at her packet. "There's a story is section B-1 you really need to read. It should be highlighted in red."

"Red was Aphrodite?" I tried to remember the color scheme.

"Hades," Zo corrected. Though she wouldn't have admitted it under threat of torture, Zo was better at following her cousin's endearingly anal organization techniques than the rest of us. It must have been something in those Porter genes.

"It's a story about how exactly Hades got his bride," Annabelle said, and it occurred to me for the first time that somewhere out there, Xane probably had a mother.

"I know this one," Zo said. "So-and-so kidnaps such-and-such and brings her to the underworld." Zo's grasp of Greek mythology was shaky at best. She had this theory that the whole thing was one giant soap opera.

Not that I could disprove that particular point, based on everything I'd seen.

"Hades kidnapped a girl named Persephone and

took her to the Underworld as his bride," Annabelle said. "While she was there, she ate some pomegranate seeds, and because of this, she was trapped there for a certain number of months each year, unable to return to the world above."

"Okay," I said, thinking of Drogan and Xane and the underworld I hadn't seen. "No pomegranate seeds."

"No food," Annabelle corrected. "Nothing to drink, either. It's another one of those overlaps between Celtic and Greek mythology. Several sources I found mentioned that if a human eats or drinks in the Otherworld, they can never leave. Ever. In the rare instances in which they do leave, they starve to death, because mortal food never tastes the same again."

For a split second, a jolt of something akin to fear passed through my body as I realized how close I'd come to drinking the night before. I stared down at my hamburger, and the bite in my mouth seemed to turn to sawdust. I was objectively lucky that I hadn't had anything to drink last night, but I could still almost taste the air, the mist, the place itself on my tongue. I put my burger down, my appetite gone.

"In Greek mythology," Annabelle continued, uncharacteristically oblivious to my train of thought, "if a mortal drank ambrosia, the nectar of the gods, he or she became immortal, like the gods themselves. It's unclear what happened after that, or if something like that could actually happen to you, because you're not entirely human to begin with, but either way, I don't think you should eat or drink anything while you're there, just in case."

I glanced at Zo. Following Annabelle's dictate would have been much harder for her than it would be for me.

"I have two questions," Delia announced from the backseat.

"Shoot," Annabelle said.

"First question is for Bailey. This Hades guy, the one who kidnapped Persephone?"

An image of Drogan—pale skin, hair the color of midnight—filled my mind. "Yeah?"

"Is he hot?"

It was such a Delia question to ask. Next, she'd be asking me what Eze had been wearing.

"He's old," I said. "Really old." That was probably an understatement. I wasn't sure how many thousands of years Drogan had been ruling the Unseelie Court, so I put it in terms I knew Delia would understand. "He looks at least thirty."

"Oh." Delia got over her disappointment surprisingly quickly. "My second question is for Annabelle."

Annabelle tilted her head to the side, waiting.

"Are we done with the research stuff yet? Because lunch period is already half over, and I'm going to need at least twenty minutes to bring you guys up to speed on Geek Watch."

Good old Delia. If you needed someone to break up solemnity, Delia was your girl.

"I'll run some searches on crossing over and the

mythological significance of shadows tonight," Annabelle said, "but for now, I'm done. It's all you, Dee."

Zo leaned around her seat to meet my eyes. She said nothing out loud but sent a thought my way: *I knew letting her near poster board was a mistake.*

Chapter 13

Delia had Annabelle and me get out of our seats so that she could fold them down as well. Then she instructed the three of us to sit on top of the folded seats so that we could see the display she'd set up on the others. The centerpiece was the poster board I'd caught a glimpse of this morning. Delia had written GEEK WATCH in scripty, all-capital letters at the top. Underneath, in a variety of colorful markers, she'd provided pictures, statistics, and commentary on the top four chic geeks at our school. There was Jared Sands, aka Music Geek, under whose name she'd written:

*Moody and deep
*Needs a haircut—in a good way!

*Writes his own songs
*Doesn't talk much, but when he does . . . wow!

She'd listed similar attributes for each of the others: the math genius who'd probably grow up to be the next Bill Gates (with better fashion sense, Delia insisted); Lit Geek, who Delia was pretty sure was the kind of guy to quote Shakespeare to a girl and actually mean it; and Cryptic Geek.

"His name is Alec," I told her. "Alec Talbot-Olsen."

Delia grabbed a marker and wrote that down. Whereas she'd printed out pictures for all of the other guys, Alec's profile was mainly question marks, though she'd ascertained that he was "adorably shy," "really, really smart," and "mysterious."

"You know, if a bunch of guys put our pictures on a poster and sat around discussing the way we look and act, we'd call them pigs." Zo made this comment in a completely neutral voice, and without taking a peek in her mind, I couldn't tell whether she was bothered by this fact, or amused.

"It does seem kind of . . . wrong," Annabelle said meekly.

Delia waved their objections away. "One: We're only saying good things about them. Two: We're barely talking about the way they look. If a bunch of guys were doing this, it would be all about our bodies, which is why they'd be pigs. And three: These guys are totally unappreciated at our school, and we're appreciating them. Do any of you really think they'd mind?"

Clearly, Delia had put a lot of thought into this. Underneath all of the fashion and boy talk, she was actually one of the nicest people I'd ever met. She'd been popular for as long as I'd known her, but she'd never ditched the rest of us, and she didn't seem to care about popularity at all. While the rest of the girls at our school were tearing each other down, Delia was earnestly bestowing fashion advice upon the masses. The worst thing anyone could say about her was that she was shallow, and those of us who knew her knew she wasn't even that. Long story short, Delia wouldn't have been doing this if she'd thought there was a chance of hurting somebody.

"Here we are," Delia said, gesturing to a small stack of poster-board squares about an eighth the size of the first.

"We?" I asked. Delia nodded and then proceeded to hand us each a square with our picture on it. All four pictures had been taken the same night, two years ago. I wondered if Delia had done this on purpose, or if seeing Morgan the day before had just brought sophomore year and that particular dance up in her subconscious mind. More likely, she'd chosen these pictures because it was the last time Zo had given Delia complete control over her appearance: dress, makeup, hair, and all.

"We've got four *possibilities* here"—in a rare show of tact, Delia very pointedly did not call them geeks— "and four of us. Now we just have to decide who the best match for each of us is, and then we'll pin our pictures on to indicate the pairings. We'll reassess later in the week, and if us or the guys aren't feeling it, we'll scramble and try again."

"You've got to be kidding me," Zo said. "This isn't a game show, Queenie."

Delia dazzled us with a brilliantly white smile. "But it could be."

Zo rolled her eyes, but she gave in, because as much as she played the martyr, she and Delia were in a constant process of making each other's lives interesting. Without Delia around, Zo would probably be too busy beating guys at soccer to ask them out, and without Zo to argue with, Delia might have gotten caught up in the fact that with almost everyone else, her charm got her whatever she wanted. They were both extremes, and they balanced each other.

So why weren't either of them more worried about the four of us splitting up?

Even in the middle of Geek Watch, after a morning of boys and psychic conflict, I couldn't quite keep from thinking about it, and this time, the thought was accompanied by another pang of sheer yearning, for the Otherworld. For no reason that I could see, my longing for the Otherworld and my fear of losing my friends were tied together in my mind. I turned this realization over, unsettled and wondering if I'd ever be able to separate the two.

"Pay attention, Bay." Zo poked me in the side. "You don't want to miss the rules to Pin the Girl on the Geek."

"Now, to determine compatibility, I ran a few analyses. . . ."

Zo and I stared at Delia. I wondered why Annabelle didn't seem taken aback, and then I did the math.

"And by 'I,' you mean 'Annabelle,' right?" I said.

"Natch."

I didn't question how exactly Annabelle had had time to do all of the research she'd done for me *and* come up with some kind of compatibility matrix for Delia. The two of them had computer class together, and knowing A-belle, in that single period she'd probably also discovered a mathematical equation for world peace and cured puppy cancer.

If I hadn't known her middle name was Elisabeth, I would have sworn it was Multitasking.

Unable to resist playing along, even though part of me refused to let go of the longing and the worry that colored my thoughts, I accepted the compatibility charts from Delia. The first thing I noticed was that Annabelle scored high on compatibility with Alec, due to their joint interest in ancient languages. The second thing I noticed was that I scored pretty much the same across the board, whereas Zo and Delia both had obvious counterparts.

"Bailey gets Alec."

Despite my having sworn her to secrecy the day before, Zo wasn't taking any chances on somebody else getting dibs on the first guy I'd shown interest in since Kane. I'd never been great at sticking up for myself.

So what was going to happen when I didn't have anyone to stick up for me?

Darn those thoughts and the way they just wouldn't leave me alone! Darn the fact that everyone else could enjoy Delia's matchmaking machinations, while I just kept thinking that a year from now we probably wouldn't even be living in the same city, let alone attending the same school. And most of all, darn the mental image of the hills and the colors and the feeling of belonging I associated with the Otherworld, a place where I instinctively knew that I'd never be lonely or scared or alone.

"Of course Bailey gets Alec." Delia tossed her ponytail over one shoulder. "As we've already established, she's going to be his *bodyguard* and *pump him for information*. Plus, he totally likes her already. I can tell."

As far as I knew, Delia had never even met Alec, but she sounded so sure that he liked me and, honestly, I trusted her guy radar a lot more than mine.

"I'm fine with Bailey getting Alec," Annabelle said. "I really don't have a preference."

Since I'm not going to ask anyone out anyway. She didn't mean to send the thought to me, but I caught it anyway. *They probably wouldn't even say yes.*

"I think Annabelle should go with Lit Guy," I said. Of all the photos on the poster board, his looked the nicest, and sitting there, listening to her thoughts, I couldn't help but think that Annabelle could use someone to quote a little Shakespeare to her. Of the four of us, she was probably the prettiest, the one who'd grown into her looks the most over the past few years,

164

but trying to tell her that was like putting a piece of chocolate cake in front of Zo and telling her not to eat it.

Futile.

"Okay," Delia said, consulting her charts. "If Bailey takes Alec and Annabelle goes with Lit Guy, then that means I get Math Boy, and Zo, you're with the quiet, broody one."

Zo and her boy would probably just sit around for hours, glaring at each other. I wondered if in some crazy way that actually made them a good match. It was certainly easier to imagine than picturing Delia with the captain of the math team.

"Now, come on, pin the girl on the geek!"

Annabelle, Zo, and I obeyed, and our pictures stared back at us.

We aren't really going to do this, are we? Zo asked me silently.

I glanced at Alec's name, smiled, and shrugged. "Why not?"

Remind me to kill you later.

"Sure," I said, "but seriously, given the creepy voice thing, you may have to get in line."

Annabelle and Delia, who had no idea what Zo was silently saying to me, didn't pay much attention to the audible half of the conversation; Delia just gave me a look, which I interpreted to mean quite clearly, "You'd better not be mind-talking about my boobs."

"So . . . what now?" I asked. I'd told them everything I knew about the mystery that was Alec Talbot-Olsen. Annabelle had shared the fruits of her research labor with us, and Delia had divided the school's most

165

eligible geeks among the four of us. As far as lunch periods go, this one had been pretty productive, except for the fact that I'd barely eaten anything at all.

"Now we go back to school," Annabelle said. "If we wait any longer, Zo will have to speed to get us back in time."

Poor, deluded Annabelle seemed to think that if she could keep Zo from running perpetually late, Zo would stick to the speed limit. Clearly, A-belle didn't know her cousin as well as I did.

Zo tossed the keys in the air and caught them. "We've got a few minutes," she said. "You got any other wisdom to impart on the geek front, Delia?"

Delia just about died of shock at the question. For once, she was stunned into silence.

"What about you, A-belle? Any more graphs?" Content to bide her time, Zo tossed the keys into the air again. Annabelle, moving with surprising speed and grace, grabbed them and then scrambled for the driver's seat.

Zo's mouth dropped open. "No fair."

Annabelle started the car and buckled her seat belt, quite pleased with herself. "All's fair in love and war. And car pools. Now, flip the seats up and buckle your seat belts. I don't want to be late for calculus."

Delia and I obeyed, even though we had to nudge Zo to her seat in order to flip the others up. One of these days, Zo was going to learn to stop underestimating her cousin.

It's the quiet ones you have to watch out for.

*   *   *

It took us almost twice as long to get back to school as it had to get to Fifties in the first place, and by the time we returned, Zo had finally recovered.

"Next time," she told Annabelle, "I'm going to Coney, and we're going to leave you in the parking lot."

Annabelle snorted and pocketed the keys.

How could the two of them even think of splitting up for college? They were like two halves of the same Porter whole! Besides which, Annabelle was even shier than I was. Who was she going to steal keys from if Zo wasn't around?

Sidhe. Home.

The image came as a reminder, in equal parts bitter and sweet, that there was a place where I wouldn't have to worry about these things, a place where my connection to my friends was a memory, instead of a living, breathing thing capable of making my stomach turn itself inside out.

I don't have to sit around waiting for them to leave me, I thought. *I could leave them first.*

Where had *that* come from? The whole point of my senior-year angst was that I didn't want the four of us to split up; why in the world would I even think of bringing everything to an end sooner?

Sidhe. Home.

No, I thought violently. *This is my home. These are my friends. Leave me alone.*

And just like that, the image and the longing were

gone, and I zoned back in and slipped out of the car before the others could notice something was up.

I shut the car door behind me, and as the four of us started walking toward the school, I realized that my right hand had Morgan's necklace in a death grip. I loosened my hold and allowed the pendant to fall back on my chest.

"You guys ready to get your geek on?" Delia asked.

Annabelle, Zo, and I looked at one another. "Maybe?"

Chapter 14

"Okay, folks. You need to find a partner and a lab station. The directions for your assignment and all of the supplies you'll need for the experiment are on your tables. I expect your completed reports on my desk by the beginning of class tomorrow."

Normally, finding a partner in physics class was an excruciating experience for me, but this time the teacher's assignment wasn't the only one I was working on. Delia would kill me if she found out I had an opportunity to work with my geek and was too chicken to actually pursue it. And given the fact that he knew about my tattoo and was somehow at the center of some Sidhe shenanigans, I really didn't have much of a choice. I needed to know who he was, what he knew, and why one of the Sidhe would care whether I spent time with him or not.

169

Also, he was awfully cute. . . .

I stood up and took a step toward Alec, who was sitting a couple of desks down, trying to gather his notebooks. He dropped his pen, and I bent down to pick it up. Unfortunately, he bent over at the exact same time, and the two of us bonked heads. Either he and I were a match made in heaven, or we were destined for the emergency room.

"Whoa . . . I'm so—"

"Sorry!" I blurted, interrupting his apology with my own.

"No, it's totally my fault. I'm just so . . ."

"Yeah, me too."

I went for the pen again, and this time managed to grab it and hand it to him without taking any blows to the head. "Here," I said, and the moment I got the word out of my mouth, I was overcome with a bout of spontaneous shyness. In some ways, being the type of person who was sometimes shy and sometimes not was worse than being like Annabelle, who was always reserved around anyone outside of our group. At least she knew what to expect. I could never predict whether I'd be Shy Bailey or whether I'd actually manage to be halfway articulate. I just had to open my mouth and wait to see what came out.

Right now, the answer was a whole lot of nothing.

"Do you want to . . . ?" Alec didn't manage to finish the question, but it was enough to unfreeze my tongue.

". . . work together?" I finished.

He nodded and then I nodded, grateful that we'd both managed to nod without hitting foreheads.

By this time, there weren't many lab stations left, so we had to make our way to the far side of the room to find one that wasn't already occupied. As a result, Alec and I ended up wedged between two of the most popular guys in our grade and two of the least popular girls.

"Okay," Alec said, wrinkling his forehead as he read the instructions. "Apparently, we're supposed to figure out the coefficient of friction for this." He gestured to a large metal ramp on the table in front of us.

"And we would do that . . . how?" I asked.

He held up several blocks. Gingerly, he set one on the ramp, and we watched it slide down. When it hit the bottom, I reached for it, and his hand brushed mine as he did the same.

"Sorry," he said quickly.

"No. It's okay," I said. "I mean . . . I don't mind."

Could this conversation get any more awkward? Could *I* get any more awkward? Things were not going according to plan. I was supposed to be probing his mind, not my limits for humiliation.

"I . . . ummmm . . . I think we're supposed to weigh the blocks," Alec said, and the way he stumbled over the words reminded me that I wasn't alone in my awkwardness. Whether or not geeks were chic, they were definitely less intimidating than boys like Kane, who couldn't even define the word *awkward*, let alone imagine what it felt like to personally embody it.

Thinking about Kane had me glancing at the guys

on the other side of Alec, who were tossing their wooden blocks back and forth as they verbally appraised the popular girls on the other side of the room.

Ugh.

"We need to weigh the blocks," I said, forcing myself to pay attention to the nice boy right there in front of me. "That's because mass is part of the friction equation, right?"

He nodded. "And we've got a stopwatch, so we can time how long it takes the blocks to slide down the ramp."

"And that should give us the acceleration." I picked up where he had left off. I wasn't A-belle–level smart, but when I wasn't zoning out, I had my moments, and Alec seemed to bring my inner Smart Bailey out to play.

"And with acceleration and mass, we can calculate the force vector," Alec continued.

"And we've got a protractor," I added helpfully.

He smiled. "Cool."

This was probably the first time in the history of the world that anyone had ever called a protractor cool.

"Cool." I decided to become the second person in the world to do so.

"Do you want to do the stopwatch or slide the blocks?" Alec asked.

"The watch?" I said, somewhat unsure what the right answer to that question was. What if I picked the job that he wanted? Was that a turnoff? Before I could worry too much about my decision (or remind myself that in the grand scheme of things I had much bigger concerns), he slid the stopwatch my way, and I picked it up.

Alec grabbed the first block and weighed it. Then he set it on top of the ramp and raised his eyes to meet mine. "You ready?"

I nodded and smiled, and as he let go of the block, I hit the start button on the stopwatch. We wrote down the time and then moved on to the second block. Soon we'd acquired all of our data and just had to figure out how to get from there to an answer.

"It's got something to do with vectors," Alec said. "Gravity is pulling the blocks down, and friction is fighting it."

"Two forces," I said, "opposite directions."

"And in the end, the stronger one wins," Alec said softly. "The friction slows the block down, but it can't fight gravity. Sooner or later, the blocks are going to end up at the bottom." He paused. "Friction isn't enough to stop the inevitable."

"It could be," I found myself saying. "If it was strong enough."

Was it sad that I found myself relating to a wooden block? This whole year was a ramp, and I was sliding slowly but surely toward the end.

Nothing will stop your friends from leaving.

It took me a second to recognize that the voice in my head wasn't actually my voice, that the hated words weren't my own thoughts. Maybe because I'd thought them before; maybe because they were true.

Everything is ending, and there is nothing you can do

to stop it, nothing you can say that will make your friends care about you as much as you care about them. There's nothing you can say to make them stay.

Stop, I thought, too sucker punched by the words to erect any kind of mental barrier to block the intruder from preying further on my fears. *Please stop.*

They're leaving you in little ways already, you know. Anyone could see how excited they are about their futures without you. Do you really think they could be that excited if they cared about you?

Get out of my head, I begged, still only half sure that there was an intruder and that my subconscious hadn't just decided to lay the smackdown by giving voice to every paranoid thought I'd tried not to think since the end of junior year.

We aren't telling you anything you don't know, Bailey. Your friends betray you every day. They betray what you foolishly thought the four of you had every second that they drift farther away. They don't even realize they're leaving.

You don't even realize they're already gone.

"Bailey?" Alec said my name in a way that made me think that he was repeating himself, but I couldn't force my way through the horrible, horrible truth to reply.

They're already gone. The onslaught was endless. *Betrayers!*

Not the truth, I chanted silently. I tried to cling to that. I tried to believe it.

We could punish them for you. We could make them stay.

Could they? Could they really keep things from changing?

The answer to my question came in a purr, and for the first time, I processed the "we" part of what had already been said and realized that there wasn't just one person, being, whatever in my head.

There were two. Maybe more.

Yesssss, the voices said. *We could make them stay. Punish them for wanting to leave.*

Punish them?

It's only fair, Bailey. They hurt you. We hurt them.

"Bailey." Alec's voice was more forceful this time, and he put his hand on my arm. I jumped and accidentally relaxed the death grip I had on the stopwatch, which fell from my grasp and clattered to the floor. Shaking, I bent to retrieve it, and realized on the way down that my head was finally, blessedly quiet. The voices were gone.

"Thanks," I whispered to Alec's shoes, knowing that he couldn't grasp what I was thanking him for. My mind my own again, I straightened up and placed the watch on the table.

My friends *did* care about me.

They had *not* betrayed me.

And I would never let anyone hurt them. Ever.

"Are you okay?" Alec asked.

Because the alternative was to openly admit that I was a total freak of nature, I nodded.

"So," I said, attempting a subject change. "How 'bout that friction?"

The two of us went back to working on our physics project, our hands brushing every now and then as we recorded data and manipulated the experimental setup to get additional readings.

"Do you want to . . ." Alec choked on the words, and when he tried to continue, I thought that I'd have to do the Heimlich maneuver just so the second half of the sentence would stop blocking his airways. ". . . with me . . . I mean us . . . we could . . ."

What, I prodded him silently, careful to keep the words in my head, lest I psychically broadcast them to him. *We could what?*

Was Alec, in his own adorably awkward way, trying to ask me out?

Before I could get any kind of answer to that question, I felt a ripple of power, a wave of familiarity that had my stomach flip-flopping so hard and fast that it hurt. Pulled by some kind of magnetic force—or possibly instinct—I looked down at our feet. The shadows near our shoes shifted colors, giving them the appearance of movement even though they remained stationary. The presence—because that was, without question, the right word—moved from shadow to shadow, zigzagging its way across the room until finally it came to the popular girls' lab table and stopped.

Turn off the lights, I thought, but I couldn't seem to vocalize it, and even though I knew getting rid of the light—and therefore the shadows—was the only thing that could stop whatever was about to happen, I couldn't talk my feet into moving toward the light switch by the door. Instead, I just stared at the popular girls, like the driver of a passing car craning my neck to get a better look at a head-on collision.

Everybody loves a train wreck.

"I mean, honestly, who do girls like that think they're kidding? This isn't a movie; we're not going to, like, adopt them, and I'm sorry, but there are some things that makeovers just can't fix." Not realizing she was being watched (by Alec, by me, and, most important, by the presence in the shadow), Jessica (who was really pushing for a promotion to Meanest Mean Girl) continued her diatribe on the audacity of unpretty people. As sugary venom dripped from her glossy lips, Jessica tapped her fingernails on the edge of the wooden block she was supposed to be studying.

Tap. Tap-tap-tap.

Tap. Tap-tap-tap.

My senses heightened and on absolute edge, I felt and heard each tap like a gunshot.

Stop, I told her silently, trying to focus my power enough to get the message across, but either popularity was its own kind of psychic shield, or something (or someone) between the two of us was interfering.

"You should have heard those girls talking this morning. They were all, 'Oh, he's just sooooo dreamy. Do you think he loves me? Will we go to the big dance together? Will they make a Disney Channel Original Movie about our fuzzy-wuzzy puppy love?' Puh-lease."

Just shut up, I thought in Jessica's direction, hoping

she'd get the memo, as much for her own benefit as because she could have easily been talking about me and saying the exact same thing. As I repeated myself over and over again on the off chance that I'd break through, the shadow moved from the floor up to her legs, snaking its way along the shadows cast on her body by the lab table and experimental apparatus.

"I have three words for girls like that." Jessica, completely unaware of her own peril, tossed her hair and gave the girls at the table behind me a pointed look. "*Pa, thet,* and *ic.*" She faked a shudder. "Heavy on the *ick.*"

You don't know what you're doing, I shouted, putting so much psychic juice into it that I thought I might give myself an aneurysm. *You don't know what you're doing to those girls or to yourself.* But it was like screaming through a wall of water—my warnings went completely unheeded and, in all likelihood, completely unheard.

"Move," I said, switching tactics and speaking out loud, but the word emerged as a whisper. Beside me, Alec shuddered violently, and I wondered if he felt the wave of power—ancient but adolescent, angry but pure—that surged through the room as Jessica shifted in her chair, inadvertently throwing her head completely into shadow.

Like the evil-girl disciple that she was, Jessica didn't stop slinging cutesy insults until the very end, when without warning, every strand of hair on her head fell to the floor.

That haircut is just adorable . . . maybe next time you can just shave your head. Believe me, bald is beautiful, at least compared to that. The taunt Jessica had thrown toward one of the I-Want-To-Be-Mrs.-Him girls from study hall echoed in my ears, as the quiet *shhh-shhh-shhh* of hair hitting the floor, lifeless and wispy, spread through the room. The rest of the class finally noticed what was going on, and then there was chaos.

Oh . . . my . . . gosh . . .

Is she . . . ?

Thank you, God, for this glorious . . .

What the . . . ?

Jessica's shrill scream distracted me from the barrage of my classmates' thoughts long enough that I managed to slam up some hard-core mental barriers. Beside me, Alec had gone completely white. I didn't blame him. Maybe he somehow knew the same thing I did.

Whatever Sidhe were doing this, they weren't done yet. Not by a long shot.

As the tittering and anxious mumbles all around me built to a low roar, the veins on Jessica's bald head began to bulge. They moved erratically back and forth, jumping all over her naked scalp in a rhythm reminiscent of the way evil sometimes moves in scary movies—jagged and staccato, like someone had edited out parts of the path the veins should have taken to get from point A to point B.

Jessica screamed like a banshee and clawed at her own head, French-manicured nails scraping against

179

skin. The girl next to her chimed in with a few screams of her own, even as she backed frantically away from her so-called friend.

I was petrified by the half-formed idea that Jessica's head might start spinning all the way around. Or worse, explode. Instead, her hair started growing back at high speed, bursting out from her scalp like a living creature. And that's when I realized it was. A living creature. Or, more correctly, creatures, plural.

Have I ever mentioned that I really, really hate snakes?

Apparently, the rest of the class felt the same way, because they didn't bother waiting on the final bell before rushing the door in a mad dash to exit first. The teacher, to his credit, didn't abandon ship with my fellow students. On the other hand, I wasn't about to give him too much credit, given that the second the snakes had appeared he'd fainted dead away.

Unconscious teacher. Panicking classmates running into the hallway. I needed to put an end to this, and I needed to do damage control. Unfortunately, I couldn't move. The snakes, hissing and writhing around Jessica's head, turning her into an unwilling high school Medusa, kept me frozen in place.

You have to do something, I told myself sternly. I was one hundred percent sure that the snakes weren't earthly in origin. They were Otherworldly, and that made this my problem. Unfortunately, knowing that and attempting to give myself pep talks did absolutely nothing toward freeing up my bound-by-terror muscles. Knowing that something had to be done, I opted for a course of action that didn't require moving.

Stop this! I sent the order to the being or beings in the shadows, channeling every ounce of power my voice had carried in the Otherworld into those two words.

The reply came in a set of spine-chilling giggles.

Punish.

Punish.

And then, *Justice.*

Justice? I thought. Seriously? They thought this was justice? I thought of every pointed stare and whispered word and completely unsubtle giggle from girls who laughed at me and not with me, and still I couldn't wrap my mind around it.

Jessica had snakes on her head. Snakes. On her head.

"Make it stop," Alec whispered beside me. I wanted, more than anything, to comply, even though he seemed to be talking to himself more than to me, his words a plea against the twisted horror of what we were witnessing. I felt for him and wondered what it would be like to watch this from the perspective of someone who couldn't see what I could, someone who saw the outcome but not the shadows. All he could do was watch and whisper. I was the one with powers. I was the one who could do something. I toyed with the idea of using my pyrokinesis to set the snakes on fire, but I wasn't sure how Jessica's head would fare with the flames. Thinking of my alarm clock that morning, I decided not to risk it.

"Stop," Alec said again, and this time, his whisper seemed to be the magic word. The snakes disappeared. The shadows quivered and became just shadows once more, and the voices in my head returned only long enough to issue one final warning.

Stay away from him, or next time, we'll be punishing you.

The bell did ring then, but I barely heard it over Jessica's continued shrieking. When the snakes disappeared, they'd left her bald again, and I had a feeling she wouldn't stop screaming for a very, very long time.

"Let's get out of here," Alec said.

I looked back toward Jessica and considered approaching her, trying to comfort her in some way, but decided against it. Instead, I sent a soothing psychic command in her direction. *Stop screaming. You're okay. You won't remember what happened. You feel safe. You're okay.* I repeated those sentiments a few times, and then Jessica stopped screaming, letting me know that my mind-control powers were—if anything—stronger than ever.

At this rate, I thought, *I'd better hope that they're* really *strong.*

Making Jessica forget what happened wasn't enough. Real damage control would involve mind melding everyone in my class—and everyone they'd told about what happened.

"Bailey, let's go," Alec said again.

I sighed, and started my massive memory-rewriting

attempt with him. I didn't try to hear his thoughts and tried to keep mine out of his head as best I could, but I sent the compulsion to forget toward him. His mind felt cold to my mind's psychic touch, like a wet wall, slippery and slick. For a second, I wondered if my attempts had failed, but then Alec screwed up his forehead and asked, "What's going on? Did the bell ring? Where did everyone else go? And what happened to *him?*"

Following Alec's gaze, I turned toward the teacher, who'd just recovered consciousness. I couldn't help but marvel at the convenient timing of that one—he passed out at the first sign of trouble and woke up just as I started cleaning it up.

"He got sleepy," I said, answering Alec's question with what was, quite possibly, the worst cover story of all time. Then I went to work on my teacher's memory. Compared to Alec, he was a snap.

"Is class over?" Alec asked again.

I nodded, feeling more than a little guilty for messing with his memory and more than a little headachy, because I really wasn't accustomed to using this particular power to this degree.

"Class is over," I told Alec, content that at least he, Jessica, and the physics teacher wouldn't remember what had gone on in this classroom. "Let's get out of here." I really didn't want to be around when Jessica rediscovered that she was bald. I also didn't want Alec to look at Jessica—half because he'd probably give away the game by asking me what had happened to her hair, and half because I didn't want to have to make up an answer to that question just yet.

Luckily, Alec and I managed to make a quick exit, and he didn't so much as glance at Jessica. When we stepped into the hallway, I half-expected Alec to ask me what had just happened in there, even though he gave every appearance of not having even the smallest clue that anything *had* happened. Some small, niggling part of me just kept whispering that—altered memories aside—maybe I should be the one asking him questions. Looking at Alec, I couldn't believe that he was somehow at the center of anything, but the voices in my head had warned me to stay away from him. He'd known what my tattoo meant. He was important.

"Are you okay?" he asked, and I realized he was shaking, just a little.

I nodded. "I'm fine," I said. "Are you okay?" I paused, measuring his response as if I expected it to tell me everything I needed to know.

"If you're okay, I'm okay," he said. "I think." He looked so utterly confused as to why he might not be okay, and whether or not there was a reason why he might feel mildly disturbed that I felt a smidgen of guilt. Playing with people's minds wasn't something I enjoyed doing. My own guilt, along with the hesitance in Alec's voice, and the way he looked at me, made me push down any questions lurking in the corners of my mind about whether or not he knew more than he was letting on. He just wasn't the kind of guy who hid things: not his own nervousness, not that whether or not I was okay was important to him, not the fact that he'd known what my tattoo meant. His whispers in the room had been just that: whispers. The two of us stood in the hallway, looking at each other, and I felt a second twist of guilt somewhere in my abdomen. After what had just happened in physics class, I had no right to be standing here, thinking about how he was kind of adorable, when something Otherworldly had just attacked one of the most popular girls in my grade in a very personal and sinister way.

"OMG. How cute are the two of you? I swear!"

Either I was in a complete daze or Delia was having a particularly good day when it came to stealth, because I didn't see her coming down the hallway until she was standing right next to me, sounding way perkier than usual. I recognized her tone of voice: it was the one she used for flirting with boys . . . or flirting with boys on my behalf.

"Hey, Delia," I said, prepping myself to tell her that now might not be the best time to move on her Geek Watch plan. After what I'd seen, after what had happened to Jessica . . .

"So, Alec, are you free right now?" Delia didn't give me a chance to call the plan to a halt. She just proceeded, like the *Titanic* barreling toward an iceberg.

"Free?" Alec repeated. "Right now?"

I wondered what he was thinking, but held back. *Thou shalt not mind-read thy love interest* was the most important psychic commandment I'd come up with in the past few years, and I wasn't going to break it, especially not with Alec, who was shy enough that poking around in his mind would feel like an incredible violation of his privacy. I'd messed with his head enough as it was—I wasn't going to make things worse by probing his thoughts for a clue about his feelings toward me, even though I really wanted to.

"You *are* free right now?" Delia asked, as if Alec had responded in the affirmative to her first question. "Good." She clapped her hands together in a display of unholy glee. "Bailey's free right now too." She shoved the two of us together. "You two crazy kids have fun."

Delia, I said psychically, *you don't understand. Something just happened. I have to take care of it.*

My friend's response was immediate. *Jessica Moore. Bald. Snakes on her head. I got the memo.*

I actually felt my jaw drop a little. In the past few minutes, the hallway around us had gone from eerily quiet in the wake of the snake incident to absolutely vibrating with varying degrees of hysteria. There was crying. Yelling. Lots of talking. I'd assumed that Delia hadn't heard about the snake incident— partly because it had just happened, but also because she wasn't reacting in the way I would have expected her to.

You know? I asked.

Natch, she replied. *I mean, hello, gossip mill, founding member, right here.*

I tried to reconcile myself to the fact that Delia knew about the snakes but wasn't freaked out in the least. In a sick way, it made sense. Everyone had their

186

priorities. Snakes and the supernatural weren't Delia's. Right now, boys and my love life were.

Look, Bay, Annabelle's already on her way to Zo's house to work on figuring out who was behind the hair thing, and I'll put together a 'bald is beautiful' trend book or something tonight. We're all doing our part here. Yours is the cute boy—he might have information, remember?

Bits and pieces of other people's thoughts made their way into my head with Delia's mental words, and I reminded myself that my part in all of this wasn't just pumping "the cute boy" for information. The snake news was spreading like wildfire, and I had to get a handle on things before it was too late—if it wasn't already.

Ignoring Delia and Alec, I took one deep breath and opened my mind to everything around me. I concentrated on a single image, a single thought—the snakes—and let the thoughts that matched up to that image come to me. It was everywhere. Everyone was thinking about it, everyone was talking about it.

Going into an altered state of being that resembled Fate Bailey so much it disturbed me, I pulled that thought toward me, applying so much mental pressure that I yanked it out of everyone else's mind and into my own. I let my mind venture farther and farther—outside of the school, miles away, searching for more, pulling thought after thought out of foreign minds and into my own. For one terrifying moment, all I could see or think about was snakes, but then, like the person I was in the

Nexus weaving life, I pulled the thought apart, into tiny, threadlike pieces, and it crumpled to dust.

All around me, the hallway went from an atypical, supercharged buzzing to a rather confused calm, and then the buzzing started up again, but this time it was regular gossip feeding the rumor mill.

"You okay?" Alec asked me. "You look kind of pale. Not that you don't look nice pale. I mean . . . not that I'm trying to say you look nice, but you do, and . . ."

Ah-dorable, Delia told me silently. *Also, is it me or did everyone just stop talking about the snake thing?*

Even though I hadn't meant to leave the thought in Delia's head, and even though I'd torn it out of everyone else's (except, I would have been willing to bet, for A-belle's and Zo's), it didn't surprise me that even in a trance, I wouldn't have messed with my friends' brains that way.

There were some lines you just didn't cross. Mind-melding a friend as a joke and letting them know you were doing it was one thing. Taking their memories was completely another.

That thought led me back to feeling bad for messing with Alec's mind again, and about then, I realized that I should probably say something in response to his (almost) saying that he liked the way I looked.

"Thanks," I said. "For saying I look nice. Not that you said I look nice, but . . ."

Delia didn't comment on whether or not my babbling was as adorable as Alec's. Instead she gave me very explicit instructions.

Zo's going to follow you and your boy—discreetly, of course—in case something else happens and you guys need some muscle. In times of crisis, it's important to keep a clear head.

Zo versus Evil Fairies, part two. I couldn't wait to see how that one turned out. Not.

And I'll be close by too, Delia continued. *For advice, emotional support, etc, etc.*

"Do you . . . ummm . . . want to?" Alec finally worked up the courage to ask. "You know, what your friend was saying before, about us both being free. Do you . . . ummm . . . want to go someplace?"

"She'd love to," Delia said. Her words left Alec hanging, so I agreed. I couldn't not, and as Delia had pointed out, as weird as this was, we did need more information, and Alec was somehow involved in what was going on—even if he didn't know it. Besides, after the psychic trick I'd just pulled, I deserved it.

"Okay," I said finally. "Yeah."

Alec smiled, like I'd just recited poetry. I wondered if the happy, dizzy feeling that had taken up residence in my entire body was the result of Alec's smile or if it was because I'd used way more power than my earthly body was probably meant to use.

"Okay. Yeah." Alec repeated my words with no small measure of awe in his voice.

I am so good, Delia congratulated herself silently, and then flounced off, expertly navigating around the everyday chaos, completely and freakishly unfreaked, even though she—unlike my slightly amnesiac classmates—

had every reason to be creeped out by the day's happenings.

"She's . . ." Alec started the sentence but wasn't sure how to finish it. I obliged by adding the perfect word.

"She's Delia," I said, and, I thought, *It's going to take a lot more than snakes and vicious Otherworlders to knock her off her game.*

Before I knew it, Alec and I were walking out of the school together, hand in hand, neither one of us entirely sure how this "date" had come about.

Chapter 15

I didn't know what to expect out of my "date" with Alec. We'd spoken for the first time less than thirty-six hours earlier, and if Delia hadn't been on a geek kick, I might not have even noticed how absolutely adorable he was. Add to that the fact that the sum total of our interactions included falling out of our chairs in study hall and witnessing some kind of utterly bizarre mystical attack in physics class (which he didn't even remember), and my mind couldn't find a next logical step.

Not that logic had ever been my forte.

For that matter, stepping wasn't really my strong point either. I proved this as I stepped out of my car. My ankle twisted beneath me, but I managed to regain my balance. "Walk it off," I mumbled under my breath.

To my great relief, Alec didn't say, "Walk what off?" There were definite benefits to hanging out with someone who really got what it was like to be a teensy bit clumsy. Then again, other than asking me if I could drive because he didn't have a car, and he knew that sounded lame, but he'd give me directions, because he knew this great place, Alec hadn't said much. I wondered if he was thinking about the "nap" our physics teacher had taken during class, or the way Delia had bulldozed us into this date. Then I wondered if he was thinking about me—even a little bit.

My mind flitted to James then. I'd only met him once, but we'd talked a lot more than Alec and I had, and with James, I'd felt like everything was funny, even the fact that I was probably the least perfect person to ever set foot on Otherworldly soil. James was laughter. Alec was shy smiles.

Why couldn't I have both of them? And really, why did I want them both so badly, when I barely knew either of them at all?

"It's just a little walk from here," Alec said, stuffing his hands into his pockets. "I think you'll like it."

I didn't ask what "it" was. I probably should have, given the fact that there was a distinct chance that Alec had somehow stumbled across something that had brought him to the attention of the Sidhe. I couldn't imagine what he could have found, or what knowledge he could have gleaned, that would have made him so important to the beings that had warned me away from him.

The same beings, coincidentally enough, who'd turned Jessica into an unwilling high school Medusa.

"Ummm . . . where did you say we were going again?" I asked as I followed him through a park I'd been to before, up to the edge of a forest I hadn't. I couldn't help thinking that the mental interlopers had promised me similar "punishment" if I didn't stay away from Alec. For our first date, I was hoping for somewhere well lit and open, where we could be seen by dozens of people and there were no shadows.

That wasn't too much to ask for, was it?

"It's just this place," Alec said. "It's really pretty." He paused and gave me that trademark shy smile. "It reminds me of you."

Awwwww, I thought.

Keep all awwwww's to yourself, Zo grumbled. I knew she'd been following us for a while and, as a side effect of keeping my mind open to her thoughts and Delia's, that there was a risk that some of my thoughts would travel in the other direction. Apparently, my *awwwww* had been one of those.

Where is Geek Boy taking you, Bay?

Somehow, I didn't think that "someplace pretty" would satisfy Zo's curiosity. I may have been Alec's "bodyguard," but Zo was mine, and she took protecting me very seriously. Following a guy who I knew to be at the center of some kind of Sidhe something-or-other into the woods probably wasn't my smartest move ever. But, hey, it's not like it was *my* idea.

"I can't believe you're here," Alec said as we

stepped into the woods and started walking down a small stone path. I felt distinctly uncomfortable at the number of shadows all around us—to the point that I was ready to set them on fire with very little provocation. Thus far, however, I hadn't heard even a hint of a voice, hadn't felt or seen anything out of the ordinary, other than the gentle tug of attraction that made me want to tousle Alec's hair.

And maybe bury my hands in it for a while.

I can't believe I'm here either, I thought.

That makes three of us, Zo told me. *Somehow, I don't think this is what Delia was picturing when she set the two of you up. Dee's idea of a "date" usually includes food or a movie.*

Luckily, Delia couldn't hear Zo the way I could, or I would have gotten a lecture on dating right then and there. Up to this point, Delia had been pretty quiet, waiting patiently for me to psychically send her any questions I might have about flirting or mussy hair or the seduction of geeks.

"There," Alec said. It took me a second to figure out that he was pointing toward a clearing. As we walked closer, our steps in rhythm except when one of us stumbled over a lump of grass, a rock, or nothing, I saw what Alec was really pointing to.

A bridge.

He looked at me, gauging my response, and I looked at him, wondering what my response was supposed to be. The grass was green here, and there was a small creek with surprisingly clear water running underneath the bridge. A weeping willow on the bank put half of the bridge in the shade, and the other side, covered in sunlight, looked downright cozy. It looked like the kind of place Delia, Zo, and I would have gone when we were little. I imagined dangling my legs over the edge of the bridge as Zo tightrope-walked along the railing and Delia co-opted the nearby flower blossoms as hair accessories.

"Do you like it?" Alec asked, and I knew from his voice alone that his palms were sweating. If I'd wanted to, I could have probed his mind more, could have poked around and seen what he was really thinking, but as previously discussed, I so was not going here again.

"I love it," I said quietly. And I did. It wasn't beautiful in the way that the Otherworld was. The colors of the flowers were shades I'd seen before, every day, in the most commonplace objects. The bridge was made of the same color wood as my kitchen table. But the fact that I could picture myself loving this place as a little kid made me like it now. If I weren't Sidhe and hadn't seen the things I'd seen, the way that the ordinary fit together into something extraordinary here would have blown me away.

Instead it made me smile, even as I wondered if anything in this world would ever match what I'd seen the night before. Would I ever be in awe of earthly beauty again? Or was this feeling—warm and right and happy—the most anyone could ask for, especially of a first date?

"You want to sit?" Alec asked, nodding toward the bridge.

"Okay," I said, glad that the weeping willow (and its shadow) was on the far side. Alec and I walked up to the bridge and I pulled him to a stop before he crossed out of the light. "Let's sit here," I said.

Ohhhhhhhh!

Along with the mental gasp, I heard an audible one in the distance and came to the conclusion that Delia had used up her stealthiness for the day, and that she was in awe of this place as well.

"So," I said, as Alec and I let our legs dangle off, "why haven't I seen you before this week? Are you new?"

That wasn't exactly what I meant to ask, especially because I had the feeling that Alec wasn't new, that I'd seen him around before, but hadn't noticed him. There was something familiar about him that I couldn't quite place, something that couldn't be explained away if he was new.

"I'm not surprised that you haven't noticed me before," Alec said. "But I've always noticed you." He mumbled the next bit into his shirt. "Always."

Oh. And also, wow.

Everything all right up there? Zo asked. *Delia and I can't hear anything.*

Everything's fine, I replied, secretly glad that I'd managed to keep my more private thoughts from bleeding over. *Great, actually.*

How great? Delia asked smugly. *And how much do you love me?*

196

I didn't answer, and as the minutes passed lazily by, I found that I didn't need to consult with Delia to find something to say to Alec. It's not like I poured my heart out to him, or him to me. We didn't even talk that much, but being quiet with him felt good. After we'd been sitting on the bridge for more than an hour, I found myself telling him things I hadn't told anyone.

Things my friends would have called moping.

Things that might have hurt them if they'd heard me say or think them.

And then I told him stories about everything the four of us had been through together. Or almost everything.

"They're really important to you," he said.

I nodded.

"You're really going to miss them," he said, his voice even softer.

I nodded again.

"You like nodding," he commented.

I nodded. He nodded back. And then, I finally got him to talk for a while about something that wasn't me. Of course, the topic he chose to talk about was the bridge, which was apparently a scale model of a bridge in England that was designed by Isaac Newton so that all the pieces fit together to support weight without needing any nails or screws to join them.

"It's about the angles," he said.

"What about you?" I asked.

"My angles?" Alec frowned, as if doing some mental calculations.

"No," I said. "Just . . . what about you? What's your family like? Who are your friends? What do you like doing when you're not sitting on bridges?" I was already babbling, so this seemed as good a time as any to get in a few of the questions I was supposed to be asking. *"How did you know what my tattoo meant when you saw it yesterday?"* and *"What's the weirdest thing that ever happened to you, and oh, by the way, did it involve any supernatural fairy types?"*

And where are the voices that keep warning you away from me? I added silently, knowing that I couldn't voice it out loud without really giving the game away.

Alec blinked several times at the sheer number of questions that had left my mouth in a blur of words.

I think I broke him, I thought to Delia.

Were you babbling? she asked.

Ummm . . . maybe.

He'll be fine. Just give him a chance to process.

In the back of my mind, I heard Zo mentally grumbling about how my physics class had turned into a battleground, yet her stakeout was yielding a whole lot of nothing. According to her, I had all the fun.

"Sorry," Alec said, though I wasn't sure what he was apologizing for exactly. Being scared by my babble? Sometimes, it even scared me. . . .

"I zoned out there for a second," he continued. "But . . . ummm . . . your questions. Well, my family. I have two . . . ummm . . . sisters. We get along okay, I guess. Most of the time anyway. Sometimes I think that they don't really get me. The things I like. The things I say. Well, you know how sisters are. . . ."

198

Actually, I didn't, but I wasn't going to risk scaring him into silence again.

"My friends are kind of like yours. They're more like family—even when I don't want them to be. Let's see . . . what else . . ."

As he murmured to himself, going back over my list of questions, I saw a flash of color in the corner of my eye and turned my head, half-expecting to see something freaky. Instead, I saw a butterfly, brighter-colored than any of the nearby flowers. I watched as it flew by Alec, and I found myself hoping the little guy would stay out of the shadows. I was pretty sure the Sidhe didn't have anything against butterflies, but I wasn't what I would call positive.

But before the butterfly got anywhere near the shadow, it disappeared. One second it was there. The next it wasn't.

"Bailey?" Alec must have noticed that my facial expression didn't match up to whatever he was saying. "Are you okay?"

"Yeah," I said, staring hard at the place the butterfly had been a moment before. "I'm fine."

"We should probably go anyway." Alec looked disappointed. I didn't need psychic powers to tell me that he didn't want this to end.

"We don't have to go yet," I said quickly, but given that the last thing I wanted to do was disappear, à la the butterfly, I didn't sound as convincing as I otherwise would have. Alec stood and held out a hand to help me up.

"It'll be dark soon," he said. "We should go."

I took his hand, and the connection between us tickled my fingers. After a long moment, he let go, and the two of us walked off the bridge and back toward the woods.

I glanced over my shoulder, looking for the butterfly one more time, and then I actually stopped and turned around. "I'll be right back," I called to Alec. "I forgot . . . something." I ran back to the bridge and, as casually as I could, brought my hands to the necklace around my neck and lifted the charm so that the mirror was angled toward the bridge.

The reflection showed swirls of blue-green, and when I looked harder, I saw—just for a second—a place of extreme beauty, larger and bolder and more magical than life.

Bay?

Zo's thought, tinged with worry, brought me back to the present, and in the mirror, the Otherworld faded away.

Knowing that Alec might get suspicious if I stayed any longer, I headed back, with an excuse prepared about how I'd wanted to look around the bridge just one more time. The two of us settled back into silence as we walked through the woods and to my car, and we drove without talking until I dropped him off at the high school and then headed for home.

I was almost halfway there when I realized that either Alec hadn't answered my question about him knowing the meaning of my tattoo, or he had, but I'd been too zoned out to hear him.

Chapter 16

I drove home on complete autopilot, parking my car at my house before walking across the street to Zo's. I didn't bother ringing the doorbell; none of us had bothered with knocking for years, and our doors were almost always unlocked. Oakridge was the kind of town where nothing ever happened. It was safe—or at least it had been until something had brought the Sidhe here. First Alecca and now this. I wondered if this was just the way things were going to be from now on. The biennial fairy fight: keeping the Otherworld in the Otherworld for the protection of this one.

I so didn't want to have to do this again in another two years. Especially if I'd be doing it alone.

Anyone could see how excited they are about their future without you.

This time I didn't have to question whether or not there was a foreign presence inside my head. There wasn't. This was all me. My memory. My issues. I just couldn't forget the things my attackers had said, and every time I let my guard down, my memory took me to the one place I didn't want to go.

I actively redirected my thoughts toward what the mirror had shown me on Alec's bridge. I would have preferred to think of just Alec, but beggars can't be choosers, and anything was better than giving time and space in my mind to irrational fears I shouldn't have had to begin with.

"Good. You're here." Zo must have heard the front door open, because she walked out of the kitchen to greet me in the foyer. "I was starting to worry that we had left you and lover boy—lover geek—whatever—alone too soon. I don't trust him."

Zo didn't trust anyone outside of our group. She just wasn't built that way.

"You can trust Alec," I said, knowing my words would be completely lost on her. "I think I do."

Zo was skeptical. She tossed me a Twinkie and I scrambled to catch it.

"Eat this," Zo instructed sternly. "It's good for you."

"Is not!" Delia yelled from upstairs. "She lies!"

The acoustics at Zo's house were perfect for yelling. Zo did her best to look mortally wounded by Delia's assertion that Twinkies did not equal health food. "Would I lie about something as important as Twinkies?

They represent at least three food groups: cakey, creamy, and . . ." She racked her brain for a third.

"Yummy?" I suggested. There was nothing for bringing me out of a funk like a conversation on the nutritional benefits of junk food. Of course, that didn't change the fact that my friends and I had much more serious things to discuss.

"You hear that, Queenie? Twinkies are yummy! Boo. Yeah."

Zo didn't seem to realize how ridiculous the contrast between her tough-girl tone and the content of her speech really was. I didn't want to be the one to break it to her that the word *yummy* wasn't exactly intimidating.

"Come on." Zo nudged me with the Twinkie box, and I noticed that she was carrying a bag of baby carrots in her other hand. "A-belle's in heavy research mode, and she's doling out jobs."

"Is your job snack patrol?" I asked as the two of us made our way up the stairs toward her bedroom.

Zo shrugged. "It's better than making charts."

Why was I completely unsurprised that Annabelle's research regime relied heavily on visual aids?

As I found out when I entered Zo's bedroom (aka Research Central) a few seconds later, the charts were very big. Poster-board-sized, as a matter of fact. And from the looks of it, Delia had been in charge of making them. As if Geek Watch weren't bad enough. This was just tempting fate.

Which was, technically speaking, tempting *me*.

Funny that I didn't actually feel tempted. Mainly, I was just really tired. Tired from a long day of first dates and supernatural mysteries, and tired of feeling a noticeable pang of sadness with every private joke that passed between the four of us unsaid.

They don't even know they're leaving.

You don't even know they're already gone.

"Tell us absolutely everything about your date." Delia greeted me with a high-speed demand. "Was it absolutely amazing? What did you guys talk about? Was he really deep?" She paused, reflective. "I bet he was deep."

Even though we had much bigger things to talk about, I knew that holding out on date details was completely futile. "I think he was deep. The two of us talked . . . about everything. Well, not *everything*."

It wasn't like I could tell Alec the truth about me, or about the Otherworld, or about the fact that he had Sidhe stalkers.

"We talked about almost everything," I said.

"Like what?" Zo was less into the dating scene than Delia was, but still curious enough to oblige with a question.

"We talked about you guys and growing up and our plan for next year." That was as close as I could come to telling my friends that I'd told Alec things that I didn't necessarily want to repeat to them. "And sometimes we'd just sit there, not saying anything. It was nice."

"Did you find out anything that explains why the

Sidhe would be interested in him?" That came from Annabelle, who just couldn't push down the desire for more information to index and factor into her equations.

"I asked him about my tattoo, but then I got distracted." With the image of the butterfly fresh in my mind, the whole story came spilling out, from the eerie disappearance of aforementioned butterfly to what I'd seen when I'd viewed the bridge through my mirror. Just talking about it was exhausting, but at the same time, getting it off my chest made me feel lighter than I had all day. There was definitely something to be said for sharing a burden.

My friends listened patiently as I rambled on, and it only took about three seconds after I stopped for Annabelle to assimilate all of the information and come to a bunch of conclusions. "If the bridge served as some kind of portal to the Otherworld, that would explain what you saw in the mirror, Bailey. It would also explain what happened to the butterfly: it simply passed from this world to the next. Plus, if the bridge really is some kind of hot spot and Alec hangs out there a lot, it makes sense that he might know things that normal humans wouldn't and that he might have attracted the Sidhe's attention."

I didn't follow any of Annabelle's conclusions one hundred percent, but interrupting her at this point would have been like jumping in front of a moving train and trying to bring it to a stop by blowing on it with breath after puny breath.

"This actually makes perfect sense with my prelimi-nary search results on crossing over to fairy worlds. There were a few different options before, but if I add in the bit about the bridge, in conjunction with the role that Mabon has played in all of our encounters with the Otherworld . . ."

Annabelle trailed off, and Zo rolled her eyes. "Carry the one," she said, in imitation of A-belle's distinct brand of academic murmuring.

"Shut up." Annabelle made a face at her cousin, but then carried on with her musings without missing a beat. "This new information also gives us another ex-ample of one of our necklaces being used to show Other-worldly things that aren't visible to the naked eye. I'm still not exactly sure of the mechanism. . . ."

"Have you guys seen things?" I asked. "In your necklaces, have you seen stuff?"

Their silence told me that they hadn't.

"If I'm the only one seeing things, then why did Morgan give the necklaces to all four of us?" I asked.

Annabelle tilted her head to the side, her eyes going wide and vacant as her brain went to her happy place, where theories bounded around like puppies. "Maybe the necklaces only function in a set. Perhaps ours ground yours in some way that lets you channel the power. It makes sense that if only one of the necklaces was to work as some kind of conduit, it would be yours, given that you're part Sidhe. . . ."

"Interesting," Zo murmured, still imitating her cousin. "This is just . . . fascinating. And the appendices of the algorithms of . . . Yes, yes, this is it!"

This time, Delia threw a pillow at Zo on Annabelle's behalf.

"Thank you," Annabelle said primly. "But since the natives seem to be getting restless"—she cast a pointed look in Zo's direction—"maybe a few visual aids are in order."

It was official: A-belle was in full-on chart mode. Delia pranced over to the poster board and, with a gesture reminiscent of Vanna White, she presented Exhibit A for Annabelle.

"This is a list of all of the questions we're still trying to answer," Annabelle said, slipping from musing mode into lecture mode with little warning. "Right now, there are three big areas to discuss. First, how do people cross from our world into the Otherworld and vice versa? Lore seems to indicate that it can be done, and Bailey said that James mentioned having done it at some point in his past. This is pretty firm evidence that crossing over does happen, especially if you take into account the incident at school this afternoon."

Annabelle made a face, and I felt somewhat comforted that, unlike Delia, Annabelle wasn't completely unimpressed with the whole snake thing. That said, she recovered quickly, continuing with her verbal dissertation on the questions she still needed to answer. "What kind of rules govern crossing over, and how strong is the barrier? Another, related question: What exactly happened to make Jessica Moore's hair turn to snakes this afternoon?"

So I was right that Annabelle and Zo had maintained their memory of the event, even though I'd stripped it away from everyone else. It was just as well—I would have told them about what happened anyway.

Annabelle cleared her throat, and I knew her well enough to know that the sound was aimed more at getting my attention than at unblocking her airways. "It seems likely that something mystical happening at our school is in some way related to Bailey and the Sidhe. So who are the likely candidates to have orchestrated that kind of display, what do they want, and how do we stop them if they try to do something like that again? And, assuming that some Sidhe did cross over to torture Jessica, did their crossing follow the rules we think govern the relationship between the worlds? And if it didn't follow these rules, how is this possible?"

Annabelle took a breath, and I swear that other than the one she'd used to facetiously clear her throat, it was the first breath she'd taken since starting to explain the questions written in bullet-point form on the chart. If she'd held her breath that long under water, I would have checked her for gills.

"The final question on the table right now revolves around our necklaces. We know they show us things we normally couldn't see, but that's it. Digging deeper might give us important insight." Annabelle paused, waiting for comments, but the rest of us were kind of dumbstruck and didn't manage so much as a single word.

Annabelle was undeterred by our silence. "I started with the first question because crossing over seems to relate to what happened to Jessica and maybe even to what our necklaces—or possibly just Bailey's necklace—can show us, if they can really be used to see the Otherworld in this one."

"What did you find?" I was almost afraid to ask, but I wanted Annabelle to get to the point. Surprisingly, this time when she started speaking, I found myself understanding what she said.

"I actually found a lot," Annabelle said. "There are a lot of different stories about beings from some kind of Otherworld crossing into ours. The gist of it seems to be that there are certain places and certain times when the barrier between the worlds is particularly thin. Equinoxes and solstices, for example."

"Days of power," I said softly. Those were the words Adea and Valgius had told me when they'd called me from study hall to the Nexus. "Mabon's tomorrow," I added.

Mabon was an equinox. A day of power. A time when, according to Annabelle, the barrier between the worlds was thin.

"And if what had happened with Jessica today had happened tomorrow, that would make perfect sense, but an almost-equinox isn't a day of power. So that leaves special places where the worlds come together."

"Like the bridge," I breathed, doing the math and for once coming up with four when I added two and two.

"Exactly. There are all kinds of stories about magical places that serve as doorways between the worlds.

The fairy mounds of Old Britain. Circles of flowers or mushrooms."

Zo wrinkled her forehead, as confused as I was about that last one, but Annabelle just held up her hand. "Don't ask."

"Are there any other places?" I settled for another question instead. Was the bridge I'd seen that afternoon really the key to everything, or were there more?

"There might be other places," Annabelle replied. "There's a theory."

Delia, Zo, and I exchanged looks. Annabelle saying *theory* was the equivalent of Delia stumbling across a fifty-percent-off sale or Zo finding an all-you-can-eat buffet.

"This theory posits that the places and times where the barrier between the worlds is thinnest follow a unifying principle called liminality."

"English, please?" Zo prompted.

Annabelle obliged. "The theory of liminality says that there are certain places and times where you can cross from one world to another. These places are *liminal,* which basically means they have a quality of in-betweenness to them."

"English, please?" I echoed Zo's request.

"A liminal state is something that exists between two other states. It's a transition. Doorways exist between one room and another, so they're liminal. Same goes for windows. Midnight is liminal, because it exists between two days. Twilight is liminal, because it occurs between daytime and nighttime."

This was almost making sense to me. Key word: almost.

"Bridges," Annabelle emphasized the word, her eyes locked on mine, "are liminal, because they're literally the connection between here and there."

Bridges. Like the one Alec had taken me to.

"Ding ding ding," Zo said dryly. "We have a winner."

Annabelle nodded. "Think about it. Bridges are liminal. So is an equinox—it's the time when day and night are the same length, which means it's between the time when days are longer than nights and the time when nights are longer than days."

Mabon.

The bridge.

Doorways. Hadn't I felt something weird when I'd stepped through the door to study hall that morning?

All of this led me to just one question. "What about shadows?"

Annabelle leaned back against the wall. "In everything I read about liminality, I never saw a reference to shadows, but if you use a loose definition, it fits. I mean, isn't a shadow what exists between light and dark?"

I thought of James telling me about how in the Otherworld, nothing is lukewarm. Things are hot and cold at the same time, light *and* dark. There is no in between.

Except for me.

I wasn't human, and I wasn't Sidhe. I was in between.

"So if the Sidhe can use shadows to cross over, why

211

aren't they here all the time?" Zo's question was one that probably should have occurred to me. "I mean, it's not like there's a shadow drought. If they work as some kind of portal, isn't that pretty much a free pass to the mortal world?"

"That's the problem with this theory," Annabelle acknowledged. "If you take a loose definition, liminality is everywhere, and if crossing over was really that easy all the time, then why does all of my research suggest that it happens a lot more often on certain days?"

"Maybe something has to be *really* liminal to work," Delia said. "If you think about it, it's kind of like popularity. Everyone's popular with somebody, but not everybody has the power that goes along with being really popular."

"That is a good, albeit disturbing, analogy, Delia," Annabelle said.

Delia preened. "Why, thank you."

"But if only really liminal things weaken the barrier between the worlds enough for the Sidhe to cross over into ours, why do I keep hearing voices in the shadows?" I very carefully did not mention that the voices had taken to telling me things other than to stay away from Alec. "Why did whatever mojo they pulled on Jessica actually work?"

Annabelle inclined her head toward me, acknowledging my questions with a tiny bow. "Nice segue into Question Two, Bailey. Can you tell us exactly what happened to Jessica?"

Now it was my turn to talk without breathing. I

told the story quickly and in gruesome detail, but I did leave out a few tiny bits of information. My friends didn't need to know about the mind games the Shadow People were playing on me. I didn't want to talk about it, and I didn't want them to think that I doubted our friendship—and them.

I didn't.

Not really.

"So, to summarize, Jessica made fun of some girl's hair this morning, and then the Sidhe in the shadows brought her words back to haunt her this afternoon. And after all that happened, you changed everyone's memories but ours so that they remember nothing of aforementioned event." Annabelle condensed my five-minute-long story into fifteen seconds.

"Pretty much. Got any light to shed on this?" When I said *light*, I found myself glancing around the room to look at each and every shadow. Nothing. They were all just shadows. We were safe.

For now.

"Given what you said about the voices mentioning punishment in particular, I do have a theory about who they might be mythwise." Annabelle's words broke into my thoughts. "But I need to check up on a few things before I'll know for sure."

"Hallelujah," Zo muttered. Secretly, I kind of agreed. I loved Annabelle to death, we all did, but I wasn't mentally prepared to take on another theory just yet. This liminality stuff was about as much as I could reasonably handle.

"Hey, Zo. Can I have some carrots?" Delia didn't bother with segues. It just wasn't her style.

Zo shrugged and threw Delia the bag. Their exchange reminded me that I had an uneaten Twinkie in my hand. Without another word, Zo handed Annabelle a Twinkie and grabbed one for herself. She held it up like she was toasting with fine wine. "Bon appétit."

And with that, the four of us ate our snacks and got down to work.

Chapter 17

Annabelle always seemed to take charge when the situation called for organization, planning, or alphabetical order, so I wasn't at all surprised when she started doling out assignments. All three of my friends could lead our group given the right circumstances, and we always seemed to collectively know whose turn it was to take the reins. I was the lone exception to the leader rule, though, because I was either in perpetual follower mode, or I was actually the real leader no matter what. I couldn't tell which.

In any case, Annabelle began by assigning me a job, and I knew without question that I'd take it, even though in this case, following orders felt almost sacrilegiously unproductive. While the rest of my friends were hard at work researching and whatnot, my job was to sleep. Obediently, I lay down on Zo's bed and tried to clear my mind, but the ridiculousness of the situation did not escape me. Still, as much as I hated to admit it, when it came to solving Otherworldly mysteries, I was worth more to the group asleep than awake. I couldn't hold a candle to Annabelle's research prowess, and I'd already caught the others up on everything I'd seen and felt, from study hall right on through my date with Alec.

"Delia, do you think your bald-is-beautiful search could wait a few minutes?" Annabelle asked. I sent out a mental probe to figure out what she was talking about and realized that in the approximately three minutes since we'd eaten our Twinkies, Delia had co-opted the computer to run a search for information she could use to comfort Bald Jessica, once Jess had rediscovered her new hairstyle. It was official: Delia Cameron had twisted priorities and a heart of gold. And right now, based on the vibes I was receiving from A-belle, she was about to get an assignment.

"I've got a job for you."

"What kind of job?" Delia was rightfully suspicious. When A-belle assigned you a job, there was at least a ten percent chance it had something to do with color coding.

"While I'm trying to correlate what happened at school today with aspects of Greek and Celtic mythology, I need you to see what you can find out about our necklaces. Do an internet search on mirrors, magical pendants, anything you can think of."

"Delia Cameron, accessory sleuth." Delia smiled brightly. "I like it." With those words, she refocused her Googling skills on our necklaces, and I made another attempt at blocking out the noise and making my way to the land of slumber.

"You asleep yet, Bay?" Zo asked.

I groaned. At this rate, I'd be better off leaving the rest of them here at Zo's and trying my luck with my bed at home.

"Zo, leave Bailey alone." I could tell by the distracted tone in Annabelle's voice that she hadn't even bothered to look up from her notes to issue the order.

You asleep, Bay? Zo tried again, silently this time, and as always, she was able to work her way past my shields just by concentrating her thoughts in my direction.

Not yet, I said silently back. *I'm starting to think I might never fall asleep again.*

Does this help? Zo asked, leaving me wondering what she was talking about in the split second it took for her to continue her train of thought. *You are getting sleepy. Veeeerrrrryyyyyy sleepy. Listen to the sound of my mind-voice. Hear the waves of the ocean.*

The waves of the ocean? I asked. If my eyes had been open, I would have rolled them.

Go with it, Bay. Embrace the hypnosis. Count backward from one hundred. Things are starting to get fuzzy. Your eyelids are heavy. So heavy.

My eyelids were already closed. It was official: Zo was definitely not allowed to watch late-night television anymore. This had two a.m. public access channel written all over it.

We could always have Annabelle tell you about the themes of Beowulf, Zo offered silently. *Puts me to sleep every time.*

I snorted, and even with my eyes closed, I could feel Annabelle look up from her papers.

Is she mind-talking with you? Annabelle asked me. *She is, isn't she?*

I wonder if these things have matching bracelets. . . .

Now all three of them were in my head. On one level, it felt good and familiar and like something I knew I would miss. On another, it was starting to give me a headache, and I had to get to the Otherworld ASAP. Annabelle's liminality theory was great, but it didn't tell me exactly what had happened to Jessica today, and it didn't tell me how to stop it from happening again. We were on the cusp of something big, and I couldn't take it lying down. Even if my way of figuring things out involved, you know, lying down.

"Here, Zo. I have a job for you."

I opened my eyes. Delia's assignment fit her talents so well that I wondered what our resident strategist had in mind for Zo.

"Does my job involve color coding?" Zo asked suspiciously.

"Yes," Annabelle said, staring Zo down. "Yes, it does."

Zo stared back, but after a few seconds, she sighed and accepted a highlighter from A-belle's outstretched hand.

"It could be worse, Zo," I said. "You could be on bald-celebrity detail."

Delia was so absorbed in her "research" that she didn't even hear me.

After ten more minutes of failing to fall asleep, I sat up. "I hate to say this, guys, but I think I need to go home."

It hadn't been dark for more than an hour, and I was in a room with my three best friends, all of whom could make it past my mental shields with very little effort. Me falling asleep just wasn't going to happen here, as comfy as Zo's bed was.

"That's probably a good idea," Annabelle said, handing Zo a stack of things to color code.

"Do you know if our necklaces are silver or white gold?" Delia asked. I was pretty sure the question was aimed at me, but it might have been to the room as a whole.

"No idea," I said.

"Silver is fairly common in fairy myths," Annabelle said. "It's thought to have mystical powers that repel members of the Otherworld." She paused. "Then again, golden objects play significant roles in several Greek and Roman myths, such as those involving Phaëthon and the Argonauts, respectively."

"Allow me to translate on A-belle's behalf," Zo volunteered helpfully. "She has no idea."

A-belle threw another highlighter at Zo, but didn't look up from her work.

"Leaving now," I told them.

"Bye, Bay!" Delia and Zo chorused, taking me back

219

to when we were little and saying goodbye that way cracked the two of them up. Annabelle murmured her own goodbye, and then I left. As I walked down the stairs and let myself out Zo's front door, I kind of wished one of them had walked me out, or that they'd seemed sadder to see me go.

They're leaving you in little ways already.

I breathed through the remembered words, willing them to leave me alone. Why did I keep dwelling on this? I knew that somebody was messing with me, knew that I shouldn't take it seriously, but my brain was conspiring against me.

Sidhe. Home.

This memory contrasted sharply with the taunting words I knew would haunt me for weeks. That one hurt. This one felt peaceful. It felt right. The two sides of my mind warred with each other, one telling me that everything I loved on this earth was falling apart, and the other reminding me that there was another world.

A perfect world.

"Argh!" I grunted my frustration as I shut the door behind me, pushing back the desire to slam it. Why was it that every time I felt even the slightest twinge of sadness in this world, the Otherworld was there in my thoughts, waiting with promises of something greater? I loved my life. I didn't want another one.

Not even when I felt like maybe Delia, Annabelle, and Zo meant more to me than I did to any of them.

Not true, not true, not true. It was my mantra, but

even as I chanted silently, other words played over and over again in my mind.

We've missed you.

This time, I didn't push down the memory, and the words James had spoken to me the night before eased their way into my head.

We've always known you. All Sidhe know all others: We're born with the knowledge of those who came before us and those who will go after. It's obvious when someone is missing, when our world is unwhole.

Maybe it was petty and paranoid and a million other bad things that start with a *p,* but part of me couldn't keep from wondering why it was that Sidhe I'd never even met longed for me, but my three best friends in the world didn't even have the decency to dread life after high school and the end of an era. Of course, if it hadn't been for some of the Sidhe messing with my mind, I might not have felt that way. I knew that.

Or at least, I wanted to know that.

I just kept telling myself that the whole reason for my early bedtime was Otherworldly sinisterness. Annabelle had said that the otherness of myths was sometimes dark and sometimes twisted, and my serpent-happy "friends" from physics class had proved that. It seemed wrong that I couldn't shake the feeling of belonging that came every time I thought of the Otherworld, even when evidence suggested that maybe it was one place where I shouldn't want to belong.

I opened my own front door and made it halfway to the stairs when my mom poked her head in the entryway. "How was your day?" She pounced on the opportunity to ask questions.

"It was good," I said, trying for a relatively benign and noncommittal answer. I didn't want to get caught up in any kind of extended conversation, so I made the executive decision not to tell her about my date with Alec.

"You're home early." My mom pursed her lips, a domestic detective fishing for a clue. "The Fab Four not hanging out today?"

"No," I said, "they are. I just wasn't feeling very well."

I should have had the presence of mind not to utter such a thing in front of my mother, who immediately attempted to gauge my temperature using the back of her hand.

"You don't feel warm," she said.

Playing sick had never been my strong suit.

"Is something wrong?" my mom asked. "You girls didn't have a fight, did you?"

"No," I said quickly. "I just need to go lie down."

And then, I did a horrible thing. I closed my eyes and allowed the heat trapped deep inside of me to trickle out to the rest of my body. Not enough to start a fire—I'd learned that lesson the hard way this morning—but just enough to raise my body temperature a few degrees.

"Are you sure I don't have a fever?" I asked, trying to sound pathetic.

My mom rolled her eyes heavenward, so sure was she of her temperature-reading capabilities, but to placate me, she placed her hand on my forehead again and frowned.

"You do feel a bit warm," she said, sounding puzzled. "Why don't you run up and change into your pajamas, and I'll bring you some chicken noodle soup and a Sprite."

I'd used my powers on my mom. I was officially going to a very bad place. Just not literally, I hoped, or at the very least, not soon.

Despite the nagging guilt at mojo-ing my mom, I couldn't help but feel a tiny bit proud of my ingenuity when, fifteen minutes later, I finished my soup and closed my eyes. I'd come up with a valid excuse for going to bed when it was barely dark outside, and I'd made it fly with my mom without putting a mind meld on her. That was a definite improvement over my past efforts at parental subterfuge.

Without my friends nearby, I didn't have to worry about others' thoughts in my head. Unfortunately, my own were enough to keep anyone awake at night. My mind bounced back and forth, from the extraordinary to the mundane, from the image of bald Jessica to Alec smiling to Delia presiding over our Geek Watch proceedings with typical flair. Images of my meeting with Mr. McMann mingled with my recollections of the Otherworld landscape. I thought of James, and that made me think of Alec again, and thinking of the two of them made me think of Kane, which made me think of Alexandra Atkins, which led me right back to Jessica, the snakes, and the voices in my head.

I thought of my bleeding finger and of the pendant

223

I wore around my neck even now. I thought of blue-green color seeping into my world, touching everything and leaving nothing unmarked until every last bit of normality had been sapped from my life. I thought of physics and friction and what it felt like to be caught in the middle of two force vectors, competing with each other for the right to tell you what to do.

I thought of my friends and Drogan and Eze and the way the vampire girls had slid their hands up and down James's body, eyeing me possessively all the while.

And then, for a split second, there was nothing, and in that single moment of peace, my breathing evened out and consciousness ebbed slowly away.

This time, I woke up facedown, my nose smushed up against the Seal in a position that was neither comfortable nor flattering. I pushed myself to a sitting position and pulled my legs in close to my body.

"You're here early," Adea commented, her tone that very distinct kind of neutral that says "I know you, and I know you're up to something."

"I have questions. I need answers." I didn't beat around the bush. "What can you guys tell me about what happened at school today?"

The two of them exchanged a glance, and I didn't like the look of it. At all. They knew something, but they weren't telling. I hated being kept out of the Other-worldly loop.

"*Your powers have matured even more than we had realized,*" *Valgius said. It took me a second to get that he was referring to the giant memory-rewriting fest I'd gone on that afternoon.*

"*What else can you tell me?*" *I said.* "*I don't want to hear about my powers. I want to hear about what happened, who did it, and how.*"

"*There's nothing we can say that we haven't told you already,*" *Adea said softly.*

"*There are limits to what may be said, rules that govern the sway we hold over your choices.*"

I hadn't heard Valgius sound that serious since the fight with Alecca.

I knew Morgan showing up wasn't a good thing. And if that hadn't tipped me off, the thing with the snakes might have.

"*She interferes,*" *Adea said.*

"*Who does?*" *I asked, but I had a pretty good feeling that she was referring to Morgan and not snakes and that she'd somehow read my mind. How had she managed that one? I wondered. It had been a long time since my thoughts were transparent to the other Fates.*

"*Sometimes you shield your thoughts,*" *Adea said, answering my unasked question instead of the one I'd voiced.* "*Sometimes you broadcast them. It's a very human trait, Bailey.*"

She reeks of mortali—

I didn't let myself finish that thought. All I reeked of right now was a need for answers. And I was going to get them.

225

"What does she interfere with?" I asked. I knew instinctively that I shouldn't say Morgan's name in this place. I wasn't sure why, but right now that particular why didn't matter, and for once, I heeded the little red flags in my head and played it cautious.

"She interferes with the Reckoning," Valgius said.

"What is a Reckoning?" I said. "And don't just tell me it's my introduction to the others. I met them last night, and I don't feel Reckoned."

Adea chose her words carefully. "For most Sidhe, the Reckoning is a time of acceptance; a time when they come before the court they've chosen and pledge their allegiance to our way."

"It's a transition into adulthood," Valgius said. "It is a choice."

"What kind of choice?" I asked suspiciously. Adea and Valgius were silent. "Let me guess: You can't tell me, because there are limits to what you're allowed to say and telling me would break the rules."

I chose my next question carefully.

"Whose rules are we playing by here?"

"To be Sidhe means to be connected. Even as separated as this place is from Home, we are connected. To the Others. To the land. To the courts."

Another nonanswer. Yay. I tried to wade my way through to their meaning. "The Others, the land, and the courts." The first part was simple enough. "The Others" referred to the other Sidhe, a number of whom I'd met the day before and some of whom had made my head their second home. "The land" meant the Otherworld itself, which *pulled at my soul even now, calling me Home. "The courts," however, was what I zeroed in on.*

Seelie and Unseelie.

Light and Dark.

Eze and Drogan. They were too old and too powerful to be the young-sounding ones who'd threatened me that afternoon, but that didn't mean that they weren't behind it.

"There's something going on here," I said. "And they won't let you tell me what." I refused to say Eze's or Drogan's name, because I hadn't and couldn't say Morgan's.

"Some of what will happen is their doing," Adea said, keeping her words as vague as mine had been, "and some of what will happen is not. The Reckoning represents a decision. For most Sidhe, that decision involves the court to which they pledge. Light and dark, male and female, hot and cold: all things in the Otherworld exist in balance, and the Reckoning serves that balance as much as either court."

I wasn't exactly comforted by the fact that they were throwing around the b-word. Balance (or lack thereof) was what had allowed Alecca to gather enough strength to try to end the world two years ago. Balance was the purpose of the Seal, and once upon a time, Morgan had told me that I was a balance unto myself.

And—though I couldn't remember exactly what they'd said before—I was about ninety percent sure that the spell Adea and Valgius had used to call me to the Seal the day before had somehow involved balance.

Was that what Adea meant when she said that they'd

already told me all that they could? If so, I seriously needed to pay better attention the next time someone used mystical chanting to pull me out of study hall.

"Is there anything else you can tell me?" I asked.

Adea and Valgius looked at each other and then they spoke as one. "Be careful." Their warning was so soft that I had to strain to make out the words, yet the combined effect of their voices was powerful enough to make me take a step backward.

I had to remind myself that I wasn't afraid of them. The three of us had a bond that went back centuries longer than I'd even been alive. We were the Fates, as connected to one another as birth, life, and death themselves.

And yet . . . they had secrets, things that they couldn't or wouldn't tell me. Things that I needed to know.

"When are we going?" I asked. I didn't have to specify where.

"Later," Adea said. "They aren't expecting us until long after your nightfall. You have time, Bailey."

Time for what?

"Time for answers," Valgius said. He held out a hand and I took it, allowing him to help me to my feet.

"Time for answers," I repeated, hoping that I'd find something in the words themselves. No such luck. "And where might those answers be?"

Adea gave me a look, the meaning of which was as mysterious to me as the workings of the average male mind. "Trust your instincts," she said.

The last time I'd acted on my instincts in the Nexus, I'd ended up in the Otherworld and my most basic and *primal self hadn't wanted to leave. "Trust" was not some-thing I should probably be applying to my instincts any time soon.*

I waited, figuring that given enough time, Adea and Valgius would find another loophole and give me a nudge in the right direction, but instead the two of them went to work. Valgius walked toward the Seal and, as his eyes bore into it, light surged into his hands. Soon, he was holding a sphere so bright and pure that it made the fabric I worked with look gray and dingy by comparison. He took the light, molded and cajoled it, whispering words whose meaning I'd never been able to grasp. I couldn't even replicate the sounds in my mind and, no matter how hard I'd tried over the past two years, I'd never been able to carry any part of his whispered words with me back to the mortal realm.

As Valgius whispered and moved his hands back and forth over the light, a tiny string emerged, stretching out from the ball in a timid, elegant line until, after a mo-ment, it broke free and flew back to the Seal.

Val's murmurings continued, but I turned my atten-tion to Adea, who'd gathered a square of light from the Seal. It stood in the air before her, moving on its own, in-terconnected with thousands of others, and Adea, perfectly serene, began to sing. Her voice was low and melodic, and there was something hauntingly beautiful about the song. It was the last thing a mortal heard before the end, and I got the feeling that when a person had a near-death expe-rience and they talked about the light at the end of the tunnel, what they were really talking about was this moment, this song. It was too big for just one of the senses, too old for anyone, even Adea, to really understand its tune.

The light in her hands grew brighter as she sang. It expanded, stretching and fighting against the confines of its physical form until it broke free, splitting into thousands of pinpoints of light that twinkled and then disappeared.

Birth was a whisper. Death was a song. And all of a sudden, I knew what Adea meant by telling me to trust my instincts. The two of them couldn't give me answers, but there were some things beyond the control of the Otherworld courts. What had happened at school today had been part of the mortal realm, part of human life.

And if it was part of life, that meant it was part of me. I might not have been able to conjure up cabana boys or control my own future, but there was one thing I could do to find answers.

I could weave.

I turned to the Seal, my body already beginning to move in tandem with Adea's song and Valgius's rhythmic, whispered words.

Life.

Life.

Life.

The souls of the world rushed into my body, and the force of it threw my head back. I couldn't breathe, but I didn't need to.

Life.

Life.

Life.

This was my oxygen. This was my purpose, my connection, my everything. I felt the souls of the world, felt them everywhere in every aspect of my being, and I couldn't stand still.

Life.

Life.

Life.

I had to weave. The web appeared before me, thousands of overlapping fabrics whose threads arched toward my fingertips. My fingers grappled with the fabric. Like a spider, I wove, my movements hardwired into my nature.

Life.

Life.

Wrong.

And there it was, a twinge of wrongness, fingernails on the chalkboard inside my mind. I forced myself to concentrate on that feeling, and the dance grew more frantic, my movements frenzied and unpredictable.

Wrong.

I couldn't stop to wonder at the wrongness or to force it into a more familiar form. All I could do was feel it and keep weaving.

Weave. Life. Wrong.

Wrong. Life. Weave.

My connection to the mortal realm lived on my skin and in it, but buried deeper in my being, there was something else, another connection, and as I worked my way through the wrongness, it separated into two feelings, one that danced along the surface of my body and one that burrowed deeper, like to like.

And then the fabric in front of me folded and changed, until I was looking at just one life, intertwined with thousands upon thousands of others. I stared at it, trying to find its rhythm, its reason for being here at this moment, demanding my attention more than the rest of the world's souls combined.

As I stared at it, my movements slowing, I saw the briefest flash of a pattern in the fabric, an image I knew as well as my own face.

My tattoo.

I continued weaving, each motion deliberate and slow, though I couldn't read meaning into the movements, no matter how hard I tried, and I watched as my life twisted and turned, as the threads that made up my past and my future unraveled and my fingers nimbly wove them back together.

Wrong.

The feeling surprised me, and as I turned it over in my mind and worked my hands over it in the flesh, the knowledge I'd been waiting for came to me. I felt my own life on my skin's surface and deep inside, and this time, the meaning of the wrongness was clear.

Mortal and Sidhe: two things that weren't supposed to mix. I'd realized earlier that the theory of liminality could be applied to me, as a person. I knew that I existed in between that which was human and that which was Sidhe. I just didn't know what that meant and, until this second, I hadn't realized how very wrong it seemed.

Almost as wrong as what had happened in my life that afternoon. The Otherworld and the mortal realm were

232

separated. The Sidhe were not meant to cross over to my world, and humans were not meant to cross into theirs, except at special times and special places. Annabelle was right. There were rules, and the rules were being broken, and something was allowing that to happen.

Something liminal.

Something wrong.

Me. My life. My destiny. I was human, and I wasn't. I was Sidhe, and I wasn't. I was both and neither, and as I wove, the words of the forgotten spell echoed as music in my mind.

To you we call,
Our third of three.
Child of power
Who set us free.

Blood in your veins,
The barrier holds.
If balance wavers,
The bridge unfolds.

We call you now
With earth and sea,
Air and fire,
So mote it be.

"So mote it be." I whispered the words, and as I did, the pull of the soul fabric finally let go of my body and it was my own again.

I couldn't pretend to understand everything that had happened while I was weaving, but I did manage to hold on to two things. The first was that the wrongness I'd felt in the world's web mirrored the wrongness I saw in myself. This afternoon, one or more Sidhe had crossed into the mortal realm, disrupting the pattern I wove, but the break in the pattern had been there before.

It existed in me.

I was mortal, and I was Sidhe. Once upon a time, I'd been a balance unto myself, but now, for whatever reason, that had changed. Maybe it was because I'd been to the Otherworld. Maybe it had to do with just how much my powers had grown over the past two years. Or maybe it was because senior year had thrown me off balance as a person and that had worked its way into my mystical makeup. Maybe I'd become a double liminality: half human, half Sidhe; half child, half adult. My whole life was one giant transition state, and I wasn't, by any meaning of the word, balanced.

Repeating the words of the spell over and over again in my mind, I fought my way to the connection between what I'd felt in myself and what I'd felt in the rest of the world.

Blood in my veins,

The barrier holds.

If balance wavers,

The bridge unfolds.

Somewhere there was a bridge that connected the Otherworld and the mortal realm, and because of me, because of my imbalance and the forty million transitions in my life and mind, that bridge was open for business. The rules to crossing over were changing. It was becoming easier. Shadows, doorways, bridges . . . what was next?

I could only hope that by the time I woke up tomorrow morning, Annabelle would be able to tell me who was taking advantage of these new rules, and that I'd figure out how to stop them.

Beside me, Adea stopped singing and Valgius whispered his last life into being.

"It's time," Adea said. "Are you ready?"

Ready to see the others again? Ready for the beauty and the power and the feeling of being exactly where I belonged?

Ready for Reckoning, Part Deux?

I was and I wasn't, and it didn't matter either way. I stepped forward and took their hands in mine, and as heat surged between us, I allowed myself to Remember.

Feral beauty. Unforgivable power. Everlasting light.

That was what it meant to be Sidhe.

Chapter 18

I was running, and it felt so good that I couldn't remember despising every lap I'd ever been forced to run in gym. I was fast and the world around me little more than a blur, but with each step I took, my heightened senses picked up on every sound, every color, every smell. I might as well have been blind and deaf in the mortal realm for the vastness of the differences between my perceptions there and here.

We ran through rivers.

Ran through forests.

Ran through colors.

Ran through sound.

We ran up mountains, but this time they did not grow beneath our feet and we did not stop when we reached their summit. The three of us kept running and I closed *my eyes, savoring the feeling of the moment: the taste of the air, the way my body burned hot and cold at the same time.*

I didn't want to stop running, ever. I didn't want to see the Others and wonder whose hit list I was on. I didn't want to go home. I just wanted to run and hear and taste and see and smell forever.

There were more rivers and more mountains, more cliffs that posed no threat to us as we leapt off. There were beaches and oceans, and I didn't stop even once to wonder at the way my feet beat against the water's surface.

And then we hit land, and things grew darker. The trees grew bigger, their bark like onyx and their leaves the darkest shade of green. The air became thicker, the taste closer to dark chocolate than cotton candy, and the earth beneath our feet gave way. The land tore itself apart so that we could fall and, even with nothing to stand on, still we ran.

And then we were there.

"Welcome, Bailey."

It was hard to pay attention to my surroundings in the presence of a voice that embodied everything I should have been looking at: endless caverns made of black diamonds, darkness tinged with every color of the rainbow.

"Where am I?" I asked.

Drogan stepped forward from the glittering shadows. "Welcome to the Unseelie Court," he said.

"This place may not suit you as well as the mountains," Eze said, shining as much in the darkness as she did in her own terrain, her pink hair standing out in

sharp contrast to the deep richness of the black all around her. "But it does have its charm."

"We'll leave it to Bailey to decide which side of our world suits her better," Drogan said. "You are Sidhe, child, and until this moment, until you stood here in this place, you had but scratched the surface of what that means."

He said surface with just the slightest twist of his lips. The day before, on the mountaintop, the two of them had presented a united front, but today, I could sense the undercurrents of tension between them. Maybe it was because of the things Adea and Valgius had told me, because I knew that the Reckoning meant choosing between Seelie and Unseelie, the mountain and the depths.

"You'll make no choices tonight," Eze said. "Do not worry about such things, Bailey. These decisions often make themselves. We only ask that you stay here for a while. Make yourself comfortable. Talk with the other younglings. Your Reckoning will be here soon enough."

Drogan flashed me a kind and blindingly white smile that scared the crap out of me, and then the "adults" excused themselves and left me alone with the next generation of Sidhe once again.

Only this time, I knew that somebody here had it out for me and that whoever it was had taken full advantage of the changing rules governing the separation between this world and the one I had, at one point in time, considered my own.

"Heya, Bailey," James said, waving to punctuate his words. "How's it going?"

I immediately scratched him off of my suspect list—not that he'd ever been on it. James's presence put me at ease, and I stepped toward him. Unfortunately, my ease didn't last as I closed the distance between us, because I made the mistake of glancing around. I was standing in a place that made darkness a counterpart in beauty to light. My body was glowing like a night-light, and I found myself strangely compelled to reach out and play with the shadows. They weren't earthly shadows. Like everything in this world, instead of existing between two states, they existed in both at once. There was light in the shadows, and darkness. They were both and neither, but absolutely nothing in between, and I pushed down the urge to run my fingertips along them, stroking them as if they were alive. Given my experiences with earthly shadows lately and the fact that, for all I knew, these Otherworldly ones were the means through which the Sidhe had traveled to the ones in my world to begin with, wanting to pet the darkness wasn't exactly what I'd call a logical reaction.

"How's it going?" I repeated James's greeting, settling for familiarity since it seemed that logic was completely out of my grasp.

"It's amazing, isn't it?" James asked. "I mean, who knew there were so many shades of black?" He lowered his voice and, even though his words remained completely casual, something about his tone made me shiver—in a good way. "Do you see what I mean about things existing in balance here, Bailey? In this world, even dark can be light."

His words were so close to my thoughts that he may as

well have been flashing a neon sign that said I GET YOU. I
GET YOU. I GET YOU. *Now if only he'd tell me to stop thinking about him and start concentrating on the problem I
came to the Otherworld to solve.*

"It's good to see you again, Bay."

Beside us, Xane stiffened, clearly not liking James's
casual tone. "You are welcome here," Xane told me for-
mally. "As the heir to the Unseelie throne"—that got eye
rolls from both Axia and Lyria as they appeared on either
side of him—"I bid you welcome to the Unseelie Court."

The three of them were heirs, the biggest political power
players of my generation. If the attack on my world (and
on me) had in any way been orchestrated by Drogan
and Eze as part of some as-yet-unseen plan, Axia, Lyria, and
Xane were all prime suspects.

At that point, I registered that I had been welcomed
and tried to generate a proper response. "Thank you," I
said, my voice coming out as powerful and ancient as it
had the night before, with just the slightest husky hint of
things I knew nothing about. It echoed up and down the
caverns until the walls absorbed it and my words became
part of this place forever. The darkness called to me,
pulling at the ink on my tattooed skin and the sometimes-
blue, sometimes-red blood in my veins.

"We've brought guests to meet you, Bailey." Axia's
voice was measured and her words were deliberate.

"Someone to meet me?" I repeated. I still couldn't
quite grasp why it was that I'd merited so much attention
(both positive and negative) from Eze and Drogan, their
offspring, and the rest. I wasn't even full-blooded Sidhe. I

240

reeked of mortality. Why would anyone who lived in a place like this want to meet me? Why would anyone even take the time to threaten me?

I just wasn't that important.

Was I?

"Girls," Axia called, and immediately, I was surrounded by a flutter of motion and greeted by nine voices speaking as one. I felt vaguely like I'd been caught in a field of massive butterflies, but when I managed to concentrate on the girls' features, I realized that they looked as human as I did. Granted, at the moment, that wasn't incredibly human, but despite the fact that these girls moved so quickly and fluidly that it seemed like they were flying, there definitely wasn't a set of wings in sight.

"Hello, Bailey," the girls greeted me, and no matter how hard I tried, I couldn't seem to concentrate on just one of them. Their voices were hypnotically musical, and all nine of them seemed to exist in a state of perpetual motion.

"Muses," James said wryly under his breath, as if that single comment explained it all.

"Muses," I repeated.

James rolled his eyes.

"I've brought a guest as well." Xane was not about to be outdone by a gaggle of females.

"Hello."

I turned toward the sound of the greeting, and for a split second, I balked.

Okay, I thought, scratch the part about there not being any wings in sight.

"Eros," James murmured in my ear.

"Yeah," I whispered back. "I got that much."

His wings were black, the exact same shade as the diamond-lined walls of Hades' caverns. Somehow, I'd never pictured Cupid looking quite so imposing. Or quite so shirtless.

Or, you know, quite so much like an angry Abercrombie model with wings.

Suddenly, my suspect list had just gotten much, much longer. I'd been working off the assumption that I'd already met all of the younger Sidhe, and my instincts told me that the people who'd attacked Jessica were young. But if it turned out that there were many more that I hadn't met, more where Eros and the Muses had come from . . .

I might never figure this thing out.

"Would you like to dance?" Eros extended one hand, and I had to remind myself that he was potentially evil.

"You can always dance with me instead," James told me. "I promise not to step on your toes." There was nothing special or flirtatious about his words, but his tone and his eyes held something else. His boyish charm and borderline-human appearance were completely at odds with everything else around us and with the power I felt in his presence, but I found myself drawn to him.

"Sure," I said.

Eros—if that was his real name, which seemed doubtful—accepted my decision with a nod and took a step back. Xane frowned. Beside him, Axia and Lyria showed no emotion, but I got the distinct feeling that they were pleased with this turn of events.

I also got the distinct feeling that I had no idea what was really going on here. And that whatever I was doing, it probably wasn't a good idea.

"Just follow my lead," James said, and I found myself desperately wanting to, even when he grinned broadly and added, "I've always wanted to say that."

He took both of my hands in his and nodded to the muses. "A little music please, ladies?"

Music isn't *the right word for the sounds that followed. My flimsy grasp of Greek mythology told me that only some of the Muses had anything to do with music, but all nine of them contributed to the melody that filled the air, and I couldn't shake the feeling that what they were doing here—what they were making—was every bit as complicated as the web that I wove with my dance each night.*

There was magic in this song and in this place, and the combination of the two did something to me. It was as if the Muses had constructed this song—deep and sad and a little bit dark—with this place in mind, and as James and I swayed back and forth, our movements fit so perfectly to the tune that I couldn't shake the feeling that I belonged here too.

Even stronger than that was the feeling that I belonged with James. He'd always known me. He'd missed me before we met, and I felt like we'd danced together a million times before. This didn't feel like a date, and it certainly didn't feel like a first one.

It felt like forever.

The song became faster, and the hint of sadness faded away to reveal something in equal parts urgent and exquisite underneath. James let go of one of my hands and spun me around with the other. I could barely remember the mortal realm, and even as the dancing grew faster, the moves more complicated, I flew through them effortlessly.

Apparently, dancing was right up there with running (and possibly James) on the list of things that my Sidhe body was made for.

The song changed again, and we slowed for a bit, our movements perfectly in sync as the others joined us. The music continued, and we never stopped, never paused, never even spoke. We didn't need to. Every spin, every step, every tilt of the head was its own language, and the message this dance communicated was plain as day.

Sidhe.

Sidhe.

Sidhe.

This is where you belong.

This is what you are.

This is the dance you are meant to dance. We were meant to dance it together. Each moment here is worth more than an eternity on Earth.

Sidhe.

James tossed me into the air, and I arched my body, throwing my head back. The thick air of the underrealm caressed my body, holding me aloft long enough that I wondered if I was flying. Seconds ticked by, and still my feet didn't touch the ground. My pose became more extreme, until my head and my feet nearly touched each other behind my body. Finally, I sank down and James caught me again.

"You're very flexible," he whispered.

I wasn't. Not really. But in the Otherworld, I was many things that I really wasn't. Or maybe, *a small voice whispered inside my head*, on Earth, I wasn't many things that I really was.

That thought was so confusing that I couldn't even begin to make sense of it and, as the dancing continued, I didn't try. The song became even faster and more layered, and I concentrated on the steps, the elaborate, interconnected motions that I somehow knew by heart, even though I'd never danced them before.

The Muses' singing changed from sweet to bittersweet to something else altogether, and I could feel the emotions building up inside of me. Each note was torture and ecstasy, and I wanted—needed—to do something. I just had no idea what. The dancing continued, until finally it was too much for me, and I just started laughing.

And soon everyone was laughing and dancing, and the song turned sweet again. It slowed, until James and I were swaying once more, both feet planted firmly on the ground.

"You're a good dancer," he said.

"Something tells me that everyone here is a good dancer," I said.

"Aha!" he said jokingly as he brought his hand to my chin in a gesture that was anything but jesting. "I told you that you belonged here, that you were one of us."

I got the feeling that he couldn't have given me a higher compliment, but at the same time, the words made me feel a little queasy. Was I one of them? Could I be?

Hadn't I just come to the realization that I wasn't any-thing anymore? I wasn't human, I wasn't Sidhe, I wasn't in balance. I was liminal, and I was me, and I knew, just knew, that wasn't going to be enough.

Dancing with James hadn't brought me balance. It didn't solve my problems. But it felt so right that the ten-tative grasp I had on my own doubts and what I'd learned floated out of my head, banished by the movements of our bodies and the sound of the song.

"You okay?" James asked, and I was struck again by how utterly familiar the expressions on his glittering face were. If I'd been dancing with anyone else, if I'd felt this way about anyone else here, I was pretty sure that queasy would have progressed to nausea, and quite possibly to "being the first Sidhe to barf during the Reckoning process."

"Bay?"

The nickname made me smile. Something about being near James just felt so right. My mind flitted briefly to Alec, back on Earth, but I couldn't picture his face in James's presence, so I came to the very logical conclusion that there was no reason for me to try. I had my very own hot—but adorably human—Sidhe boy right here. What more did I want?

"I'm fine," I said. He moved a little closer to me, and we continued to dance to the slow, rhythmic music, our movements gentle and perfectly matched. "Just a little overwhelmed."

"You?" James said, his voice full of faux shock. "Never!"

"Shut up."

"As you wish," he said, but the grin was back on his face with a vengeance.

"So," I said, searching for a topic of conversation.

"So," he returned.

I wondered if he was having as much trouble as I was reconciling the sound of our voices, powerful and old, with our conversation, which sounded pretty much like every awkward conversation I'd ever had with a boy.

"So," I continued, "who are you?"

Until I asked, I'd completely forgotten that I wanted to know, but as was so often the case, my brain ended up playing catch-up with my mouth.

"Feeling philosophical?" James asked. "I think, therefore I'm James."

And I'm yours. *That addition was silent, but I felt it in his smile and his tone.*

"You're James," I said, and for a second I wondered if I'd accidentally replied, "I'm yours, too" instead. I covered quickly, aiming for the goofy, casual tone he sometimes used with me. "You're the 'first James,' I know, but that wasn't what I meant. Axia is Artemis. Lyria is Aphrodite. The Muses are . . . the Muses. So who are you?"

"What if I told you I was nobody?" he asked.

"I wouldn't believe you," I said softly. *If anybody here was nobody, it was me, and given that I was one of the three Fates, I just couldn't picture James as not playing his role as well. It was much easier to picture Xane as "nobody" in Greek myths, because so much of his identity was*

247

tied up in being his father's mini-me. James, on the other hand, had to be someone. I was sure of it.

"I am a man of mystery," James said, striking a James Bond–esque pose. "Plus, I kind of don't want to tell you."

He made me laugh. It was so strange: one second the two of us were connected on some deep and mind-blowing level, and the next, he was a goofball and I was a goofette. It was so completely odd, but so right.

"It can't be that bad," I said, searching his eyes for confirmation. "Right?"

James looked a little bit sheepish.

"Fine," I sighed. "In that case, tell me about the others."

He raised one eyebrow quizzically. "The others? I already told you most of what I know."

"Not who they were in Greek mythology," I said. "Tell me about who they are now. You know . . . normal stuff." He seemed to have no idea what I was talking about. "Like who's dating who. Or who the cool kids are. Or what their powers are."

Okay, so maybe that last one wasn't entirely normal, but I was curious. I wasn't exactly sure why I was curious, and I got the feeling that there was something I should have been remembering, something that this place and this moment and James were keeping me from thinking about, the same way it made my thoughts fuzzy whenever I tried to think about my friends.

Hadn't I come here for a reason?

Hadn't I been scared of something?

I couldn't quite remember, which was strange, but

not quite as strange as the fact that I suddenly didn't want to.

"Powers?" James repeated.

I gave him a look. Even when my mind was fuzzy, playing dumb didn't work on me. I was friends with Delia, and she made pretending to be more clueless than she was an art form. Or at least I was pretty sure that I was and that she did, but under the influence of the rainbow of blackness here, I couldn't have sworn to it. Strange feeling, that—being unsure of the one thing in life that I'd always known was true.

"What can you do?" I said. "What can anyone here do? Like . . . Eros. Does he really have a bow and arrow? Does he make people fall in love?"

Is he the reason I feel this way with you? I thought. *It made no sense. None of it made any sense.*

"There was a time when Eros interfered more in the lives of mortals," James said. "There was a time when we all did, but then the worlds began to separate, and later . . ." He trailed off. "Later, things changed."

My best calculations said that "later" corresponded with the establishment of the Nexus, the Fates, and a new connection between the two worlds.

"How did things change?" I asked, feeling on some level like I should know the answer, but unable to access it.

"Crossing over became rarer," James replied. "It became possible only at certain times, certain places."

The fuzziness in my head kept me from figuring out why that sounded familiar. The inside of my skull itched, and I found myself wondering how to make it stop and whether or not my powers in this realm extended to reaching inside my own brain to scratch.

There was something I was forgetting.

The thought was fleeting, sucked out of my head by the air around me and the gentle movement of the other dancers through this magical space. With deliberate effort, I finally remembered that I'd been asking him about powers and, despite feeling a little light-headed, I continued on that path.

"What can you do?" I asked.

"Me personally, or the Sidhe in general?"

"Either," I said.

James took my hand and spun me. "I can do this."

I laughed. "That's not a real answer." I waited for him to tell me what his powers really were, but no answer came.

"Tell me about someone else then," I said. "Like . . . what about Lyria? She's Aphrodite, right? But what does that mean? The Greeks thought she was the goddess of love. She's the heir to the Seelie throne. So what can she do?"

"Lyria is highly empathic," James said carefully. "She has the ability to feel others' emotions as her own."

"That's it?" I was skeptical. Eze was powerful. I could feel that much, and I doubted that her daughters were any less powerful. And for some reason, the question felt more important than my mind told me it was.

"She's also an expath," James continued. "She can manipulate the emotions of others, though she rarely chooses to do so. There are strict rules governing the

250

manner in which we use our powers on one another. Lyria knows them well."

Rules that govern . . . *The phrase sounded familiar.*

"Okay," I said. "So Lyria's emotion girl. I guess that makes sense, with the whole love thing."

It didn't exactly make sense considering that I hadn't seen Lyria display any emotions, but close enough.

"Anything else?"

"She's very strong in the glamour," James said. Seeing that I didn't understand, he elaborated. "Changing what other people see when they look at her. It's a skill we all share, but some are better at it than most."

"And that's it?" I asked. I wasn't actually all that in-terested in Lyria's powers specifically, but I wanted to get a sense for exactly how outclassed I was here. I was psychic, but if that worked on other Sidhe, it certainly didn't work the same way, because I hadn't caught a stray thought in the Otherworld. Not one. As I waited for James to reply, I tested my pyrokinesis, concentrating just long enough to reach for the fire inside me, verifying that it was there, ready to spark to life the second I called it.

I couldn't manage a glamour. I wasn't an empath or an expath, but as far as power went, I wasn't doing half bad for someone who only half-belonged here in the first place. Now, if only I could put my finger on why it seemed so important to match my powers against theirs.

"Lyria does have a few other powers," James admitted. "She can call forth certain emotions in their physical forms—fire for passion, ice for fear. Nothing too out of the ordinary."

So much for my extraordinary fire powers.

But if my powers weren't "out of the ordinary," then why were Drogan and Eze bothering to woo me? Why did anybody care about the result of my Reckoning? Why bring me here at all?

And what was I forgetting?

"Song's over." James's mild comment broke me from my thoughts, and I realized that we'd stopped moving. I had no idea how long we'd danced, but as I stood there, the stillness jarring my muscles, I couldn't shake the feeling that it had been hours and that my time here tonight was almost done.

"Thirsty?" James asked.

I nodded. Putting heart and soul into unearthly movements for extended periods of time had a tendency to do that to a person.

James reached out to the shadows, and as I watched, he pulled at its edges, and the darkness complied, stretching and molding itself into two cups, one for each of his hands.

"Water?" he said, offering me one of the cups.

I took it and smiled at the feel of the shadow, metallic yet silky. I raised it toward my lips and glanced down at the water. It was clear and there was light in it despite the darkness of its container. It smelled fresh and sweet, like dew, only more so. I lifted the cup to my lips, and as I did, a reflection danced along the water's surface.

My necklace.

Without warning, the necklace grew very hot against my skin, and I reached for the chain, to snatch the pendant away before it burned me. My fingers grazed the side of the pendant, and it was only through luck that it didn't cut me again. My contact with the charm was brief, but in that instant, Annabelle's voice flashed into my head, clearer than any Earth-related thought I'd had since we'd started dancing.

"No food. Nothing to drink, either. It's another one of those overlaps between Celtic and Greek mythology. Several sources I found mentioned that if a human eats or drinks in the Otherworld, they can never leave. Ever."

I dropped the cup as if it had scalded me the way the pendant had a moment before. I expected it to shatter, but instead it dissolved, losing its shape as the darkness swirled and fled back to the living shadows. As for the water, it lay at my feet, sparkling in a way that looked sinister to me now.

Water wasn't supposed to be that clean or that pure or that anything. It wasn't supposed to be beautiful or smell divine. This wasn't my kind of water, and I wasn't supposed to drink it.

"What's wrong?" James asked, but the moment before the words left his mouth, I saw something flash across his face—a split second (or maybe not even that) of disappointment—and I lowered my shields in hope of hearing his thoughts.

So close.

I took a step back.

"Bailey?"

He'd tried to make me drink. He'd tried to trick me into drinking. He'd offered it up so innocently, but if

Annabelle was right, then there was nothing innocent about it. Once I ate or drank something here, I wouldn't be able to go back, and if I did, I'd waste away, longing for what I could never have again.

With James's horrible thought still echoing in my head, I knew beyond all knowing that was what he had intended. A-belle had wondered if that kind of trick would work on me, because I was part Sidhe, but what she'd forgotten, what I kept forgetting, was that I was part human, too.

They'd brought me here to seduce the Sidhe in me, and barring that, to fool the human.

And James was at the center of it all. The connection I'd thought there was between us. The way he'd made me laugh.

"Bay?" James wrinkled his forehead, confused.

Oh, I just bet he was.

"Don't call me that," I said. "You don't get to call me that."

He'd been so nice. So friendly. He'd been glad to see me. He'd acted like he'd spent his whole life missing me, like all of them had, when really, he'd been trying to get me to drink. I went over every word he'd spoken, and realized that from the beginning, his words had been crafted with one goal in mind.

He wanted me to stay here.

"That's what this is about, isn't it?" I asked, my voice ancient and small and shrill all at the same time. "That's why you brought me here, that's what this Reckoning is. It isn't just choosing sides. You don't care if I choose Seelie or

254

Unseelie. You just want me to choose. You want me to stay here."

But why? I was one of the Fates. I couldn't stay here. I belonged to the Nexus and to Earth. I couldn't live in the Otherworld the way the others could. So why the persuasion? Why the tricks?

Maybe, *I thought slowly,* it's not so much that they want me here as it is that they don't want me anywhere else. Maybe they don't want me in the mortal realm.

The ideas were fleeting, wisps of smoke that slipped through my fingers again and again, but I clutched at the pendant, not caring whether it cut me or not, and things grew more concrete in my mind.

"We do care which court you choose," Xane said. "My father and I would very much like you to pledge yourself to the Unseelie. There's a greatness in you, Bailey. You could be great here."

Xane was oblivious to the fact that I was freaking out—that, or he just didn't care. Axia showed slightly more tact.

"You're confused," she said, "and that's our fault, but we play by rules not our own. You speak truly enough. You weren't meant for the mortal world, and we do want you to come home, where you belong. But as Xane said, the choice offered to you at your Reckoning tomorrow night is an important one. The Seelie Court would be honored to have you."

"Tomorrow night," I repeated. "My Reckoning is tomorrow? And you expect me to choose courts?"

"You must choose," Lyria said softly. "That's what a Reckoning is."

"That's what a Reckoning is," I repeated. "A choice that's not really a choice. You pick one of two options, and you're stuck with it for the rest of your immortal life."

"It's our way," Axia said, her voice louder, but as gentle as her sister's. "There comes a time when all Sidhe must choose. For you, that time is tomorrow. For the rest of us, it could come any day."

"You mean none of you have been Reckoned?" I asked. I'd been operating under the assumption that I was the only un-Reckoned person left. They were thousands, maybe even tens of thousands of years old. I was a senior in high school, yet somehow I was the one on the chopping block?

"You've lived in mortal years," Axia said. "We have not. We're considered young still. Our time will come, and when it does, we—each and every one of us—will choose, just as you must choose tomorrow."

"And if I choose, what then?"

The three heirs looked at one another.

"Then all will be as it should be," Axia said finally.

"I'll be stuck here," I said. I couldn't drink the water. I couldn't eat the food. Somehow, I severely doubted I could pledge myself to either of the Otherworldly courts and expect to be allowed to go home.

"Would that really be so terrible?" James asked. I couldn't let myself wonder at the tone in his voice and what it meant. "You love it here. Think of the way it feels to run. Think of the singing and the songs and the burning and the cold. Think of your connection to us and ours to you."

256

Gone was the awkward goofball, and in his place stood someone far more eloquent, someone who didn't seem nearly as human as he had moments before. Someone I still felt connected to nevertheless . . .

"You played me," I said. "This whole time, you've just been . . ." I trailed off. I couldn't even say it.

"I haven't told you anything that wasn't true," James said. "I want you here. We all want you here. You're amazing, Bailey. I don't think you understand just how special you are."

"Why?" I asked. "Why am I so special?"

"Because the power comes through you." James's words were followed by the loudest silence I'd ever heard. I inferred that whatever he'd just told me, it wasn't something that I was supposed to know.

"The power comes through me," I repeated. "Of course. I'm your connection to the mortal realm. I weave life, it fuels your power. That's how the story goes, isn't it? But I'm not like Alecca. I don't live in the Nexus. I'm human—"

"Part human," Xane corrected. "And not even that for long."

Axia gave him a sharp look, and he shut his mouth.

"You guys want me to pledge so that I'll be trapped here. No, not even here—you want me with the Seal, all the time, because the more I'm there, the more power I feed into your land."

"It's your land, too, Bailey," Axia said. "There are those of us who believe that the Old Ones were mistaken in separating the Three from the rest of us. You would be welcome in the Otherworld, whenever you wished to come."

In her own way, she was trying to be nice. Considering her mother was probably the mastermind behind this whole setup, I wasn't sure I could expect much more from her. But James . . . I'd thought he was my friend. I'd thought he was interested. For a split second, I may have even been ridiculous enough to think on some subconscious level that he was my soul mate.

I was an idiot. Boys like James . . . Sidhe like James weren't interested in half-mortal girls like me.

It didn't matter how right this felt. It didn't matter how beautiful darkness was here, or how much I longed to stand in the Otherworldly light. The running, the connection, the intense sense of belonging and the fact that this place ran in my blood—none of it mattered.

I didn't belong here.

No matter how much I wanted to, I couldn't. Why hadn't I seen that before?

"I won't stay," I said. "I won't choose. You can't make me."

"Can't we?"

The voice sounded something like Axia's, but older, cooler, and I didn't allow myself to turn around, because the last thing I wanted to do right now was face down Eze.

"You have some power, Bailey, but here, you are not as powerful as you believe. There are rules, and you will abide by them. This is our land, Drogan's and mine. We rule here, and you will choose."

I didn't want to listen to her words. Instead, I told myself a story, one that Annabelle had told me. After the Olympians had defeated the Titans, the three brothers had divided the world between them. Zeus got the heavens. Hades got the underworld. Poseidon got the seas.

Drogan and Eze weren't the only ones who ruled here. I may not have been as powerful as the two of them were, but Morgan was. She could help me. She had to.

"You dare think her name in our presence?" Drogan asked. "She is a traitor to her kind. She betrays us by living among them. She travels freely through their waters and ours as if they were one."

Clearly, that was the Sidhe equivalent of blasphemy. Or maybe, given what James had told me about the difficulty that most Sidhe had crossing over most of the time, it was something to be coveted.

"She cannot help you now, Bailey," Eze said, her voice gentle and kind again. I wished it weren't. She was scarier this way. I would have rather she glared at me than smile.

"You think us villains, but we're not, Bailey. We're just trying to save you—from yourself and from what that world would do to you. You would grow old there. You would die there. And what would happen to the world then? You spin their lives. What will happen when you stop?"

I'd never thought of my own death before, not in any kind of concrete way. Even in the moments when I'd absentmindedly wondered who would come to my funeral, I hadn't thought about what my dying would really mean. I was the Third Fate. What would happen to the world when I died? Even if I lived to be a hundred, eventually I'd die.

Who would be Life then?

The guilt trip hit me like a cement truck, and Drogan, sensing weakness, picked up where his sister had left off. "You see the wisdom in my sister's words, but soon you'll convince yourself that that may be a risk worth taking, that you won't die for years, that perhaps your immortal blood will sustain you or that you may pass it on to the children you will someday bear."

I had to wonder why he was talking me out of my guilt as easily as Eze had talked me into it.

"But there are other things that staying in the mortal realm would do, Bailey. Things that will happen to your world if you insist on staying there." Drogan smiled, his white teeth nearly reflective in their brightness. "There is a balance to be maintained. You know better than anyone how delicate that balance can be."

I'd felt the imbalance in the world's web and I'd traced it back to myself, back to my mixed blood. Suddenly, everything I'd discovered earlier in the night, everything I'd wondered before crossing over, came back to me. There was some magic in this place, some dampening charm that left my mind fuzzy and made it hard for me to concentrate on these thoughts, but looking at Drogan, it became all too clear.

They'd tried to tempt me here.

Eze had added guilt to the mix.

And now we were dealing with blackmail.

"What happened in school today," I said. "That was you."

James had told me that crossing over was ordinarily very difficult for Sidhe. There were days when they could *cross, and Morgan obviously didn't have trouble with it, but there were limits, limits that were in place for good reason. Because when something happened to lift the limits and Sidhe could cross over at will, things got messy.*

Especially if things getting messy was the point.

"For a short period of time, your own balance—half human, half Sidhe—was enough to set things right," Eze said, her voice kinder and more horrible than ever. "But that time has passed. Now the greater balance is at stake. There have always been Three, who live in between the worlds. Now there are two in the Otherworld and one in yours." She paused and then laid it out for me. "As long as you live in the mortal realm, the gateway between realms will remain open."

I'd thought it myself, before I'd come to the Other-world and forgot why I was here, I was liminal. I was in transition. I was off balance, and that had very real consequences.

"And as long as that gate remains open," Drogan said delicately, "we have no way of ensuring that others of our kind don't use your world to . . . play."

No way of ensuring, my butt. They'd probably ordered the others to attack Jessica. That was a demonstration. They were showing me what could happen, what they could do. That was the whole point, wasn't it? They'd found a way to use the imbalance to suit their whims. As long as I lived in the mortal world, they'd be free to mess with it, and until I agreed to stay here, they wouldn't stop.

Maybe they were lying to me, maybe I could call their bluff. . . .

"Bailey." James whispered my name into the back of my neck. "What happened to that girl today was nothing compared with what it could have been. Drogan, Eze, the others of their generation . . . they can do much, much worse than any of us could or would." He swallowed hard. "Some of them would enjoy it."

This could not be happening.

As I was trying—desperately—to talk myself out of this, the Muses collectively decided that now would be the proper time to start singing again. Maybe they thought that if we could dance, we'd all just get along. But I wasn't going to get pulled into it. Not this time. I wasn't going to be seduced by the music. Or by James. I thought of Alec and tried to remember what a human crush felt like. What it felt like to have feelings for someone real. With what I'd been through tonight, who needed forever?

Pushing the thought out of my mind, I glanced from Lyria to Eros and back again, wondering which one of them was responsible for that.

"Children do love to play," Eze said fondly. Then she met my gaze with her deadly blue eyes. "Imagine what would happen to your world if the adults began to cross over."

She wasn't just threatening my school. She was threatening my entire world, and I most definitely and without question did not want to imagine anything.

"We'll expect your decision tomorrow night," Eze said. "Seelie or Unseelie, the choice is yours."

I caught the meaning of her words: that was the only choice that was mine. Beyond that, I was trapped.

"You could let the world—"

"—suffer, but that would be—"

"—so wrong."

Kiste and Cyna appeared on either side of me, doing their creepy talking-in-turns thing. Kiste lightly stroked long fingernails over my skin, and one look at her eyes told me that she'd love nothing more than to use those nails as if they were talons and tear into me.

"Leave her alone," James said. I tried not to be surprised that he was standing up for me, but I couldn't help myself. "She hasn't done anything wrong yet."

"Do as he says," Axia told the vampire twins sharply.

Eze raised a single eyebrow, and Axia met her eyes. "Do you disagree, Mother?"

Eze smiled. "No. Of course not. My daughter and James speak truly. Bailey has done nothing wrong, and you are forbidden from attacking your own kind."

"She is—"

"—mortal."

"She can be—"

"—punished."

Punished. *The same word the synchronized voices in my head had used. Kiste and Cyna were the ones who'd attacked Jessica. It seemed so obvious now. There were two of them. They were Otherworldly Mean Girls. How could I not have figured them for the most likely suspects in a case that involved two sinister voices, threatening me and terrorizing my high school? I felt incredibly stupid. And then I realized that if Kiste and Cyna were the ones who had attacked Jessica, they were also the ones who had warned me to stay away from Alec. . . .*

"Now, now, girls," Drogan said, smiling indulgently

at the girls, who I was absolutely positive would pledge themselves to the dark court when their day of Reckoning came. "Bailey might not remain mortal forever. And if she chooses to remain that way, she will be punished."

Kiste and Cyna preened, and I swallowed hard, wondering what exactly they'd do to me (and, for that matter, why they were so obsessed with keeping me away from Alec).

"We must take our leave of you now." Adea's voice was quiet but strong, and when I realized she was there, I wondered why she'd stayed silent so long. She was my ancestor, my Otherworldly mother. Why hadn't she stood up for me? Why hadn't she rescued me?

"Very well," Eze said, and her tone was sharp enough to cut flesh. Adea did not visibly wince, but I could feel her doing so. Valgius laid his hand lightly on hers. In all things, the two of them were united, and he wasn't about to let her suffer by herself.

As the three of us took our leave of this place, I tried to push down the truth that just wouldn't leave me alone as we ran.

Adea and Valgius hadn't protected me because they couldn't. Nobody could. I was on my own, and no matter what I did, this was not going to end well.

Chapter 19

When I woke up, it was still pitch black outside. I turned to look at my clock, but then realized I'd scorched it the day before.

"Doesn't matter," I said softly. No matter what time it was, I wasn't going back to sleep. I needed to think. I needed to plan. I needed to find some way around the trap that had been laid for me. One thing was certain. I couldn't do it alone.

I slipped out of bed and threw on a white T-shirt and jeans. I had much bigger things to concern myself with than fashion. Say, for instance, the utter chaos that would soon engulf the world if I didn't agree to leave it.

And yet even with the threats the Sidhe rulers had made fresh in my mind, I couldn't help the pang of sadness, loneliness, and longing that hit me when I consciously realized that I wasn't in the Otherworld anymore. Would it always feel like this? Like somebody had suctioned out the vast majority of my heart? Like my body was just a mask I had to wear on this plane because mortal eyes couldn't handle my true form?

Stop it, I told myself silently. *This is your true form. You're human.*

But that was the problem. I wasn't human, and I wasn't Sidhe. I was both of them, and I wasn't either of them. I was completely imbalanced, and if the world became a playground for beings who made Kiste and Cyna look like Girl Scouts, it was going to be my fault.

Trying to banish the thoughts, I pulled my hair into a ponytail and looped it through the tie again, leaving all but a few stray strands in a loose pseudo-bun. Delia would probably have a conniption when she saw it, but I just wanted my hair out of my face and out of my eyes. I didn't want to look at the dual color and think about what it meant.

"Okay," I said in what I hoped was a firm voice. "No more thinking about what not to think about. I need a plan, I need help, and I know exactly where to go to get both."

Annabelle was spending the night at Zo's house. With a little luck and a lot of stealthy maneuvering, I could wake the two of them without Zo's dad knowing I was there at all. Once I made it in, it would be simple enough to get Delia over there. Together, the four of us would find a way to stop this. They wouldn't let the Sidhe blackmail me into leaving this realm. We'd taken down one Sidhe. Now we just had to find a way to out-smart the rest.

Piece of cake.

Unfortunately, my mom wasn't nearly as deep a sleeper as Zo's dad was, and the second I started walking down the stairs, she woke up and tiptoed into the hallway to check out the noise.

"Bailey?" she said, her voice a whisper even though my dad, like Zo's, could have slept through a chain-saw massacre. "What are you doing up?"

"I have to go to Zo's," I said.

My mother stared at me incredulously. "Do you have any idea what time it is?"

Actually, no.

"It's four-thirty in the morning. You're not going anywhere except back to bed."

"Actually," I said softly, "I am."

"Bailey Marie, I don't know what you think you're doing, but . . ."

I sighed and then bit the bullet. There was no way around it. I needed my friends, and I couldn't afford to get myself grounded in the middle of an apocalypse—or something close to it. It was wrong, and I felt like a horrible daughter, and I was sure the heavens them-selves were going to smite me for it, but my chances of escaping the next twenty-four hours without being smote were looking pretty slim as it was.

"You want me to go to Zo's," I said, letting down my shields and allowing my will to bleed over to her mind.

"I want you to go to Zo's," my mom said, the intonation totally her own even though the words were mine.

"You won't worry about this at all," I continued. "You're not angry."

"You go on, sweetheart," my mom said. "I'll get right back to sleep."

"You won't freak out when you wake up in the morning and I'm not here," I said, and then, because I felt like I had to do something to atone for mind melding my own mother, I added one last instruction. "You're going to sleep late and take a nice, long bath when you get up," I said. "You don't need to worry about me, and you can have a day completely to yourself."

"You know," my mother said, her voice contemplative, "I think I'm going to take a Me Day tomorrow. Sounds nice, doesn't it, Bailey?"

I smiled. "Yeah, Mom. It does."

A moment later, she wandered back to bed, with no idea that I'd been in her mind, molding her thoughts into what I wanted them to be.

"I am a bad, bad person," I said as I walked to the front door. "Zo will be so proud."

As it turned out, Zo was a little too grumpy to be proud. When I let myself into her house using the key in the empty flowerpot and then made my way up to her bedroom to wake her, she was less than amused.

"The world had better be ending," she grumbled the second she realized that I was not, in fact, a dream. "Because if it's not, I'm going to kill you."

268

I didn't say a word in reply; I just looked at her.

Zo narrowed her eyes. "Awww, man. The world is ending?"

I shrugged. It wasn't like the Sidhe were out to destroy the world the way that Alecca had been. They were just out to use it and the mortals who lived here for a little fun.

Lethal fun.

How had James phrased it? The adults could do much, much worse . . . and some of them would enjoy it.

"Maybe we should get A-belle," Zo said. "This is more her deal than mine."

I nodded, and the two of us crept down the hallway and into the guest bedroom, which Annabelle used as her own whenever she spent the night. I reached out to touch A-belle's shoulder, but Zo stopped me.

"No," she said. "Let me."

Even in the midst of a crisis, Zo couldn't turn down an opportunity like this. She climbed onto the bed, put her face right next to Annabelle's, and then waited.

"What if she doesn't wake up?" I asked as Zo inched closer, until her nose was almost touching her cousin's. Zo didn't reply, she just gave me a toothless smile that said "She will."

Annabelle's eyelids fluttered. She shifted in her sleep and then opened her eyes. When she saw Zo, directly on top of her and grinning like a madwoman, she opened her mouth to scream, but Zo muffled the scream with her hand.

"My work here is done," she said.

269

I rolled my eyes. "We have a problem," I told Annabelle. "A big one."

A-belle managed to regain her wits, and she glared at Zo. "Is my cousin altogether necessary for solving this problem?" Annabelle asked. "Because I really do think killing her would put me in a more problem-solving mood."

"I need you guys," I said. "All of you guys. Speaking of which, we need to get Delia over here, stat."

Zo lit up like a kid on Christmas morning, and I was positive she was thinking of creative ways to wake Delia up, but we didn't have time for fun and games, so I concentrated on Delia and cast out my mind-voice, using all of my psychic power to penetrate her dreams.

Delia, you need to wake up.

But I'm wearing Chanel, Delia complained silently. *I never get to wear Chanel.*

You need to wake up. I need you.

Those words brought Delia back to consciousness, and I sent her a mental picture of the three of us sitting in the guest bedroom at Zo's, hoping she'd get the point and sneak over here ASAP. Delia's mother wasn't nearly as with it as mine was. She wouldn't miss her.

"What's going on?" Annabelle asked, reluctantly abandoning all thoughts of killing Zo. "If it wasn't bad, you wouldn't be here. What did you find out?"

The story came spewing out of my mouth. I couldn't even make myself wait for Delia to get there, and when she arrived five minutes later, I was just coming to the part where Eze and Drogan had finally laid all of their cards on the table. Delia didn't interrupt me. She just listened, and when I was finished, she looked to Annabelle for a summary.

"Bailey being who and what she is and living here has thrown off the world's balance," Annabelle said succinctly, in a tone that would have been more appropriate for discussing the quadratic equation than my future in this realm. "This imbalance has somehow caused the barrier between the realms to break down, allowing the Sidhe to travel freely into our world. They're the ones behind the chaos at school yesterday, and the King and Queen of the Sidhe told Bailey that the only way to keep it from happening again, the only way to keep it from getting worse and spreading to the whole world, is for her to leave it." She nibbled on her bottom lip, deep in thought. "If we try to fit this in with what we were talking about yesterday, it seems like Bailey herself is liminal, and combined with an imbalance between the worlds, her presence on Earth increases the liminality of things around her."

"Bailey's not going anywhere." Zo's voice was implacable, and just listening to it told me how much she wanted to punch something—or someone—right now.

"Of course not," Annabelle said. "There must be another solution. If there wasn't, Morgan never would have gotten involved. From what Bailey says, it seems like Morgan is key in all of this. She's the only one who has as much power as Drogan and Eze, and somehow, she's not subject to the barrier and the balance the way the others are. She dwells in our world, at least some of

271

the time, but her presence doesn't seem to have the kind of adverse effect that Bailey's does." Annabelle paused and then shot me an apologetic look. "No offense, Bay."

"None taken." How could I take offense when everything she was saying was true? Morgan could somehow travel between worlds at no cost to the balance, and she wasn't even Liminal Girl. There was no doubt in my mind that Morgan had known what Drogan and Eze had planned for me, and that, just like last time, she'd armed me as best she could.

"The necklaces," I said. "They do more than just show us the true nature of things in the mirror. When I was . . . there . . ." I couldn't bear to say the name of that wonderfully horrible place out loud. ". . . James offered me something to drink, and I forgot and almost took it, but then I touched the necklace and it stopped me. It's like, in this world, it shows me the Otherworld, and in the Otherworld, it connects me to this one. It clears my thoughts."

But how was that supposed to help me find a solution that didn't involve me leaving the mortal realm forever and didn't involve the mortal realm being irrevocably changed until I caved?

"I'm confused," Delia said, wrinkling her forehead in deep thought. "Why is Bailey being here such a big deal?"

Annabelle grabbed a sheet of paper and a pen from her bag and started drawing a diagram. "It's like osmosis," she said.

The three of us stared blankly at her.

"Come on, you guys took chemistry," Annabelle prompted. "In a solution, things move from areas of high concentration to areas of low concentration until they're equally distributed." She drew a bunch of dots on the right side of the page and only a few on the left, and then scrawled in an arrow showing the direction of movement from the dot-heavy side to the side with barely any dots at all.

"And this has to do with Bailey, how?" Delia was not shy about asking questions when she didn't understand something. Sometimes it made her seem ditzy, but the real idiots were the ones who pretended to understand, but didn't.

Annabelle drew a line down the page. "Okay," she said, "this is the mortal realm, and this is the Otherworld."

"There's something in between," I said. "The Nexus."

"Right," Annabelle said. "That said, however, the in-between space is still in the Otherworld, right?"

I nodded. It wasn't an earthly place, that was for sure.

"So you've got three Fates," Annabelle said, "and two of them are on one side of things, and one of them is on the other. That's not balanced. Plus, Bailey's only half Sidhe, so there's basically a four-times-higher concentration of Sidhe Fates in the Otherworld than there is here." Annabelle drew many, many more dots on the Otherworld side of the page. "And there are a ton of

Sidhe on the other side, and just half of Bailey—and maybe Morgan—over here. That's a major imbalance, which is okay, so long as the barrier between the worlds is impermeable to Sidhe in most places, but once it's not . . ."

"Our world becomes fairy central," Delia said. "Gotcha."

"So what do we do?" I asked. "Me being in this world is what made the barrier permeable to begin with." I felt weird using Annabelle's vocabulary, but it was a familiar kind of weird, the kind I was used to. "Is there any way to stop it? To keep them in their world? Because if they can cross over, they will. Eze and Drogan want me in the Otherworld. They want the power I can bring them, and they won't stop until they get it."

"Or until we make them," Zo said darkly.

"They're stronger than Alecca," I said, even though I hadn't seen a real demonstration of that strength. "I know they are, and it took four of us, with powers, to beat her. So how do we take down all of the Sidhe?" I closed my eyes and left them that way for several seconds. "It's hopeless."

Zo grabbed the front of my shirt and pulled me to her until her face was as close to mine as it had been to Annabelle's a few minutes earlier. "It's not hopeless. If those *fairies* think we're letting you go anywhere, they're out of their little Otherworldly minds." Zo narrowed her eyes, and I got the feeling that she wouldn't hesitate to beat the crap out of me if I argued. "You got that?"

"Yeah," I said, wrapping my arms around her and hugging her hard. "I got it."

"We need a plan," Annabelle said, not trying to spoil the moment, but unable to contain her thoughts. "And to make a plan, we need to know what we're up against. Bailey, you said that so far only the other young ones had crossed over?"

I nodded. "Two of them. Kiste and Cyna."

"I think it's safe to infer that the key to sorting out more about exactly who and what they are is the circumstances surrounding the attack on Jessica. Bailey, you said that James indicated that crossing over used to occur more during the heyday of ancient Greece. If this is the case, then I think it might be safe to assume that whatever Kiste and Cyna did to Jessica was part of their Greek MO."

I wasn't sure we could believe anything James said. Every interaction between the two of us had been based on a lie.

Zo had a different reservation. "I'm all for figuring out exactly what it is that the scary chicks do, but I'm not crying about bald Jessica. How many times has she made fun of other people's hair? If you ask me, the girl deserved what she got."

"And that's the crux of it," Annabelle said. "This wasn't just random malice. This was *punishment*."

I swallowed hard at the words. What was it Kiste and Cyna had said the night before?

She is mortal. She can be punished.

And the others kept telling them that I hadn't done anything wrong. Yet.

275

"The Furies," Annabelle said. "They're either vengeful or just, depending on your perspective, but in Greek mythology, they punished evildoers and brought justice to murder victims."

Our high school wasn't exactly ripe with murderers, but we had jerks aplenty, and apparently that provided Kiste and Cyna with suitable targets, too.

"They threatened me," I mused out loud. "Kiste and Cyna. They said that if I stayed in this world, that would be a selfish decision, and that as a mortal, I could be punished."

"So they're blackmailing *and* threatening you?" Zo asked. "Have I mentioned that I really hate the Sidhe lately?"

On the one hand, I was Sidhe. On the other hand, I completely concurred with Zo's statement. Even Adea and Valgius, who were supposed to be my family in that world, hadn't tried to help me the way my friends were helping me now. And maybe that wasn't fair, maybe they couldn't help me, but still, I wasn't feeling happy, fuzzy feelings toward any member of my ancient race.

Annabelle pulled a notebook out of her bag and began to flip through one of the packets she'd handed out the day before. "The Furies," she said, scanning her notes. "Also known as the Erinyes. They're the daughters of Ouranow, and there are thought to be three of them: Tisiphone, Megaera, and Alecto."

"Three?" I said, but seconds later I came to the conclusion that I'd just wasted a question mark. Of course there were three Furies, just like there were three

Fates and nine Muses. Three was a number of power in the Otherworld, and I didn't have to think for very long to figure out who the third Fury was.

"James."

The others looked at me.

"He's the third one," I said, my voice dull. He'd already lied to me and used me. Why should the fact that he was evil come as a surprise? "James and Kiste and Cyna are bound together somehow. They act like they own him, and he wouldn't tell me who he was or what his powers were."

If he was a Fury, no wonder. "I extract vengeance in the cruelest of ways" wasn't exactly what I'd call a good pickup line.

"Remind me to hurt that guy later," Zo said, and I wasn't sure which had inspired her wrath more: the fact that he'd tricked me, or the fact that I'd actually liked him. It definitely wasn't Jessica's baldness, which Zo still seemed to think was brilliant, even now.

"We don't just need to hurt him," Annabelle said. "We need to stop him, stop all of them. If we can figure out a way to combat the young ones, that will buy us some time to try to fix the barrier."

And if we could fix the barrier, I filled in silently, *if we could fix* me, *I might not disappear from this world and my friends' lives . . . forever.*

Chapter 20

"So let me get this straight," Zo said, once I'd given them an overview of the major players. "We're supposed to find a way to attack the Muses, the Furies, Aphrodite, Artemis, Cupid—"

"Eros," Annabelle corrected.

"—and whoever this Xane guy is supposed to be, and we have to figure out a way to do it in the next . . ." Zo checked her watch. "Half an hour."

"Don't forget the adults," Delia chimed in. "That's going to suck even more than the rest of it."

It was hard to believe we'd been talking for so long. It was light outside, and we didn't have much time before school. There was no doubt in my mind that Eze and Drogan would launch another attack today. The only question was how far they'd be willing to go and how many humans they'd be willing to hurt to gain my compliance.

I had a sinking feeling that the answers to those questions were too far and too many. Yesterday had been bad, but no one had died or anything like that. What if James had been telling the truth when he insisted the older Sidhe were more sinister than the un-Reckoned "young ones"? What happened if Drogan and Eze decided I needed more of a push? What happened when the Furies—or someone even worse—stopped making people go bald and started taking their lives?

It sounded so silly, the idea of Greek myths going on a massacre at my high school, but I couldn't ignore the possibility. I couldn't let that happen, not when this whole situation was my fault. If I'd managed to keep my own balance, if I hadn't spent weeks freaking out about college, if I hadn't been seduced by the Otherworld that first night . . .

I didn't have time for these kinds of thoughts. I couldn't help that my life was in transition. I couldn't help that I was half human and half Sidhe. I couldn't help that somehow that added up to something Very, Very Bad.

"We'll think of something," Annabelle promised, her voice quiet but firm. "We have to."

"If we still had our powers," Delia said, "I'm sure I could transmogrify our way out of this."

Zo ran her hands over her necklace and fingered the charm lying on her collarbone. "You know, Morgan may suck less than the other Sidhe, but she isn't exactly my favorite person right now either. Sophomore year, she gave us powers that we could actually fight with; this time, all she gave us were these necklaces."

"They let us see Sidhe who come into this world," Annabelle said, fair to a fault. "And they kept Bailey from drinking in the Otherworld."

"Lot of good that's going to do us when it comes to taking down the Muses," Zo said. "We'll be able to see the enemy, but what can we do to them?"

Delia cleared her throat, and when none of us responded, she cleared it again.

"Yes?" Annabelle said dryly.

"Never underestimate the power of accessories. Remember yesterday, when you had me researching the necklaces, A-belle?"

Annabelle nodded.

"Well, I couldn't find anything like them online, so I had to get creative. I think they're silver, and apparently that's, like, really poisonous to fairies and werewolves. And they're ringed circles, and circles are thought to be the most magical shape there is. In a lot of myths, circles are way more powerful than pentagrams."

"Stonehenge is a circle," Annabelle said. "So are a lot of other ancient monuments. And there's *got* to be something magical about pi."

"I'm going to pretend you didn't just say that," Zo told her cousin. Annabelle made a face. Delia, used to their antics, even in times of crisis, continued on.

"And then I looked up myths on mirrors, and there

are, like, a ton of them. There's one with that Greek guy, Perseus."

"He killed the Medusa using a mirror," Annabelle supplied. "Because looking at her straight on would have turned him to stone."

"And mirrors are used all the time for scrying," Delia continued, "like Zo used to do back when we had our powers. According to some sources, mirrors have also been used as portals to other worlds. Maybe that's why our necklaces let us see things the way they really are. They connect us to other realms. There's got to be some way we can use that. Maybe we can use our necklaces to send the Sidhe back where they belong."

That was a thought.

"And then," Delia said, on a roll, "there are all these stories about how some people used to think that your reflection in a mirror was really your soul. That's why it's bad luck to break one. You might trap your soul in the mirror forever."

"And hey," I said, "worse comes to worse, these things are *really* sharp."

Zo laughed. "Yeah, Bay, I can see it now. 'You guys may have mind-boggling superpowers, but we have the Necklaces of Doom! Beware!'"

"It's better than nothing," Annabelle said. "And right now it's all we've got."

That was a sobering thought.

"Do you think Morgan would come if you could figure out a way to call her?" Annabelle asked after a long pause. "If mirrors can be used for scrying and as portals, then maybe we can use them to communicate, too. With Morgan on our side, we'd stand a chance, at least against the younger Sidhe."

"I'll try," I said. We didn't have very long before we left for school, and we hadn't come up with any alternative plans. The others sat very quietly as I picked up my necklace and gazed into the little mirror. At first, it showed me exactly as I was, but as I stared at my reflection, it changed, until there was a sparkling undertone to my skin and my eyes had paled. What little hair I could see glowed both colors—brown and blond—instead of neither. The changes were subtle, nothing compared to the way I looked in the Otherworld, but they were there.

In the mirror, I wasn't human, and I wasn't Sidhe. I was something in between, and I had to accept the fact that this mirror showed things as they were. I could never really belong to one world or the other. I belonged to both, and as I gazed into the mirror, I was overcome with the thought that though Eze and Drogan were wrong to try to force me to choose their world over mine, I couldn't renounce the Otherworld either. There was no choice for me but to live in both worlds; it could be no other way.

I wondered if this was Morgan's wisdom, if maybe she was communicating with me through the mirror, but as hard as I tried to see her, I couldn't. Some scrying tool/window to another world this thing was.

Please, I thought, gripping my necklace tighter and

praying that Morgan would hear me. *I need your help. You're the only one who can help us.*

The surface of the mirror trembled and then a new picture took its place.

Alec.

Can he help us? I thought. *Is that what you're trying to tell me?*

The image changed again, and I found myself looking at James.

Not him, I thought vehemently. *He's the one who got me into this.*

Alec again. Then James. Then Alec. Then James. Back and forth, again and again, in the span of only a few seconds, the mirror showed me my crushes, until I wasn't sure I'd ever be able to get either of them out of my mind.

Alec. James. Alec. James.

I wish you'd talk to me, I told Morgan silently, sending every ounce of psychic power I had to the mirror. *I wish you'd tell me what I need to know. Is there a way out of this? How can there be? Would you have given me this necklace if you didn't think there was a chance?*

Why won't you help me?

Alec. James. Alec. James.

Their images faded into each other, until I was looking at both of them at once, a person who was Alec and James, but not quite either of them.

Things must unfold as they must, Bailey. Morgan spoke from the mirror to my mind, as I stared at the picture of the first two guys I'd liked in a very long time.

You know that better than anyone. Open your mind to the possibilities you refuse to see. Remember everything you've learned. I've given you everything you need. The answer is there. You must be the one to find it.

And then Morgan's voice was gone, and I found myself staring at the Alec/James hybrid again.

And that's when the little cartoon lightbulb appeared above my head.

Alec and James, James and Alec. The two of them at once. The way I'd never seen Alec before this week. The way James had seemed to know me better than he should have.

The way Alec had been present every time something weird happened.

The way James had felt far more human to me than any of the others.

The way that Kiste and Cyna had been so possessive of James. The way that they'd warned me to stay away from Alec in that same possessive tone.

It was so obvious, so crystal clear, that I wondered why I hadn't thought of it before.

Lyria's strong in the glamour, changing what other people see when they look at her. It's a skill we all share, but some are better at it than most.

I'd never once looked at Alec in my mirror. Standing there, I knew beyond all shadow of a doubt what the mirror would show me, but at the same time, I couldn't believe it.

Without saying a word, I grabbed the packet out of Annabelle's hand and started scanning the part about the Furies, looking for something that would tell me I was wrong, but instead I found the opposite.

There were three Furies.

The Greeks had called them Tisiphone, Megaera, and Alecto.

"Alec Talbot-Olsen," I said out loud. "Alec T-O. As in Alecto. Very clever, James."

The others stared at me, and I realized that they hadn't been privy to my conversation with Morgan or what I'd seen in the mirror.

"Alec is James," I said. "I don't know why, maybe he wanted to spy on me or something, but James and Alec are the same person." I shoved the paper at them. "Look."

"Your geek is a Fury in disguise?" Delia asked, wide-eyed.

I didn't reply. I was too busy thinking that my "geek" was about to get his butt kicked, Fury or no.

Chapter 21

I stalked toward study hall, armed only with righteous indignation, my necklace, and the hope that somehow, while I vented my anger on Alec/James, Annabelle would manage to puzzle out the solution Morgan had spoken of. Apparently, I had everything I needed, but the only "solution" I'd been able to come up with involved me making James/Alec/Whatever regret that he'd ever even thought of doing this to me.

When Kane dumped me, I was sad, but now I was *ticked*. My hair crackled as I walked, fury leaking out of my body in the form of tiny sparks.

The second I found James, he was a dead man. Or a dead fairy. Either way, he was going to be sorry he'd ever even thought of playing me.

"Bailey."

The fact that he was the one who found me took the tiniest bit of wind out of my sails. Luckily, I had POed wind aplenty.

"You." My voice was one hundred percent accusation as I whirled around to face "Alec." I could feel my body temperature rising, and it took everything I had not to let the fire leap from my blood to his flesh.

"You," he said, repeating my greeting and offering me a shy smile, like the two of us had just exchanged terms of endearment. I had to wonder what part of the hint of flames in my hair made it seem like patronizing me was a good idea.

Wishing my position as the Third Fate came with laser eyes as well as pyrokinesis, I glared straight through him.

"We need to talk," he said.

Oh, we'd talk all right. The palms of my hands twinged, and when I looked down, I realized that I was holding two matching flames. Each tickled and caressed my skin, and I had to actively tell myself that the hallway right outside study hall was in all likelihood not the best location for me to demonstrate the fringe benefits of my Otherworldly blood. With a great deal of effort, I clenched my fists and doused the flames.

Then, moving slowly and deliberately, I raised the pendant around my neck, angled it toward the boy in front of me, and looked down.

Even though I expected to see James's face staring back at me, I wasn't ready for it. There hadn't been any doubt in my mind, but knowing something is true and staring down the proof are two very different things, and I couldn't help the bit of fire that leapt onto his shirt, burning a small hole in one of the shoulders.

"Ow!" James, still wearing his Alec guise, jumped back. "Hey, cut it out, Bailey."

"Why?" I said. "Is it wrong? Are you going to *punish* me?"

James looked over his shoulder and then, without a word, he reached out, grabbed my arm, and dragged me into a nearby bathroom. It was uncharacteristically deserted, and the moment we were alone, James let go of my arm and shut the door behind us.

"Sheesh, Bay. Get it under control," he said, shaking out his hand. "I burned myself just touching you. If you're not careful, you'll burn down the entire school."

"Isn't that what you want?" I asked. "Don't you want me to do something wrong, so you and your little skank patrol can have an excuse to hurt me even more? And hey, if I burn down the school, I'll probably feel really bad and then I'll see that Eze and Drogan were just looking out for me when they tried to tempt, guilt, and blackmail me into leaving my entire life behind and becoming their personal butt monkey."

"Butt monkey?" he repeated skeptically.

Clearly, his crash course in human behavior hadn't included slang used by Xander on *Buffy the Vampire Slayer*.

"Bailey, I know you're angry, but—"

288

"What tipped you off?" I asked. "Was it the heat rolling off my body, or the fact that I hate you?"

"You don't hate me," he said softly. "You want to. There's a difference."

What I heard was: Please, light my pants on fire.

"Okay," I said, and James breathed a sigh of relief . . . until his pants burst into flames. He yelped, and with a flick of his wrist, the fire was gone. As the flames disappeared, so did his glamour, and as the Alec visage dissolved, the expression on James's face stayed exactly the same.

"We don't have time for this," he said. "I hurt you, and I'm sorry about that, but right now we have bigger problems."

"We?" I repeated. "There is no we. There's me, and there's you." My voice broke, and to keep sadness from encroaching on my anger, I babbled on. "It's bad enough that you lied to me, that you used me, but did you have to do it twice? As two different people?" I probably should have stopped there, but I didn't. "Did you have to make me like you twice? Was once just not humiliating enough?"

"It wasn't like that," James said. "I was following orders."

Because it made me feel so much better to know that he'd played me because someone else had told him to. This was as bad as being the girl who gets asked to prom on a dare.

"Bailey, you don't understand what it's like to be Sidhe."

How could he say that? I'd run through the Otherworld. I'd stood on the Seelie mountains and danced in the caverns of the Unseelie Court. The fact that I was part human meant that I understood what it meant to be Sidhe better than he ever could. He'd never been anything else.

I had.

"As part of the Otherworld, we're bound to the courts even before our Reckonings. The connection you feel to all of us is multiplied fourfold after several millennia in the Otherworld, and Eze and Drogan know that. They know how to use it."

"So you had no choice?" I asked. "None whatsoever? You know, you're not making a permanent move to the Otherworld sound any more tempting here."

"I had a choice," James admitted. "I didn't know that I had one, but I did. They asked me to get close to you, and I did. They told me to mention your tattoo to pique your interest, and it worked. They asked me to take a human guise so that I could play on your weaknesses in the Otherworld. They asked me to form a bond with you in this world so that if worse came to worse, I could break it and hurt you enough that you might not want to stay here."

That had been part of the plan? Make me like James enough to agree to swear off the mortal realm, or, failing that, have James-as-Alec break my heart in this one?

What Zo said about the Sidhe sucking? Triple that.

"Like I was ever interested in you," I said, even

290

though I'd already admitted that I had been. "Either of you."

"Eros and Lyria were going to work on that," James said. "If they needed to, but that's the thing, they didn't. You liked me. Both me's." He paused. "And I liked you."

Like this whole thing wasn't mortifying and painful enough, he had to say that. Sure, he liked me. Just like Kane had "liked" me. Just like nobody ever really did.

"I do, Bailey. You're funny and you're sweet and it doesn't matter which form you're wearing, you're drop-dead gorgeous."

Funny he should mention "dropping dead." The flames began to form again at my palms, nipping at my skin, begging to be set free.

"Bailey, I made the wrong choice before. I shouldn't have misled you, and I shouldn't have tried to trick you. At first, I was just following orders and then . . . I wanted you to stay. I can't be Alec forever, and I don't know if Lyria and Eros have been messing with me, too, or what, but I wanted you to stay in our world, with me."

"I'm not going to," I told him, my resolve stronger than ever. "No matter what you say, I won't go there with you. I won't give any of you what you want."

"I know," James said. "And they know it too. That's why I'm here."

I wasn't quite following his logic and I didn't particularly want to, but he kept talking, forcing his words into my ears and leaving them bouncing around my brain, no matter how much I didn't want to listen.

"They know that they haven't won yet, that the last thing you want to do is give in to their demands and threats. They know that you've had contact with the one whose name we do not speak, and they know that two years ago you and your friends took down a full-blooded Sidhe who'd already begun to harness the power of the mortal soul." James looked away. "And because of me, because of what I've told them, they know that your friends are the most important thing to you."

It didn't matter that I'd told him as much myself. Anyone with half a brain could have figured that out within a couple of hours. Kiste and Cyna certainly had. Delia, Annabelle, and Zo were everything to me. That's why I was so freaked out about next year. That's why, even in the thrall of the Otherworld, I hadn't given in to the temptation to leave.

"Your friends matter to you, Bailey, and that makes them your weakness." I was about to protest, but his next words came before I had the chance. "They also strengthen you, and that makes them a threat." He stared at me, his eyes steady, and waited for his words to sink in.

The night before, Eze and Drogan had promised me that the longer I stayed in this world, the worse things would get. Today was Mabon, and tonight was my Reckoning, when I would be forced to choose between the courts, and—if the King of Darkness and

Queen of Light had their way—to forswear the mortal realm forever.

I wasn't ready to do it. Even if they followed through on everything they'd threatened, even if my presence in this world put everyone in danger, I wasn't sure I could just walk away, and they knew it.

But what if it wasn't the world as a whole in danger? What if it wasn't the mean girls at my high school? What if it was my friends?

"They can't," I said. James caught my chin in his hand.

"As far as I know," he said, "they already have."

I'd been so set on finding James and making him pay for hurting me that I'd left Delia, Annabelle, and Zo to go to their first periods and figure things out, if they could. It hadn't occurred to me that they might be in danger or that while I was in the bathroom talking to James, someone might be out there, hurting them.

"What did they do?" I asked. "What are they doing? Why are you even telling me this? I have to go. I have to help them. I—"

"You aren't going to be able to do this alone," James said. "I know what their plans are, and I don't care if Kiste and Cyna don't see it, this is wrong. You can think whatever awful things you want about the three of us, but at the end of the day, right and wrong matter to us. They matter to me, and so do you."

I barely even heard his words. Maybe they were romantic. Maybe they were cheesy. Maybe they were true, and maybe they weren't, but right now that didn't matter. All that mattered was making sure that my friends were all right, so I didn't respond to James's confession. Instead, I turned on my heels and ran out the door and down the hall, casting my mind out for the others and hoping I wasn't too late.

Chapter 22

Annabelle? Delia? Zo? I called out their names silently, lowering my shields completely and trying to ignore any thought that came my way that wasn't theirs.

I'm here, Bay. What's the matter?

Zo. She was okay. And, if I was reading her thoughts correctly, she was dying for an excuse to skip out on math.

The Sidhe are going after you guys, I told her. *I need you where I can protect you. Now.*

I got Zo's next thought in pictures and feelings instead of words, but the bits and pieces of memories and the desire to protect me made her thought process clear. Zo would barge out of math class, completely ignoring any consequences, not because I needed to keep her safe, but because she wasn't about to let me face any danger on my own.

Annabelle? Delia?

At first, there was no reply, and I thought my body was just going to give out, that the fact that I couldn't find their minds was going to end me then and there, but the next second, two things happened to keep me together.

The first was that Zo arrived at my side.

The second was that Annabelle ran by wearing nothing on top but a neon bra.

"Okay, somebody's taking the skanky Hollywood fashion thing a little too far," Zo said.

"Somebody?" I repeated. "That was Annabelle."

"Yeah, right, Bay. There aren't enough fairies in the freaking world to make Annabelle run around topless. This whole situation is just messing with your brain."

"No," I said. "Seriously. That was Annabelle."

Somehow, this kind of "attack" wasn't exactly what I'd had in mind. I'd pictured something a little more sinister and a lot less lewd. I mean, what were they going to do, embarrass A-belle to death?

"Come on," I said, tugging at Zo's sleeve, and then I took off running in the general direction in which Annabelle had streaked a moment before.

We found her in a Spanish class. She was, to put things as nicely as humanly possible, making a scene.

"Boys! Boys! Hello, boys!"

When we walked into the room, Annabelle was greeting the entire male population of the Spanish class in an up close and personal manner. As we watched, frozen in shock and morbid fascination, she walked up to one of the most popular boys in our grade, jumped onto his lap and straddled him, burying her hands in his hair.

"This form is pleasing," she purred. "Isn't it?"

The boy, his eyes glued on the bright pink bra, just nodded, and Annabelle brought her lips to his.

"She thinks she isn't pretty," Annabelle said, dragging herself away from the kiss. "She thinks that boys don't like her." She moved on to the next boy, pulling him to his feet and in close to her body. "She's wrong."

Okay, I thought slowly, my ability to process this turn of events severely compromised by the absurdity of it all. *Annabelle's running around in a bra kissing every boy in sight and referring to herself in the third person.*

This could not end well.

"Annabelle?" Zo said, physically incapable of believing what she was seeing. She turned to me. "Annabelle?" she asked again, unable to manage more than that single, strangled word.

It must be Lyria, I said silently. *She's Aphrodite, remember? All about the lust. She must have done something to Annabelle to make her . . . ummm . . . lusty.*

Please do not say the word lust *in reference to my cousin,* Zo returned. Out loud, she just repeated herself, her voice going high and squeaky. "Annabelle?"

Annabelle didn't reply. She ripped out her ponytail holder, threw her hair over her shoulder, and moved on to the next shell-shocked boy.

"Dios mío," the boy murmured as Annabelle lifted

him from his seat and slammed him against a wall, pressing her lips hard to his.

"My eyes," Zo said, "they're burning."

"Don't just stand there," I told Zo. "Stop her."

Sidhe.

The feeling of connection and familiarity didn't surprise me. Neither did the way the hairs on my arms were elevated with a charge from the presence of another Sidhe in the room. James might have fooled my senses, but Lyria either wasn't trying to mask herself, or her ability to cast a glamour didn't extend to hiding the mystical quality of her presence.

I grabbed for my necklace, expecting to see bluegreen color permeating the air. Instead, all I saw was the reflection of one very angry teacher, who'd finally overcome his initial shock at Annabelle's lusty invasion of his classroom.

"You!" he yelled. "In the hallway! Now!"

Forget finding Lyria, I thought. I needed to do damage control. Stat.

"You're imagining things," I told the teacher, willing my words to become truth in his eyes. "There's nothing to see here."

He blinked several times and then ran a hand through his hair. "Must be imagining things," he said. "Nothing to see here."

The students looked at him like he was crazy, and as Annabelle moved on to a boy with a girlfriend in the class, things started to get ugly. I had to extend the mind meld to everyone in the room, save for Annabelle, Zo, and myself.

"Nothing is happening here," I said. "You won't remember any of this. You should go back to work."

Soon they were all scribbling on worksheets, and I approached Annabelle.

A-belle, I called out to her silently, hoping to break through whatever hold Lyria had on her. *It's me. You've got to stop this. You've got to fight it. You don't want to be doing this.*

"Oh," Annabelle said softly, "but she does. People think that just because she's the quiet one, just because she's shy, she doesn't have the same kind of feelings other girls do."

"That's not true," I said. "We love Annabelle—I mean, you."

"But who does Annabelle get to love?" Annabelle asked. "Who does she get to date? Who does she get to kiss? Too shy to ask anyone out. Too quiet to draw attention to herself. She thinks she's not pretty, but she is, and she *loves* doing this."

With those words, Annabelle sashayed up to the teacher and plunked herself down on his desk. She stretched out her long legs and leaned back on her elbows. "Hellllooooooooo, teacher," she said.

Having a nubile young girl lying across his desk proved to be too much for the mind meld I had on the teacher. He stared at Annabelle, and, lasciviously, she ran her tongue over her lips.

And Zo thought her eyes were burning before.

Annabelle! Stop it.

"A-belle, I don't care what kind of mojo you're under, that's just wrong." Zo, finally snapping out of her stupor, ran over to her cousin and tried to yank her off the desk.

"Nothing to see here," I said, reinforcing the hold I had on the rest of the class, lest they, like the teacher, break free.

Annabelle shrugged off Zo's grip, and when Zo, forceful and determined, reached for her a second time, Annabelle lashed out with her leg and managed to kick Zo clear across the room.

"Zo!" I couldn't believe Annabelle had just done that. In fact, given the fact that Zo had flown a good six or seven feet through the air, I was beginning to suspect that maybe *Annabelle* hadn't done anything at all, because the last time I checked, none of my friends had superstrength.

Are you okay? I sent the question to Zo silently as I approached the teacher's desk, carefully keeping myself out of kicking range.

"Nope," Zo said out loud. "I'm traumatized for life, and also, that hurt. Dang it, A-belle."

"That's not A-belle," I said. I'd thought that Lyria was using her abilities as an expath to manipulate Annabelle, but her display of supernatural strength had given me pause. I felt a Sidhe in this room, but I hadn't seen one in my mirror. And hadn't James said that Lyria was a master of the glamour? That meant she could make herself look like anyone at any time. And if that was the case, then maybe shirtless A-belle wasn't actually Annabelle at all.

Maybe it was Lyria. And really, what was the chance

of Annabelle actually wearing a hot pink bra? In my calculations, slim to none.

"Lyria," I said. "Stop it."

The Annabelle look-alike paused in her pursuit of the teacher. "But I like being human," she said with a pout. "It's fun."

I tried to reconcile the being in front of me with the quiet girl I'd seen in the Otherworld. Lyria was shy, apt to blush, and nearly silent. In many ways, she was A-belle's counterpart in that realm, so maybe it wasn't that surprising that she'd chosen my friend's form to wear in this one.

To confirm my suspicions, I grabbed the mirror charm off my chest and angled it toward "Annabelle's" face, expecting to see Lyria's.

I saw Annabelle, but instead of the sexy pout on her face in the real world, the Annabelle in the mirror looked shell-shocked, mortified, and dazed, all at once. I knew those expressions. They were Annabelle's, the real Annabelle's. But if the mirror showed me Annabelle, then that meant that Lyria wasn't wearing a glamour that made herself look like my friend.

It meant that Lyria was *in* my friend. And that Annabelle was, in fact, wearing a hot pink bra.

Annabelle's reflection disappeared from the mirror, and when I looked up, I realized that she'd bolted from the room.

"What is she, possessed?" Zo grumbled.

I took in her sarcastic words and then sighed. "Yeah," I said. "She is."

It was up to us to get Annabelle de-possessed, and quick.

I didn't even bother to tell Zo to follow me as I ran out after Annabelle, knowing that she'd be on my heels. By the time we got to the hallway, Annabelle was nowhere in sight. With our luck, Lyria was probably hooking up with all of the guys in AP calculus as we spoke.

"We need to find her," I said, "and find a way to kick Lyria out of her body."

At times like these, I really needed Annabelle to research the proper method for exorcising a Sidhe, but as she was indisposed at the moment, Zo and I were just going to have to do the best we could.

And that's when I remembered something that Annabelle's whacked-out sexcapades had completely made me forget.

Delia.

I'd wondered what the point of making Annabelle go boy crazy was. It wasn't life-threatening, even if it was freaky beyond all words. It didn't match up with the seriously malevolent quality of the attack on Jessica the day before or the things Eze and Drogan had threatened me with in the Otherworld. Something wasn't right here. But what if Lyria possessing Annabelle wasn't the point? What if it was a distraction?

Delia! I screamed her name with my mind, hoping that my fashion-loving friend would respond. Instead, Zo took in a sharp breath behind me.

"Where's Queenie?" she asked.

I closed my eyes, searching for any hint of Delia, but I came up with a whole lot of nothing. "I don't know."

"I do."

James's voice took me by surprise. "I tried to warn you," he said, "and I tried to stop it, but Xane is stronger than I am, and—"

"Xane?" I interrupted.

"He took her," James said. "We have to get her back."

"What do you mean he took her?" Zo demanded.

"He means that Xane takes after his father and that in the Unseelie Court, kidnapping is considered tantamount to wooing."

I recognized the voice immediately, and it put me on guard.

"What are you doing here?" I asked Axia. Instinctively, I placed myself between the Seelie heir and Zo. Lyria had possessed Annabelle. Xane had pulled a Hades and taken Delia to the underworld. I would die before I'd let Eze's daughter get her hands on Zo.

"I brought her," James said. "When Xane got Delia, I called Axia for help."

"Help?" I repeated. "You expect me to believe you're here to help me? This whole thing was probably your mom's master plan!"

"I didn't know," Axia said. "Not about this. My mother has ruled the Seelie Court for many of your millennia, and her methods can be ruthless." She paused. "Someday, I will be a different kind of ruler."

Right now that didn't do me a whole lot of good.

"I know you don't trust us," James said. "I know you don't trust me, but if you're going to get Delia back and if you don't want Lyria inside of Annabelle's body forever, you're going to need our help."

"I know my sister," Axia said. "She doesn't mean to do you harm. This is just very . . . liberating for her. She's never been in the mortal realm before. She's never been human, and until today . . . well, she'd never kissed a boy."

Somehow, I found that one hard to believe.

"So you're saying she turned my cousin into a kissing ho because she's too shy to kiss anybody herself?" Zo was not amused.

"I can stop her," Axia said. "She'll listen to me."

"You're not going anywhere near A-belle," Zo said through gritted teeth. "Not without me."

"She's right," James said. "Axia, take Zo with you, and the two of you stop Lyria. Bailey and I will go after Delia and Xane." James and Axia exchanged a look, and something else passed between them. "Hurry," James continued. "If Xane makes it back to the Unseelie Court, it's going to take all of us to free her."

Axia nodded and then turned to Zo, on the verge of issuing some orders herself.

"Why would you help me?" I blurted out.

"Because you're Sidhe," Axia said. "You're one of us, and where we come from, that's supposed to mean something."

James didn't respond, but the look on his face gave

me the impression that he had his own answer, one that I couldn't bear to hear.

I didn't want to accept their help. I didn't want to go along with their plan, because for all I knew, it was another trap. The Sidhe were tricksters, masters at manipulating others to get their own way. Still, I didn't have much of a choice. One of my best friends had just been kidnapped to the Otherworld; another one was currently possessed by a horny fairy. Whether I liked it or not, I was officially in over my head, and I needed backup, stat.

Chapter 23

It wasn't until after Axia and Zo took off down the hallway that I processed the fact that this plan entailed me being alone with James, but I didn't have the time or the space in my mind to complain about it. This was Delia, and some things were more important than the way my heart wrenched when James took hold of my hands.

"What are you doing?" I asked, jerking them out of his grasp. I didn't trust him. I couldn't, and I didn't want to. For all I knew, this was part of some master plan.

"We need to cross over," James said. "We can't take the chance that we'll get separated. We don't have much time, and neither one of us is a match for Xane on our own."

I didn't tell him that I had no idea how one went

about crossing from the mortal realm to the Otherworld at will. As a general rule, the only surefire way I
knew of to get from one world to another involved losing consciousness.

"Today is the equinox," James said, in the kind of
voice that someone would use to talk a puppy out from
underneath a car, "and because of your presence in this
world, the barrier is even thinner than it normally
would be on such a day. We could use the bridge I
showed you to cross over, but on Mabon, we shouldn't
have to. Especially you."

It occurred to me for the first time that the bridge
I'd visited with "Alec" on our first and only date was
probably the means through which James had traveled
between the worlds during his stint as a spy. I hated
thinking of what sitting on that bridge had been like,
hated wondering how much of what "Alec" had told
me was true.

He'd said he had sisters. He hadn't sounded all that
happy about it. Was he referring to Kiste and Cyna?

"So do we go to the bridge, or are you going to
trust me now?" James asked, holding out his hands.

Trust him? No way. Still, Delia was in trouble, and
every second I waited here was a second that Delia was
alone with Drogan's son.

"Let's go," I said. "Here. Now. Whatever. Just tell
me what to do."

James seemed to accept that. Gently, he took my
hands. "Think about the Otherworld. Think about
the rivers, and how the blood of that place flows in

your veins. Think about the mountains and the caverns, the colors that you could never find on this side. Think about light so bright that it would blind mortal eyes. Think about dark prisms full of colors. Think about the feeling you get in your gut when we're all together."

His words were soft and rhythmic, and something about the way he strung the sentences together hypnotized me. As he spoke, I felt my anger and my fear melting away until all that was left was my desire to be a part of that world. I wanted to hate feeling this way, but nothing in my mind could overcome the strength of that connection, and as I lost myself in it and in James's melodic voice, I could feel my earthly form blur, and suddenly, we were elsewhere.

The scenery assaulted my senses and soothed them at the same time, and it took a few seconds for my mind to catch up with the rest of me. My whole body buzzed with warmth, but there were goose bumps on my arms, and when I met James's eyes, a shiver ran up my spine even as the grip between our hands burned white.

It took everything I had to pull away, and he dropped my hands, averting his gaze for the smallest moment as he recovered from whatever it was that had passed between the two of us. Then his face was blank, and I wondered if I'd imagined the look in his eyes the moment before.

"Delia," James said.

"Delia," I repeated, and for the first time, my mental image of my friends and what they meant to me was as strong in this world as it was at home. "How are we going to find her?"

"Xane will take her to the Unseelie Court," James said. "For all we know, he's there already, but mortals can't travel as quickly here as we can. The two of them had to have crossed over using the bridge, and it would have taken them time to get there. We'll just have to hope that Delia is slowing him down."

Having had the experience of trying to drag Delia through the mall at a speed greater than that of a turtle, I had considerable confidence in her ability to make darn well sure that Xane was moving at her pace and not his.

"So we just head for the caverns and hope for the best?" I asked.

James shook his head. "There are too many ways to get there, and if Xane isn't a complete idiot, he'll expect us to follow him." James paused for the slightest instant. "I tried to stop him from taking her. I really did."

I didn't respond, but as much as he'd misled me in the past, I couldn't force myself to believe he was lying. What was wrong with me? Was I seriously lacking in all intelligence? James was a bad guy. He'd fooled me over and over again. He'd told Eze and Drogan all about me. For all I knew, he may have been Kiste and Cyna's source as well, and who knew what else he had told them. Besides which, he was one of the Furies. There was no way I should have believed a word he said.

"So how do we find Delia?" I asked, not trusting myself to say anything else.

James gave me a sheepish look. "Actually," he said, "there's not much of a 'we' with that one. I don't know her. She's human. I'm Sidhe. There's no connection. I can't feel her. You can."

It made sense, and I wondered why it hadn't occurred to me. Every time I'd come to this world, I'd done it by thinking about this place and my connection to it. Each night, I'd run, and I hadn't just followed Adea and Valgius. I'd known where we were going, even if I hadn't known how. Connection and instinct were everything here, and if we were going to find Delia, I needed to search for her in the same way.

"Just think about her," James said. "Cast your mind out and look for her."

Delia, I thought, unsure whether she would hear me, or if I was even really calling to her, or if I was just thinking her name. *The person who gave me my first makeover, when I was four years old. The girl who can strike fear into the hearts of an entire neighborhood just by saying "arts and crafts." The girl who's always been popular, but has never stopped being my friend. Smarter than she appears. Occasionally shallow, but always kind. Lover of sticky foods. Fashionista.*

Friend.

Images flashed through my mind, one after another, of the two of us growing up together. I saw Delia the way she looked at our baby ballet dance class, every inch the teeny-tiny diva. I saw her doing her best to climb trees, just to keep up with Zo. I saw the two of us at every age from the time we were born until now.

And as all this flashed through my mind, all of the memories and everything the two of us had shared and the way that she'd always been there for me, even when she could have had her pick of other friends, I was overcome with the feeling that nothing could take that away. Not college. Not changes. Not Xane.

Delia.

"I see her," I gasped as the power of the image washed over me. "She's with Xane." I smiled. "She's got her hands on her hips and that look on her face, the one where you know she's not going to take no for an answer." I tilted my head to the side. "They're stopping. He's not happy about it, but they're stopping."

"Where?" James asked.

"Next to a lake. It looks like she's . . . uhhhh . . ." I tried to wrap my mind around what I was seeing. "She's laying out."

Leave it to Delia to work on her tan at a time like this.

"Which lake?" James asked. "There are thousands."

"This way," I said, turning to my left. The image of Delia faded, but I could still feel her. The connection between the two of us was a physical thing, and even though I couldn't see it, there was no mistaking the incredible force of the pull. The two of us were bound together, and all I had to do to find her was follow the binding to its source.

"Let's go." The words were barely out of my mouth when I started running. This time the sights and sounds and smells of the Otherworld didn't dominate my mind. They were there and I felt them as part of myself, but Delia was there, too, and James was beside me, and those three things bled together until running wasn't about my senses or letting my hidden nature come out to play. It was about . . . everything.

This was who I was. I was a friend, and I was a fairy. I belonged here, and I belonged with my girls. We'd been friends for so long that they were part of me, and in a strange way, as I ran, I realized that this meant that they were a part of the Otherworld too.

I couldn't quite grasp the significance of that, but as I ran toward Delia and Xane and something bigger than any of us imagined at the time, Morgan's words played over and over in my head.

Open your mind to the possibilities you refuse to see. Remember everything you've learned. I've given you everything you need. The answer is there.

Time lost all meaning as we ran. Maybe it stopped altogether. I don't know, but as I felt myself coming closer and closer to Delia, I knew that the answer, the one Morgan had spoken of, the thing that could allow me to fight not just the young Sidhe but also Eze and Drogan and all of both courts, was coming closer too. ·For the first time, even though the answer was hovering just out of reach, I felt like I would find it, like reaching Delia was just a single step leading me toward the truth.

Things must unfold as they must, Morgan had told me. *You know that better than anyone, Bailey.*

Maybe I was meant to be here. Maybe Xane was meant to take Delia. Maybe James and I were meant to find them. And maybe all of this, everything that had happened—the bad and the good and even my moping—had been leading inexorably to a single point in time and destiny.

Morgan was right. I knew better than anyone that things happened for a reason and that sometimes even the person who wove the fabric of life couldn't see the forest for the trees.

Somehow, my hand—traitorous appendage that it was—worked its way into James's as we ran, and this time there was no heat between us, only color. Darkness, light, both and neither, played along the surfaces of our skin, emanating from our clasped hands. My senses blurred, but didn't become any less clear. Instead, I found myself hearing colors, seeing sounds, feeling the taste of the air everywhere but on my tongue.

Everything Eze and Drogan had done had been motivated by a desire for power, but they didn't know what real power was. Once upon a time, a million years ago, Alecca had said that Sidhe didn't love, that they didn't feel things the way that humans did, and I wondered if that was why the Sidhe needed me. Because real power, real feeling, real emotion—that was something they couldn't understand the way I did. I wondered if James could feel it too, if the oneness of this moment was the same for him as it was for me, and the second the thought occurred to me, the two of us stopped running.

We didn't drop hands, and as I glanced at him

out of the corner of my eye, I had the answer to my question.

"That was incredible," James whispered, his voice— a voice that had seen ages come and go in my world— catching in his throat.

I wouldn't look at him. Not after everything he'd done. Instead, I let my eyes go where we'd been heading all along.

To Delia.

She was stretched out on a lakeside beach, her legs tan in the Otherworld sun. As I watched she propped herself up on her elbows, and even though she looked almost plain in comparison to Xane's glittering pearl-white skin, she carried herself with the same confidence she had when she walked among mortals. She tossed her head and said something to Xane, and to my amazement, he smiled.

I'd seen that smile on too many guys over the years to wonder at its meaning.

Somehow, beyond all odds, Delia's magical C cup had done it again.

"Did Xane just . . . smile?" James was incredulous. I didn't blame him. In my experience, Xane didn't just randomly break into a grin. He bestowed each smile like it was a precious gift and like those of us who were blessed to witness it should count ourselves very lucky.

But there he was, sitting opposite Delia as she basked in the sun and tossed her thick hair over her shoulders like she was auditioning for a shampoo commercial.

Delia, I thought, calling out to her silently.

Bailey?

She sat up, folding her long legs under her, much to Xane's dismay. Immediately, she started looking around.

"Not exactly subtle, is she?" James asked under his breath.

I snorted. Delia? Subtle? I was pretty sure those two words had never even been used in the same sentence. Everything she was, she was to the nth degree, and she didn't make apologies for any of it.

Unfortunately, the moment Delia started looking for me, Xane registered that fact. Within seconds, he was on his feet, standing guard over her with a deadly gleam in his eye.

Delia, I'm here. I'm going to get you out of this.

Why? Delia sounded truly mystified. *Fairy McHot-stuff here was a little uptight at first, but he's coming to see the error of his ways. And I'm pretty sure I could teach him how to be a geek.*

I tried very hard not to sigh. Words like *fickle* were invented for girls like Delia. *He's dangerous, Delia. Do you even know who he is? He's one of the guys we're supposed to be fighting.*

Granted, technically so was James, and the two of us were still standing very, very close together.

He's the son of Hades! The heir to the Unseelie throne. And he's totally pompous.

He's a prince? Delia asked, giddy. *Sweet!*

Meanwhile, the prince in question scanned the surroundings, and his eyes quickly landed on mine. So much for the element of surprise. The only thing left to do was to confront him head-on, so that's what I did.

Sort of.

"I see you've met my friend, Delia," I said, my voice infinitely more powerful than I felt as I strode out of the forest and toward the beach. "If you wanted an introduction, all you had to do was ask."

Huh, I thought. *So this is what false bravado feels like.*

"She's mine," Xane said. "I'm bringing her home, and she's mine."

Delia cleared her throat and gave him a very pointed look. Obviously, the two of them had had this conversation before.

"I mean, she's graced me with her presence and will do me the honor of accompanying me back to the Unseelie Court." Xane made the correction through gritted teeth. Clearly, he wasn't used to taking orders from anyone, let alone a mortal. Luckily, however, Delia was enough of an old hat at being bossy to make up for it.

Not satisfied with Xane's correction, she cleared her throat again.

"What?" he asked, dragging his hand through his hair in frustration.

"You forgot to mention the part about how my impeccable sense of style and natural beauty make you want to get in touch with your feelings," Delia said.

Hehehe. Delia sent a mental laugh my way. *Isn't he cute when he gets all grumpy? See that vein in his forehead?*

I couldn't believe this. She was pushing his buttons.

On purpose. And he hated it, but was head over heels for her anyway.

If we got out of this alive, I was never again, even for a second, going to doubt any future revelations Delia might happen to have about the male race. Seriously, whatever powers Xane had as a member of the Sidhe were nothing compared to Delia's feminine wiles.

Unfortunately, that just made Xane all the more determined to keep her.

"In any case," he said, refusing to repeat Delia's line about getting in touch with his feelings, "I acted with the blessing of both courts, and she is here as my *guest*."

I took the special emphasis on the word *guest* to mean *hostage*.

"I will do as my father asked, and bring her to the Unseelie Court. Stand in my way at your own peril."

"You do realize that you sound like something out of a really cheesy movie, don't you, Xaney?"

Xaney? Seriously?

"I have asked you repeatedly not to call me that," Xane said, frowning.

"And I've repeatedly called you that anyway," Delia replied helpfully. "And FYI, threatening Bailey is a no-no. In the words of the immortal Spice Girls, if you want to be my boyfriend, you've got to be nice to my friends."

One of my best friends in the world had just quoted (or worse, *misquoted*) the Spice Girls to a modern-day Hades intent on kidnapping her to the underworld. Forget cheesy movies. This had to be a dream.

"I have no wish to hurt her," Xane said, addressing his words to me rather than Delia. "But I cannot allow her to take you back. Not yet."

I read his meaning, even if Delia did not. If I wanted Delia to be able to leave the Otherworld, I'd have to agree to stay here.

We'd just see about that.

"I'm not letting you take her anywhere," I said. "This is between you and me, or your dad and me, or maybe every Sidhe and me, but you can leave my friends out of it. They didn't do anything wrong and I won't let you hurt them."

Xane smiled, but this time it was cold and nothing at all like the way he'd grinned at Delia earlier. "That's what we're counting on, Bailey."

Beside me, James stiffened. "You know, Xane," he said, his voice silky and low, "that's just wrong."

And with those words, James leapt forward, and I watched as his body transformed itself in midair. His fingers grew long and thin, flesh giving way to metal talons. His skin turned to some kind of scaly armor, and when he opened his mouth to let loose a wailing war cry, I could just make out the outline of fangs.

Delia scrambled away on all fours. Xane didn't so much as blink as he sidestepped, but he was so focused on not being impressed by James's attack that he didn't stop Delia from moving from his side.

James moved again and this time he managed to catch Xane's side. Blue-green blood spilled from the wound. Delia screamed, but before I could so much as echo the sentiment, the wound healed and Xane thrust out both hands, shooting midnight blue lightning out of his palms.

"No!" This time my scream beat Delia's, and the second the word left my mouth, the flame left my body, throwing up a wall of fire that cut Xane off from James.

I rushed forward, hoping that James would heal as fast as Xane had. Seconds before I reached him, Xane stepped dispassionately through the flame, his sparkling skin bubbling with the heat, but setting itself right within seconds.

"Stand back," Xane told me. "I don't want to hurt you."

I stared him down, even though I couldn't get the image of that dark blue lightning out of my mind. "You just want to hurt James."

"He attacked me," Xane said. "Using his powers against one of his own kind, let alone an heir, is forbidden."

"Yeah, well, as far as I'm concerned, kidnapping one of my best friends so you can blackmail me into leaving the mortal realm forever is forbidden too."

"Forbidden by who?" Xane scoffed.

"Blackmail?" Delia repeated. She stood up, suddenly completely unaffected by the fact that her boy toy could walk through fire and mine barely looked human at all. "You brought me here to blackmail Bailey?"

Delia's temper is a horrible thing to behold. Xane actually took a step back, my wall of fire singeing his hair.

"You can't stay here, Delia," I said. "The things that happen to humans in the Otherworld . . . they aren't pretty."

I don't know how I knew that was true, but I did. Maybe I'd been listening to Annabelle's lectures more attentively than usual, or maybe it was the kind of inherited memory that came with a connection to this place.

The Otherworld was no place for mortals.

And yet . . . I couldn't shake the feeling that my revelation on the way here—that my friends were connected to this place because they were connected to me—was true.

"Don't worry, Bay," Delia said. "I'm not staying." The look she gave Xane should have melted his bones. I made a mental note to get Delia to give me glaring lessons when we got home.

"You have to stay," Xane said, his voice soft and almost apologetic. "At least until Bailey agrees. You'll like it here. Really, you will. I wouldn't let anything bad happen to you."

Delia folded her arms over her chest. "If I had my transmogrification," she said, "I'd turn you into pudding."

As a threat, it was somewhat lackluster, but I couldn't fault Delia on the delivery.

"Pudding?" Xane asked, more confused than intimidated.

"Be afraid," Delia told him. "Be very afraid."

During this exchange, James had managed to climb back up to his feet. I reached out to touch his scorched arm, and his scales gave way to skin under my finger-tips.

"I can't hold this form for very long," he told me, returning to the appearance I knew him by, save for the talons, which he kept, his eyes trained on Xane's every movement.

Somehow, I didn't think Wolverine-esque claws were going to do James much good against an enemy who could heal himself instantly. No wonder James hadn't been able to stop Xane from taking Delia.

I couldn't ignore the fact that he'd tried to save my friend again, knowing that he wasn't a match for Xane. That didn't change anything, not really at least, but as far as apologies went, this was much better than the one in the bathroom.

"I can't let you take Delia," I told Xane, staying on task. "Even if she wanted to go, I couldn't let her, not if I wasn't sure she'd be safe."

Xane glanced at Delia. "So it's okay for *her* to tell you what to do?" he asked, somewhat put out. Clearly, in their short acquaintance, Xane had already figured out that he couldn't get away with giving Delia orders of any kind.

"Bailey can tell me whatever she wants," Delia said in a tone of voice engineered to convey the maximum amount of *duh* per word. "She's Bailey."

"This is wrong, Xane," I said, and beside me, James twitched at the word, his instinct pushing him to fight again, even though he knew as well as I did that he would lose. "I never thought I'd say this, but I don't think you're evil. I don't think you want to hurt Delia." I took a deep breath. "I don't even think you want to hurt me."

Xane didn't reply, but I opened myself to his mind, and even though his thoughts were shielded by a wall at least as powerful as my own, I managed to make it far enough past to hear two words.

I don't.

Along with the words, I got a slew of feelings, all of which were rather foreign and entirely vexing to Xane. Delia intrigued him. She made him smile and made him want to rip his hair out, and even though she wasn't Sidhe and he hadn't known her more than an hour, he felt a pull toward her, a tug on heartstrings he hadn't even known he had. He wanted to own her, to keep and protect her and to make her happy, and the first of these was the only one that he could understand.

I felt Xane's confusion, the loss of his certainty that his well-being and the court he would someday rule took precedence over everything else. I felt his confidence in his father's judgment beginning to waver.

Thwack.

Xane must have sensed me in his mind, because he threw me out with such ferocity that I stumbled backward and fell to the ground, hitting my head against the side of a rock. Instantly, James and Delia were at my side, and Xane was looking down at me, something akin to horror on his face.

I don't want to hurt you.

This time I didn't have to go looking for his thoughts. He let me hear them and the puzzlement in them. He wasn't used to feeling human emotions, but Delia brought them out in him. The way that I brought them out in James.

"I'm fine," I said, addressing my words to Xane. "You have to let us go, Xane. Please. This isn't right. You know this isn't right."

Silence. I could feel Xane wavering, fighting with himself and his desires and this annoying new conscience. And then, just as I thought we might actually win, the silence was broken.

"My son knows nothing of the sort."

Drogan. Here.

"Father," Xane said, any trace of humanity I'd seen in him long gone. "I brought the girl. Unfortunately, there were some complications."

He gestured toward me and James.

"Don't worry, Xane," a female voice purred behind me. "You've done well."

Eze.

"Come, Bailey. There's much to be done before your Reckoning, and the girls have brought some friends of yours along for the ride."

Annabelle and Zo? Delia asked me silently.

My throat went suddenly and inexplicably dry. *I left them with Axia and Lyria.*

As Eze placed a hand on my arm and one on Delia's, it occurred to me that I had no idea whose side the heirs to the Seelie Court were really on. All I knew was that no matter what, Delia, Annabelle, and Zo were on mine.

Suddenly, reality blurred around us, and as everything went inky black, I felt my physical form losing shape and my control on the here and now slipping.

Huh, I thought with my last bit of consciousness. *So this is what teleportation feels like.*

Chapter 24

When I finally came to, the first thing I saw were three very familiar faces.

"Are you guys okay?" I asked, but since I apparently hadn't quite regained command of the English language yet, it came out sounding a little bit like "Arrooooookyyyy?"

"We aren't the ones who've been playing Sleeping Beauty for the past four hours," Zo said, needing no translation of my mumbling.

"Four hours?" I asked, sitting up.

The others nodded.

"Where are we?" I asked, looking around and trying to get my bearings. The walls were made of stone, and though the room was quite large, I couldn't see an entrance or an exit of any kind.

"As far as I've been able to tell," Annabelle said, "we're inside a mountain. Quite probably the Mount Olympus of myths."

"Annabelle?" I asked, searching her face for a familiar expression or something that would tell me beyond all doubt that she was really herself again.

"If only I'd brought my research," Annabelle said. "There must be something that we've overlooked. Preferably something that would get us out of here before your Reckoning starts."

"Good enough for me," I said. Everyone had nervous habits. Annabelle's involved analyzing data and making charts. "Are you sure we're inside the mountain?"

Annabelle nodded. "The girls we came here with just waved their hands over it, and the mountain opened up. They made me walk inside, and it closed."

"I'm sorry," I said, looking away from her. "I thought Axia was on our side."

Zo socked me in the arm. "Don't apologize," she said. "Without Axia, we never would have gotten the other one out of Annabelle, and she'd *still* be making out with the entire student population."

Annabelle blushed.

"Sorry," Zo said contritely. "I'm exaggerating. You didn't make out with everyone." She paused, but just couldn't leave it with that. "Just ninety percent of the guys."

Delia placed a hand on her chest. "I'm so proud."

"Can we concentrate on the problem at hand?" I

asked, saving Annabelle from further mortification. There'd be plenty of time for the others to tease her later. Right now we had bigger things to worry about.

"Where was the entrance?" I said. "Which side?"

Zo shrugged. Delia looked down at her nails, but Annabelle took several steps to her left and put her palm on the wall. "Here."

I followed and waved my hand over the place she had indicated, feeling ridiculous, but hoping that whatever mojo the others had used to stick us in here would work for me now.

Nothing happened.

"Put a little more oomph into it," Delia suggested. "Like so." She demonstrated by flicking her hand back and forth, with several dramatic gasps for emphasis.

Somehow, I didn't think that was going to work. Instead, I closed my eyes and searched for the mountain with my mind instead of my senses. I found it, and even though I was standing right next to the stone wall, the buzz in my brain was muted, as if I were very far away. I concentrated on that feel, that sound, and brought it closer and closer, until the mountain was all around me in my mind.

I was running through forests and over rivers, up mountains that grew under my feet as I ran.

The memory played against the backdrop of my eyelids, and I tried to remember what it had felt like to run over these very stones, to bid the mountain grow at my will. Then I lifted my hand and, eyes still closed, I imagined the wall rearranging itself, the stone giving way to open space.

I started walking out through the gap I'd created before I even opened my eyes. My friends followed, and we made our way out of the mountain and onto its surface. As soon as we were free and clear, I let my hold on the mountain go, and the stone fell back into place.

Thank you, I told the mountain silently, feeling as if I should offer it something, but having nothing else to give.

The stone sang back in reply, and somehow I understood that it had been a long time since anyone had spoken to it with anything other than a command.

"So this is the Otherworld," Zo said as we walked toward the edge of the mountain. "Not bad."

Below us, the land spread out, as vibrant in color as it was up close, and something inside of me fluttered.

Sidhe. Home.

Even now, when I knew that the beauty of this place hid something far more sinister, I couldn't push down the connection I felt to it, and I didn't try to. I wasn't going to hold the land responsible for the things that were done to me here, any more than I could blame the mountain for being our temporary prison.

I was a part of this, and it was a part of me, forever and ever, no matter what.

Sidhe. Home.

On a whim, I opened my mind to my friends, sending them this feeling, this image, and as I did, they gasped. For a brief second, I saw this place through their eyes, and I realized how daunting it was and how much of the beauty was in the small things: each blade of grass, each shade of purple and gray in the mountain. To them, it was beautiful and ominous. To me, it was right.

Sidhe. Home.

As much as it pained me to do it, I turned away from the landscape and back to my friends. "We have to find a way down," I said. Somehow, I doubted they could run it the way I could. "We need to go home."

Sidhe. Home.

The land called to me, and I called back, sending thoughts to it the way I'd done for the girls a moment before.

I thought of A-belle, quiet and understated and wickedly wonderful in her own quiet and understated way.

Of Delia and the way her confidence allowed her to tame even the most obnoxious, pompous beast.

And then I thought of Zo, fierce and loyal, half sister, half friend.

I sent these images out to anyone and anything who would listen, completely oblivious to the fact that I may well have been alerting the others of our escape.

Friends, I explained to the land and the mountain and everything that called me here. *Home.*

"Bailey." Axia spoke my name, but didn't say anything else. I wondered how long she'd been standing behind us and if I'd brought her here with the thoughts and images I'd just broadcast.

"I trusted you, you know," I told her, not bothering to turn around. "You were supposed to keep them safe. You weren't supposed to bring them here."

"What must be, must be," Axia said softly. "You should know that better than anyone."

There was something in her tone and in her words that was familiar, and I realized that the last time I'd talked to Morgan, she'd told me the same thing. I whirled around to meet Axia's eyes, wondering if it was in any way possible that my trust hadn't been misplaced, that maybe I wasn't the only one Morgan had given cryptic instructions.

"I'm supposed to prepare you," Axia said. "For the Reckoning." With those words, she lifted her hand and waved it at me, and my hair began intricately braiding itself.

"That," Delia said, "is almost as cool as transmogrification."

"Telekinesis?" Annabelle asked, a scholarly tone creeping into her voice.

Zo had a slightly different reaction. "Leave her alone," she said, stalking straight up to Axia and placing herself between the two of us. "Don't touch her. Don't wave your hand at her. Don't do whatever it is you're doing to her hair. Leave her alone."

"She's not hurting her," a very small voice said from somewhere to my left.

"You!" Annabelle bit out. Apparently, at some point between the time I'd left her and the time she and Zo had been escorted to our mountain prison, she'd met

Lyria, and A-belle hadn't quite forgiven her for the kissing rampage.

"I'm s-s-sorry," Lyria managed. She blushed, but instead of turning red, her cheeks began to exude light the exact same shade of pinkish white as her hair. Axia reached out to touch her sister, and Lyria managed to banish her Otherworldly blush. "I didn't mean you any harm. I was just supposed to cause a diversion. I . . . ummmm . . . I kind of got carried away."

"Kind of?" Annabelle squeaked.

Lyria looked away. "It was my first kiss too."

Something passed between the two of them, to the extent that I wondered if Lyria was speaking silently to my friend or if there was something else going on that just didn't include the rest of us.

After a moment, Annabelle nodded. I had no idea what she was nodding to, but I didn't get much of a chance to ponder, because as soon as Axia finished with my hair, Lyria tilted her head to the side, and as her eyes grew very blue, my clothes morphed, jeans and T-shirt melding together, the fabric changing to silk and growing into a simple light blue dress. As I watched, the dress molded itself to my body and intricately stitched patterns appeared on the torso.

"A Reckoning only happens once," Axia explained, her voice completely devoid of emotion. "The dress is somewhat formal."

"This Reckoning ain't happening," Zo said flatly. No sooner were the words out of her mouth than the mountain exploded under our feet, sending us soaring

331

even further upward, until the portion we'd been standing on became the apex.

Suddenly, we weren't alone.

Annabelle looked at her cousin. "I hate to say this, but evidence suggests you're mistaken."

"Silence." Eze's tone was pleasant enough, but there was so much power in her voice and in the way she held herself that there was no question in my mind or anyone else's that it was an order.

I glanced around, sure that Drogan was nearby, and he accommodated me by stepping out of the shadows. My glancing, however, told me that he wasn't the only one standing just out of sight. We were surrounded on all sides by Sidhe. Adea and Valgius, the Muses and Eros, James, Kiste, and Cyna. Xane stood next to his father, refusing to meet Delia's accusing glare, and Axia and Lyria stepped away from me to join their mother. Beyond the inner circle, there were dozens, if not hundreds of Sidhe, shining beings whose beauty should have made them stand out even more than they did.

I gazed beyond this peak and my keen Sidhe eyesight showed me others, standing on other mountains, watching from afar, lending their presence to this moment and this event.

"We have gathered. We are here. Tonight, we welcome home a daughter. With this ceremony, we honor her. We honor the blood she carries and the connection it shares with our own. We honor her as a child of this world, ready to become an adult. We come here to offer her our acceptance and to accept hers of our ways."

I'd expected something that involved a little less honoring and a little more threatening, but still—as far as I'd been able to tell—nothing in Eze's words had been a question or a request. There simply wasn't an option to decline their ways or their honor, to tell Eze that while I'd never forswear this place, this land, these mountains, she could take *her* connection and shove it.

"She is Sidhe." Drogan spoke the words. Apparently, his soliloquy was significantly shorter than Eze's.

"She is Sidhe." Every person on the mountain, save for Delia, Annabelle, and Zo, repeated Drogan's words, and the effect was so massive that even though there was no echo, and the words died soon after they were spoken, the timbre and volume of the collective voices of the Sidhe in those short seconds was enough to make me wonder if the sound of it would ever stop ringing in my ears. It was as if my brain could not comprehend the vastness of the sound, so it parsed it in stages, dragging out the noise long after it was gone from the air.

"Bailey, you are welcome at the Seelie Court." Eze took over speaking again. I opened my mouth to tell her exactly what she could do with her welcome, but no sound came out. I tried again, and she inclined her head slightly, as if to say "nuh-uh-uh," before continuing with her formal invitation to join her court. "There is a lightness in you, a desire for things to be good and right and pure. You were made to stand in the sun, and if you swear fealty to the Court of Light, you need never fear darkness again."

"Bailey, you are welcome at the Unseelie Court,"

Drogan said, and as he spoke, the scenery around us flickered and changed, until it appeared as though we were standing in the caverns deep in the Otherworldly earth. "You long for depth and truth and have learned to look past appearances. You have danced in our darkness and seen its beauty. You recognize cruelty and could not live in a world in which it is passed off as right. Swear your fealty to the Court of Darkness, and the secrets of the shadows will be yours."

As he finished delivering his speech, the world around us righted itself, and we were standing on the mountain again.

Lame, Zo opined silently. *Seriously, who's writing their dialogue?*

I smiled, and Drogan took that as an indication that his words somehow resonated with me. If he'd opened his mind to it at all, he probably could have heard what Zo was silently saying, anyone here probably could have, but to them, my friends were little more than leverage, and they didn't bother opening their minds to the leverage's thoughts.

"Adea. Valgius." Eze spoke their names, and the two of them stepped forward.

"You are our daughter," Adea said. "Blood of our blood, heart of our hearts."

"You are our child," Valgius continued, his voice oddly stiff, as if these were words he didn't want to be saying in the least. "We welcome you to adulthood and bid you choose according to what your blood and your heart tell you."

"Let the land counsel you," Eze said.

"Let the mountains and the depths implore you," Drogan added.

Let the waters guide you. Let them cleanse you of all influence and free from your mind the solution that you seek.

Morgan. She was here. She was part of this, and nobody knew it but me.

"Bailey of the Sidhe, this is your moment. This is your Reckoning. Choose wisely, child, for when the choice is made, you won't be one any longer, and the words you speak will bind you through eternity." Eze and Drogan delivered that line together, and then there was silence.

If my words were binding, I had to think of a way to phrase them very, very carefully. I might only get one shot at this, and until I knew what to do, until the pieces of the puzzle fell into place, I wouldn't say anything or choose at all.

As seconds stretched into minutes, the silence became louder, more obtrusive, and even though I concentrated on keeping my mind clear, on following Morgan's dictate and reaching out for the lakes and rivers that ran through this world and into my own, I couldn't ignore the mounting tension all around me.

Finally, Eze inclined her head toward my friends, and instantly, they were surrounded by Sidhe, each of them caught in an uncompromising hold.

Life here can be unpleasant for humans, Eze said silently, unwilling to speak aloud. *It becomes too much for them. The colors and sights and sounds of our world beat at their senses until they are dull, and the land will feed off of their life forces until they waste away, losing the will to breathe air whose taste they cannot comprehend.*

Mortals cannot resist the thrall of our people. Drogan added his mind-voice to Eze's. *Our voices will haunt them until they'd gladly claw off their own ears for the honor of hearing us speak again. They'll tear off their eye-lids so that they can gaze upon our beauty unfettered by something as human as blinking. They will be bewitched and reduced to puppets, playthings, pets.*

They will be used. Both monarchs spoke at once.

Choose, Eze told me. *We'll keep them here until you do. They'll fade, slowly at first, but within a year, they won't know or recognize you, and you won't be able to look at them.*

Choose, Drogan said. *Either you leave here tonight or they do, but you cannot have it both ways.*

Water, I thought. *Running water. Blue-green lakes, the river under my feet as I run across it.*

Blood.

That was the thought the waters sent me, and the mountains and caverns and land echoed it in my mind.

Blood. That was my connection to this place. Sidhe blood ran in my veins. Once upon a time, I'd spilled Alecca's, and through that, I'd come to take her place. Tattoos made of Sidhe blood had once given my friends temporary powers, and it was my blood through which my connection to this place ran.

My blood and the waters.

My blood and the land.

My blood and the mountains.

My blood and the depths.

Again and again, that was the answer pounded into my head. Everywhere I turned in the labyrinth of my mind, there it was.

Blood.

My blood was the reason there was an imbalance. What had Annabelle called it? Osmosis? Something about there being one Fate in my world, and two in the Nexus; one Sidhe on Earth and countless in the Otherworld. I was half human and half Sidhe, and the only way to close the barrier, to be both at once instead of lingering in between, to be balanced instead of liminal, the only way to keep the balance between the worlds was to even things out.

Blood.

And that's when I knew.

Once I begin to speak, can they interrupt me? I sent the question to Adea and Valgius, who didn't dare reply in mind-speak, but shook their heads. I'd suspected as much. This was a ceremony, and the Sidhe were all about the ritual.

Choose, Drogan and Eze urged me, and so I did.

"I will make my choice," I said. "I will pledge. I will be Reckoned."

Eze nodded, and the Sidhe guarding my friends stepped back. My word was binding. I'd said I'd make my choice, and I would. I'd said I would pledge, and I would. This was my Reckoning, and I was ready.

"Delia. Annabelle. Zo." I spoke my friends' names with the same solemnity with which Eze and Drogan had delivered their speeches. All around me, eyebrows shot up at my words. Clearly, this wasn't what anyone had been expecting.

"You're my friends, my family, the other half of myself. For the past couple of months, I've been wondering what I was going to do without you next year, and I couldn't help but feel that without our friendship, our connection, I didn't know who I was."

Zo opened her mouth—probably to tell me I was an idiot—but no words came out. They were as silent as I'd been before Eze and Drogan had yielded the floor to me, and it occurred to me that maybe right now I was the only one who actually could speak, King and Queen included.

"Earlier today, I was running through the Otherworld, and I can't even describe the feeling. It's everything. You guys and me and this world and every sensation you could possibly imagine, blending together and crossing over to something new. And it occurred to me that I've spent all this time wondering where I belong and where I'm going to belong once we graduate, and I never once realized that it doesn't matter where I am. It doesn't matter where we go to college. It doesn't matter if we're on opposite coasts or in different worlds. You are in me. You are part of me. And my choice here, right now, is to be part of you."

With those words, I reached for my necklace. For

the first time since Morgan had given it to me, I took it off and slowly, deliberately, I held up the pendant. Its dull, silver gleam wasn't anything compared to the skin of the other Sidhe, but every pair of eyes was locked onto it. I held up my left palm, and with my right hand, I angled the pendant toward it. Annabelle realized what I was doing, and her eyes grew very wide just before I pressed the razor-sharp edge of the pendant into my flesh and forced it to cut mercilessly through the length of my palm. As the razor moved, blue-green blood welled up on my hand.

In the mirror, it was red.

"Part human," I said. "Part Sidhe. Somebody once told me that the power was in the blood, that our connection to this world was in the blood." I turned toward my friends. With shaking hands, Annabelle unclasped her necklace and mimicked my actions, slicing her own palm open. I touched my hand to hers, allowing her blood to run into my wound and mine into hers.

"My power. My blood. Our connection," I whispered.

Delia was lightning quick with her clasp, and Zo didn't even bother with it at all, ripping the necklace off instead.

"My power. My blood. Our connection."

I repeated the words, once for Delia and once for Zo. The necklace grew hotter and hotter in my hand as my friends and I shared blood, and in my mind, a tiny buzz grew into something louder, until the sound of rushing water in my ears made it out of my mouth in the form of a spell.

"To you I call,
My three of three.
My blood in yours
And yours in me.

Through this change,
The balance holds.
The barrier righted,
The bridge refolds.

I give this gift
With lake and sea,
River and water,
So mote it be."

The moment the last word left my mouth, each of our wounds exploded into light and disappeared, and when my eyes recovered from the explosion, I took in the most beautiful sight I'd ever seen.

My friends were standing on Mount Olympus, just as they'd been a moment before, but now they were sparkling, diamonds sewn into their skin with the power of my spell, their hair glowing not one color, but two.

I was in them. They were in me. And all four of us were Sidhe.

Chapter 25

"How dare you?" Eze's voice was low in pitch, but big on volume. "You would defile your birthright, you would share what you have no right to claim in the first place? That your blood is muddied with mortality is something we have forced ourselves to overlook. That you would dilute it further and willingly take on more humanity to give these abominations a portion of your power is an insult that we will not bear."

Drogan did not follow the Queen of Light in her display of emotion, but rather spoke calmly and coolly. "You said you would pledge," he said. "You have not. To be Reckoned means to choose between the courts and to align yourself with one of the ancient lines of power. You cannot pledge to your friends." He spat out the last word like it was an obscenity. "Your word is binding. You must pledge, and as they carry your blood, they will be bound by your decision. We offered you a chance to choose your path. Now you will be choosing your end—and theirs, for as my sister said, this is an insult that we will not bear."

That wasn't exactly the way I'd planned on this going. I'd been so sure that this was the solution that it didn't even occur to me to wonder what would happen after I'd shared my blood. It had seemed so perfect: instead of having one half-Sidhe in the mortal realm, we'd have four, which would perfectly balance the fact that the other two Fates lived in this one. Beyond that, I was hoping that making my decision would right my own imbalance, which would put the barrier back up full force, and that meant no more visits from Aphrodite, the Furies, et al. Plus, if my friends had Sidhe blood, I wouldn't have to worry about Eze and Drogan's ominous warnings about what happened to mortals who lived too long in this realm.

See? Perfect.

Only not, because if swearing loyalty to my friends didn't count as pledging, that meant that I still had to bind myself to one of the rulers of the Otherworld, and that, apparently, meant bloody death for my entire group.

Way to go, Bailey.

"You can't kill her!"

At first, I thought someone was sticking up for me, but when I located the source of that statement, I found myself staring at Xane, who was looking at Delia.

"Another one?" Zo asked Delia. "Do you have to rack up boyfriends *everywhere* we go?"

"Silence!" Drogan yelled.

For a second, he had exactly what he'd asked for, but then a melodic voice spoke from somewhere behind me.

"You always were rather dramatic." With those seemingly benign words, the voice's owner began walking toward us, and the crowd of Sidhe parted for her. "Hello, brother."

Remember what I said about not liking Morgan? Zo said silently. *Forget that. Lady has a heckuva sense of timing.*

Personally, I could have done with Morgan coming before death threats had been issued, but at this point, I was too entranced by the interaction between the three most powerful Sidhe to care.

Eze refused to acknowledge Morgan's presence. Drogan glared at her and hissed something in a language I didn't understand.

"It's been a long time since I stood on this mountain," Morgan said. "Many millennia have gone by in the human world since I've come here to watch another choose." She smiled. "In fact, I haven't been here since my own Reckoning, the day my brother, sister, and I came into power and split our world among the three of us. They demanded your fealty, divided you between them. I chose a different path. I became one with our waters and, through them, the waters of the mortal world. I've spent these years in both worlds, allowing the courts their will in most things."

"You have no place here," Eze said. "You have no power to undo what has already been done. The child agreed to pledge. Her word is binding. She will fulfill it, or the blood in her veins will turn against her and she will plead with us for an easier death."

Okay, the Sidhe seriously needed to be more specific when they told someone that their word was binding, because I'd had no idea what I was getting myself into.

"The child has already pledged," Morgan said. "You just weren't listening closely enough. 'I give this gift, with lake and sea, river and water, so mote it be.'" Morgan somehow managed to make jovial look elegant. "She didn't pledge to the mountain or the caves. She pledged to the waters. In other words, she pledged to me."

I did? Could I even do that?

"She can't do that!" Eze said.

Drogan expanded upon his sister's objection, loathing oozing out of his voice. "You don't have a court. You chose to sequester yourself. To live in both worlds rather than allow anyone in this world to bind themselves to you. Remember?"

"And it surprises you that I would choose to begin my court with a child who belongs to both worlds? It is my right to have one. It has always been my right, and I have never forsworn it. Bailey has pledged herself, and her friends, to me, and I have accepted them. Bailey's word has been fulfilled; she has been Reckoned, and thus it will be."

344

Delia couldn't help herself. Feeling safer with Morgan here, she spoke up for the first time since the Reckoning had begun. "Take that!" Then she turned to Xane and mouthed something that looked suspiciously like "Call me."

"We will wage war on your so-called court. With four half-breeds, what hope do you have of standing against all of us?"

"Make that five." James stepped forward. "Anyone up for a double Reckoning? I'm suddenly feeling ready." Without waiting for an answer, he walked over to me and held his hand out. It took me a second to realize what he was reaching for.

My necklace.

I gave it to him and, with a huge smile plastered across his face, he cut his palm. I felt the searing pain in my own, and when I looked down, I realized that my wound had been reopened. I glanced at my friends and found them bleeding as well.

"Well," James said, "I'm not that great at the rhyming thing, but I pledge myself to Morgan's court and freely share my blood with these lovely ladies." He winked at me, and for the first time since I'd discovered the truth, he seemed more like the James I'd met than the one who'd betrayed me. He followed the wink with a shy smile, and in that second, he seemed like the Alec I'd partway fallen for as well. "Here goes nothing."

His palm touched mine, but somehow it felt like our lips were touching instead, even though a blood transfusion was a pretty weird version of a first kiss. As

James moved past me to my friends, Axia stepped forward, Lyria at her heels. They didn't speak any words out loud, but as Eze watched, her eyes deadly, they took their turns with my razor-sharp pendant.

"I used to think that when we ruled, this court would be different," Axia said. "But I don't think you'll ever willingly step down from the throne, Mother, and I don't think you'll ever change. I want to be part of the kind of court I would have led. I pledge myself to the seas, to Morgan, and to Bailey, who taught me that humanity is something worth having."

Lyria cleared her throat and delivered her own speech. "Me too."

Was this really happening? Had Eze's daughters just come over to our side? This was absolutely unreal!

"You would have killed Delia," Xane said, never moving from his father's side. "She is most annoying and quite bossy, but I find her intriguing, and I cannot abide that you would see her dead for nothing more than revenge."

"You've known him, what? Like five hours?" Zo said. "And four of those you were stuck inside a freaking mountain! Seriously, Delia, we can't take you anywhere."

Despite Xane's words, he seemed to be having a great deal of trouble actually moving, but when he finally took the first step toward me, he ended up leading close to a dozen others. The Muses. Eros. A guy I'd never even seen before.

One by one, we shared blood, and one by one, Morgan's court grew.

Kiste and Cyna stood by, aligning themselves with the old guard, their hatred for me and for what James had done clear in their every expression. Of all the un-Reckoned Sidhe I'd met, they were the only ones who stood against us.

"You planned this," Eze said, fury and—if it were possible—hurt clear in her voice. "All of these years, you've been planning to take our children from us, and for what?"

Morgan smiled, but it was a soft, sad expression on her face. "For the future. Your daughter said it best, Eze. Humanity is something worth having, and it's high time that there was a court in this world that wasn't afraid to be a little bit human."

Eze had accused me of defiling my Sidhe blood by sharing it with my friends, but in the end, it was my human half that others needed the most. I could feel the balance inside of me, could feel the blood of each of the others offsetting what I'd given away, but somehow, sharing my humanity with the Sidhe didn't lessen the way it pulsed through my own veins.

Despite everything, I was human and Sidhe, both at the same time, instead of somewhere in between. I was a balance to myself, only this time I'd been the one to find the balance, and no matter what happened, nobody could take that—or my friends—away.

EPILOGUE

Seven and a Half Months Later

"Today is a new beginning. Some people would call it the beginning of adulthood, the genesis of the rest of our lives, but I prefer to think of it simply as the beginning of now. Just as every minute of every day has led up to this moment, so this moment leads us to something new. This is not a turning point; it is neither the beginning nor the end of life as we know it. It is the continuation of everything that we've become, and the beginning of everything that we might be in the future. This moment has never happened before and will never happen again, but with each passing minute, hour, day, we will be faced with new moments, new beginnings, new opportunities to become the people that we wish to be."

Blah, blah, blah, blah.

I elbowed Zo in the side. After all, that was her cousin up there giving the valedictorian speech. The least she could do was act impressed and refrain from making grumbling comments inside my head.

Hey, just be glad I'm not shooting lightning bolts at the pep squad.

For about the millionth time, I wished that the mix of blood in Zo's veins hadn't resulted in her acquiring Xane's affinity for lightning. After years of complaining about getting the short end of the powers stick, she'd hit the jackpot this time around, with equal doses of lightning and fire. It took all three of us—and the occasional visit from Morgan—to keep her in line.

"Right now, in this second, it doesn't matter if you have plans. It doesn't matter if you're leaving home or staying close, or if you don't know what happens next at all. What matters is this moment, the decisions you make right now about who and what you want to be, about what lessons you want to take with you from this place, and what things you want to grow past and leave behind. Once this moment is gone, it will never come again. Use it wisely."

I glanced at Delia, who was using this moment wisely to braid and unbraid her hair—with telekinesis. I would have been worried that someone else would see her, but Delia was almost as strong at applying the glamour as Lyria was, and besides me, Annabelle, and Zo, all anyone else would have seen was a girl with thick hair, a perfect smile, and a graduation robe that had been accessorized to capacity and beyond.

Up on the stage, Annabelle continued her speech, perfectly in tune with her audience's emotions. Lyria said that Annabelle had always been a little empathic and that maybe that was why she'd chosen her as a target for possession to begin with, but now A-belle had surpassed the former heir in her ability to read others. Luckily, though, Annabelle didn't have to worry about manipulating other people's emotions, because the single trace of expath ability she'd gotten in the mix only showed up when she chose to take on a nonhuman form. Since Annabelle didn't exactly make maximum use of the shape-shifting she'd inherited from James, most of the time she had her powers firmly under control.

"Today is a time for remembering and a time for looking forward, but more than anything, it is a time for living, a time that exists between yesterday and tomorrow for whatever purpose you design. Somebody once asked me if I believed in destiny, and if there's anything that senior year has taught me, it's that we can make our own destinies. I believe that the extraordinary is out there, waiting to happen, and that the ordinary might be the most precious thing of all."

As for the results of me mixing blood with the rest of Morgan's court, not much had changed. I was Life, the Third Fate, and that wasn't something a little spell could alter. The only difference was that now I understood the pattern I wove a little bit better, because when it came to weaving or painting, dancing, singing, or any kind of art, I was, for lack of a better word, *inspiring*.

Unfortunately, I was pretty sure you couldn't major in *inspiration*.

"So if you only remember one thing from this

speech, remember this. For all you know, this moment, this second, or the next, or the next, could be your destiny. It's not about having plans. It's about having purpose and being who, not what, you want to be. Today is about possibilities, and even when they feel finite, I have it on good authority that they are endless. Thank you."

Annabelle walked gracefully away from the podium, just a hint of gazelle in her step.

As she took her seat at the end of our row and the principal came to the microphone and began calling out names, I wondered how I could have ever thought that this moment would be the end. A-belle was right. We made our own destinies, and even if ours hadn't included a few mystical twists, the four of us would have survived. Blood or no blood, they were part of me and I was part of them, and something as trivial as splitting up for college didn't stand a chance against everything we had shared.

A lifetime of friendship.

Four years in high school.

Hundreds of sleepovers.

Countless mall trips.

Two mystical adventures.

The list went on and on, and as Delia's name was called and she sashayed toward her diploma, I smiled. Somewhere in the crowd, Xane was probably watching this, completely Delia-whipped and significantly geekier than any former heir had a right to be. James was probably with him, magicked to look like somebody else. For all I knew, the entire court—Morgan included—

352

might have shown up. The barrier was closed again, and even the most liminal of times and places didn't allow for much crossing over, but, like Morgan, her court lived in both worlds, something that only those with a lot of power or a little humanity could do.

By the time the principal reached the *K*s, I was starting to get fidgety, but I kept myself calm, for Annabelle's sake, lest my emotions bleed over onto hers.

Just think about tonight, I told myself. *Think about weaving life. Think about running through the Other-world. Think about the party the Court of Awesome is going to throw once we get there.*

Ultimately, it was thinking the name Delia had bestowed upon Morgan's court that banished my nervousness. Officially, we were Morgan's Court, or the Court of Water, but everybody who was anybody knew that we were the Court of Awesome, no questions asked.

"Bailey Marie Morgan."

The principal called my name, and I stood up, my legs shaky as I walked forward and grabbed my diploma. This wasn't the end. This was a beginning of new adventures, for all of us, and no matter where we went in this world, Annabelle, Delia, Zo, and I would always have the Otherworld. We would always have one another.

As I turned to walk back to my seat, the cheers grew louder, and for just an instant, I saw through the glamour the other members of our court had cast. James was hooting. Xane was clapping in a very dignified fashion.

Lyria and Axia had both managed whistles, and the Muses appeared to be doing some kind of dance in my honor.

As for Morgan, she simply inclined her head as if this was what she had expected of me all along.

I sat back down next to my friends, and the Others disappeared. Annabelle got her diploma, and then Zo, and before I knew it, we were throwing our graduation caps up in the air and hugging one another.

"So," I said, "who's driving to the after party?"

"Not Delia," Zo said quickly.

"Not Zo," Annabelle put in.

"Hey!" Delia said. Zo opted for something a little less PG, and she might have added a tiny lightning shock to the mix had it not been for the fact that something about the situation struck me as so inexplicably funny that I couldn't help cracking up.

Like Annabelle had said, this was our moment, and as far as I was concerned, it was perfect.

ACKNOWLEDGMENTS

Thanks first and foremost to everyone who wrote to me after reading *Tattoo,* asking what happened next. Despite what Greek mythology has to say on the subject, I firmly believe that readers are an author's most incredible muses, and I'm incredibly grateful to mine. Thanks also to my editor, Krista Marino, who seems to have an actual sixth sense for knowing what a manuscript needs, and to my agent, Elizabeth Harding, whose support at every step in the process is invaluable. Finally, I couldn't imagine writing a book without the people who keep me sane and happy while I'm waist-deep in a process that can be a little crazy: my mother/first reader, Marsha Barnes; my roommate/sounding board, Neha Mahajan; and my friend/cheerleader/commiserator, Ally Carter.

ABOUT THE AUTHOR

Marsha Barnes

Jennifer Lynn Barnes wrote her first novel when she was still a teenager. Since then, she's written five others, including *Tattoo* and its companion, *Fate*. Jennifer spent the year after her college graduation living in the United Kingdom, so she understands what it's like to be caught between two worlds. When she's not writing, Jennifer is a full-time student, working on a PhD in developmental psychology at Yale University. Visit Jennifer online at www.jenniferlynnbarnes.com or read her blog at http://jenlyn-b.livejournal.com/.